W9-CEF-764

The Blackcoat
Rebellion Series

QUEEN

QUEEN

AIMÉE CARTER

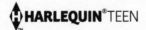

ISBN-13: 978-0-373-21161-6

Queen

Printed in U.S.A.

For Matrice

I

SPEAK

I gazed out across the gathering crowd, my heart in my throat. The citizens of Elsewhere shifted restlessly, their red and orange jumpsuits bringing color to an otherwise gray winter landscape, and I could feel them growing impatient.

They weren't the only ones.

"Knox, everyone's waiting," I said from my corner of the stage the Blackcoats had constructed over the past several days. It was made of whatever materials they'd been able to salvage from the buildings that had been destroyed during the Battle of Elsewhere. Two weeks later, they were still pulling bodies from the wreckage.

Knox Creed, one of the leaders of the Blackcoat Rebellion—and my former fake fiancé—looked up from his spot at the base of the stairs. His forehead was furrowed, and the annoyance on his face was unmistakable. "I'm aware, thank you," he said. "There's only so much I can do to hurry things along."

I hopped down the steps to join him and the other Blackcoats who lingered nearby. He'd made no secret of his distaste for my less-than-obedient attitude, and though I'd done my best to play by the rules after the battle ended, we were still on shaky ground. I wasn't so sure our friendship would ever be mended completely, no matter how the rebellion turned out. But right now, we both had more important things to worry about: he had a rebellion to lead, and I had a speech to give. As soon as the cameras were ready for me.

"Benjy said the test run this morning went fine," I said. "Is there a problem now?"

"There's always a problem," said Knox. Turning away from me, he spoke into a cuff on his wrist. "What's the holdup?"

I waited in silence as he listened to the reply in his earpiece. He muttered what sounded like a curse, and it was my turn to frown. "How much longer?"

"They're having trouble breaking through the network's security," he said. "Something about encryptions and passcodes."

In other words, nothing I could help with. Or Knox, for that matter. "Why don't we just record the speech and broadcast it once they've found a way around it? Wouldn't that be easier?"

"If it comes to that, we will, but we can give them a few more minutes." As if realizing for the first time that I was standing next to him, he did a double take, his dark eyes looking me up and down. "Did you bathe?"

I blinked. "Are you joking? I spent an hour letting them do my hair and makeup."

"What did they do, stare at you the entire time?" He ran his fingers through my hair in an attempt to do—something. I didn't know what. "You look nothing like Lila anymore."

Lila Hart—one of the founders of the Blackcoats, who also happened to be Prime Minister Daxton Hart's niece. Four months ago, on my seventeenth birthday, I'd been kidnapped and surgically transformed to look exactly like her in order to take her place. She had been Knox's real fiancée. I was only playing the part.

But now, after the dust had settled, the entire world knew there were two of us. Lila was working for Daxton, who had to be holding something over her. Whatever it was must have been a matter of life or death, because the Lila Hart I knew, while not particularly brave, would have never openly supported the government that had murdered her father and turned her mother into a fugitive rebel. Not like this. Not unless there was a gun to her head—or someone else's.

There was little we could do about Lila's sudden change in allegiance now, though, and in the meantime, I was working for Knox and the Blackcoats. He had plenty to hold over me, but none of it mattered, because Knox didn't want me here. I was in Elsewhere because I wanted to be. I was about to speak in front of countless Americans because it was the right thing to do. And no matter how many times he tried to intimidate me into leaving, nothing would make me change my mind.

"I look exactly like Lila, and everyone in this damn place knows it," I said firmly. "You're just beginning to see the differences more clearly. There were two boys in my group home—they were identical twins, and no one could tell them apart at first. But the more we got to know them, the easier—"

"You can spare me. I know how telling twins apart

works." His scowl deepened, and I wondered what I'd said to upset him. But it was gone as soon as it came, and someone must have talked in his ear, because he stopped fussing with my hair and touched the piece. "All right. Kitty—they're ready for you. Remember your talking points, and for once, would you please stick to them?"

I shook my hair out, letting the shoulder-length blond bob fall wherever it wanted. "Do I get to tell my version of events, or yours?"

"I want you to tell the truth," he said. "The entire truth. We can't afford lies and misdirection anymore, not when Lila and Daxton are the ones feeding them directly to the people."

The corners of my mouth tugged upward in a slow smile. "Really? The entire truth?"

His dark eyes met mine, and he leaned in until I could see the gray that ringed his irises. "Every last bit of it."

Whatever his reasoning was—whatever he was using me for—I didn't care. He was giving me permission to be myself for the first time in months, and I wasn't going to turn him down.

Someone had fixed a bright light over my spot behind a makeshift podium, and I climbed back up the steps and walked over, my boots thumping against the wooden planks. Hundreds of faces stared up at me expectantly, but the more I focused, the more discontent I saw in the crowd. The people of Elsewhere, who had not only survived the battle, but in some cases an entire lifetime of captivity, were less forgiving than most. During my few days here as a prisoner, I'd been beaten up and threatened more times than

I could count. They were hostile, merciless, and quick to protect their own skins above all else.

But this was different. The government had cut off several of Elsewhere's key supply lines and destroyed most of the stores in the battle, and the more time that passed, the fewer resources Knox and the Blackcoats had to take care of everyone. They were going hungry, slowly but surely, and if I didn't do this—if I couldn't convince the people to listen—then we would soon starve. And they knew it.

I cleared my throat. The microphone hooked up to the podium amplified my voice, making it echo through the square. Two weeks ago, a cage had stood in the center, and every evening, insubordinate citizens had been forced to fight to the death for a second chance. Now only a twisted lump of melted steel remained.

Things in Elsewhere weren't easy, and they wouldn't be for a long time. But at least that ruined cage was a reminder that they were marginally better than before.

In my peripheral vision, Knox stood with his arms crossed, giving me a look, and I didn't need to hear him to know what he was trying to tell me. They wouldn't be able to hold the broadcast channel open forever. If I wanted the five hundred million people who lived in the United States to hear me, I had to start talking.

I pushed the number from my mind and held my head high. This wasn't about me. This was about the rebellion, about freedom, about doing the right thing for the people— I was just the mouthpiece. Nothing more.

"Good afternoon," I said, and for the first time, I used my own voice and accent instead of the dialect I'd painstakingly learned in September. "As I'm sure you've put together by now, my name is not Lila Hart."

A murmur rippled through the crowd, and Knox took a deep breath, his shoulders rising and falling slowly. His lips were pressed together, and even from twenty feet away, I could see the fear and anticipation in his eyes. We were both keenly aware of how much was riding on this.

"My name is Kitty Doe, and seventeen years ago, I was born here, in Section X of Elsewhere," I said. "My biological mother is Hannah Mercer, and my biological father was Prime Minister Daxton Hart."

These were facts I had only become aware of two weeks earlier, when Hannah—my mother—had confessed her affair with the Prime Minister. The words stuck in my throat, and even after repeating them countless times to myself, they still didn't feel real.

"I was lucky," I continued. "Because of who my father was, he had the power to make arrangements for me outside Elsewhere, in a group home for Extras and orphans in Washington, D.C. I am, as far as I know, the only person to ever leave Elsewhere."

Once someone was convicted of a crime, no matter how innocent or small, they were sent to Elsewhere for life. Population control, I'd been told by Augusta Hart, Daxton's cold-blooded bitch of a mother. In reality, it was just one more way for the government to assert control over the people.

"I was raised in a group home with thirty-nine other children," I said. "I thought it was a relatively normal life. I went to school. I played with the other kids. We dodged Shields, snuck into markets, and imagined what our lives would be like after we turned seventeen, when we would take the test and become adults. But there was one thing no one had ever told us—that the freedom we'd imagined, getting to make our own choices and deciding what our lives would be like...that was all an illusion.

"We were naive to believe it, but we never knew to question it until it was too late," I added. "We're all given ranks based on that single test. Compared to the rest of the population and put in our place. A low II, a high VI— it doesn't matter. Our lives are never in our own hands. Our rank dictates everything. Our jobs. Our homes. Our neighbors. Where we live, what we do all day, the amount of food and care we're allowed—it can even decide when we die. Some of you have been lucky enough to have easy jobs, ones that don't take an insurmountable toll on your body. But others aren't so lucky.

"I wasn't one of the lucky ones." I turned around and swept my hair aside, revealing the VII tattooed on the back of my neck and a scarred X running through it. I let the camera linger for several seconds before I turned around. "What you see now is a VII, but the ridges underneath will tell you my real rank—a III. I was assigned to clean sewers far away from my home and the only family I'd ever known. It's good, honest work," I added. "But it wasn't what I'd dreamed of doing. I was one more cog in a machine too big for any of us to fully comprehend, and because I couldn't stand the thought of leaving my loved ones, I chose to go underground and hide in a brothel instead."

At some point while I'd been speaking, Benjy had joined Knox on the side of the stage, his red hair fiery in the sunlight and the look on his freckled face relaxed and encouraging. I flashed him a small smile. He was the reason I'd risked my life and entire future to stay, but he was mine—he was private, and while anyone in Elsewhere could see the pair of us walking around together, working on target practice or tending to the recovering victims of the battle, I wasn't going to tell the world about him. He was the chink in my armor, and I wouldn't give anyone the opportunity to use him against me.

"If you'll bear with me, I promise this all has a point," I said as more and more people began to shift and glance at their neighbors. The revelation that I was really the Prime Minister's illegitimate daughter was only good for so much rapt attention, and I was rapidly burning through it. But the Blackcoats wanted me to tell my story. I wasn't the only victim of the Hart family, but I was the only one who the people already cared about, without even realizing who I truly was.

"At the brothel, Daxton Hart bought me. But instead of—well, you know—he offered me a VII." The highest rank in our country, one you had to be born into in order to receive. "I had no idea I was actually a Hart at the time, but even then, no one turns down a VII. No one. A VII meant luxury, enough to eat, and what I thought would be a good life—it was an easy choice, so of course I said yes." I leveled my stare at a painfully thin woman in a red jumpsuit. I didn't recognize her, but I needed to look at someone. "On the way out of the brothel, my best friend saw us together by chance. Daxton Hart had her murdered in the alleyway, and while I was screaming, he gave me something that made me black out. When I woke up, it was two weeks later, and I had been Masked—surgically transformed into an identical version of Lila Hart, whom her family had secretly assassinated days earlier."

More murmurs ran through the crowd, and the woman I was watching held my stare. I had their attention again. Good.

"I was given a choice. Pretend to be Lila, or die. It wasn't a real choice at all. It never is when you're staring down the barrel of a gun and waiting for someone to pull the trigger. And I thought that was what my life was going to be—a series of dodged bullets until one day, I wasn't lucky anymore.

"But when I agreed to impersonate Lila, it opened up an entirely new world to me. Not just the unparalleled luxury of the Hart family's day-to-day lives, but a real opportunity to change things through a revolutionary group called the Blackcoats. As soon as my education on becoming Lila began, Celia, Lila's mother, and Knox, Lila's fiancé, made sure my education on the Blackcoats did, too.

"They didn't have to tell me about the injustices our citizens face day in and day out. How Shields often kill and arrest innocent people in order to meet their quotas, or because they're having a bad day and have the power to take it out on us. I already knew that—I'd been dodging Shields since I was a kid. But Celia and Knox did tell me how IIs are given rotting food, houses with leaking roofs, and no respect or support from anyone above them. How most extra children born to IIs and IIIs are sent to Elsewhere, to be raised inside a prison, and never see the outside world. How our *entire lives* are dictated by a single aptitude test that only caters to one type of intelligence, and how children who are lucky enough to be born to Vs and

VIs get certain advantages. Tutors, inside information—in fact, every single one of the twelve Ministers of the Union received VIs, not on their own merits, but because of the family they were born into. They never took the test, and neither will their heirs.

"Before I became Lila, I believed the lies the government feeds us—that we're in charge of our own lives, that if we just do well enough on the test, they'll take care of us. They'll tell us where we belong, and that every single one of us has a place in society. I believed them when they told us we were all important and needed. I may have rejected the life they wanted for me, but I still *believed* them.

"The first lesson in my education came the day I was finally declared ready to impersonate Lila. Daxton Hart brought me to a wooded area for a hunting trip. But we weren't hunting deer or quail," I added. "We were in Elsewhere, and we were hunting humans."

I let this sink in for a moment, and the crowd stared at me with slack jaws and pale faces. During my few days as a prisoner, I'd quickly discovered none of the other citizens of Elsewhere knew why so many of their ranks were plucked without warning, never to be seen again. Now they knew. Now everyone knew how VIs and VIIs had hunted humans for sport, all because there was no one to stop them.

"All of the VIs and VIIs took part in these hunting trips, and as Lila, I was expected to shut up and go along with it. And I did, because while I hated watching innocent people die, I knew that blending in and doing what was expected of me then meant a chance to help others now.

"America is supposed to be a fair meritocracy. We're all supposed to receive what we deserve based on our skills and intelligence. But unlike the rest of us, there is a small section of the population that is born into a life of luxury that they never have to work a day in their lives to earn. The Hart family included.

"But being born into a life of privilege isn't the only way to get a VI or a VII. I received a VII after I was Masked, for instance. And I wasn't the only one." I gripped the edge of the podium so tightly that I felt a splinter wedge its way into my palm. "Over a year ago, another citizen was Masked as a Hart—a man named Victor Mercer. Except he wasn't Masked as a background figure like Lila, too many steps away from power to be anything more than a pawn. Victor Mercer was Masked as the one and only Daxton Hart—Prime Minister of the United States."

An audible gasp rose through the crowd, and they began to push forward in their eagerness to hear more, jostling for a better position. Victor Mercer had been a high-ranking official who ran Elsewhere with his brother for years, and no doubt many of the former prisoners remembered his particular brand of sadism. Several shouted at me, demanding proof, and I shook my head, my voice rising.

"I've felt the V on the back of his neck myself. But he's done a masterful job of destroying nearly all of the evidence that he was Masked. Some still exists, though. And when the time is right, the Blackcoats will release it and prove that the man who calls himself Daxton Hart—the man dictating our lives, the most powerful man in the country—is an impostor."

I had to shout the last few words into the microphone to be heard over the audience's roars of outrage. Out of the corner of my eye, I saw Knox give me an approving nod, though he still didn't smile. Either way, it was enough. At last we'd agreed on something—that telling the truth, the full truth, was what would eventually help lead the rebellion to victory.

"This country belongs to the people, not to the ruling class," I called above the noise. "We're the majority—we're the ones their policies and decisions affect, while they constantly hover above the law. They kill the lower ranks for sport. They live in luxury while IIs and IIIs starve. And *we* have the power to stop them. Yet not once, in the seventy years the Harts and the Ministers of the Union have been in power, have we risen together to face these injustices. But now we can. It's our *responsibility* to stand together against these monsters—against the impostors that rule our government. This is *our* country, and we need to take it back before the man who calls himself Daxton Hart destroys it completely."

At last a rousing cheer rose from the crowd, and I exhaled sharply. My hands shook, and my heart pounded, but I felt as if I were floating. I wasn't done yet, though, and the next portion wouldn't be so easy. I'd gone back and forth with Knox, arguing about it for days, but ultimately telling the truth meant telling the entire truth—and that meant calling out the real Lila Hart.

"Daxton will try to tell you that every word I say is a lie," I said. "He'll ask for proof. He'll call this a trick to gain sympathies. He'll insist I'm only acting as a puppet for the leaders of the Blackcoat Rebellion. But the real puppet here is Lila Hart. I've seen the speeches she's given since the Battle of Elsewhere. I've heard her cries for peace. And we—the Blackcoats—will do all we can to make sure no more blood is spilled in this war. But when peace means lying down and allowing the government to execute us, for standing up for our freedom and for those who can't stand up for themselves, I'm afraid we can't do that. Peace without freedom is imprisonment. It's oppression. They can try to scare us. They can try to threaten our families and our lives, but ultimately we won't *have* lives if we can't decide for ourselves how we live.

"I don't blame Lila," I added. "I know that, if she could, she would be here with me, giving this speech much more eloquently than I ever could. And I say to her, right now—" I looked directly into the camera. "You are not alone. Whatever Victor is holding against you, whatever he's doing to make you obey—we know those aren't your words, and we know they aren't your beliefs. And we will do everything we can to help you, the way we're doing everything we can to help the people. You are one of us, and we will not forget you."

I paused to allow that to sink in. While the citizens of Elsewhere couldn't have cared less about Lila, the rest of the country did, and they had to know she was a puppet. It wouldn't completely cut off Daxton's counterpoints, but maybe it would be enough to plant the kernel of doubt.

"This isn't about Lila, though," I said at last. "It isn't about me, and it isn't even about Victor Mercer posing as Daxton Hart. This is about *you*—every single person watching right now. This is about *your* future, *your* family, *your* health and happiness and hopes. All our lives, we've been living under a dictator masquerading as a friend, with no way to overthrow him and take back the freedom Americans enjoyed a hundred years ago. But the Blackcoats have opened the door of possibility. They've paved the way for real change, and it's up to us to take this opportunity and turn it into a reality. *Our* reality. Not a dream, but something we can *live*. The chance to choose our own paths in life. To be *more* than the numbers on the backs of our necks.

"The Blackcoats have crippled the military and seized control of their main arsenals. They have infiltrated the government, and they have worked tirelessly to give us back the inalienable rights that were stolen before any of us were born. But it's up to us to finish the job. We need to stand together against the Shields, the Harts, and the Ministers of the Union. We need to remind them that *we* are the ones in charge, not them—that this is *our* country, and after all they've done to us, our families, and our friends, we are revoking their privilege to rule. Because it *is* a privilege," I added fiercely. "*Not* a right. A privilege *we* gave them through our compliance. And the time has come to take back what is ours. Together, we *will* prevail, and we *will* be free."

The cheers from the former prisoners were deafening. I could see it in their faces—for these few moments, they forgot about their hunger and their despair. They believed in what I was saying. They believed in hope, and that alone had made everything I'd been through worth it.

Knox joined me on stage, but instead of saying anything to the audience, he set his hand on my shoulder and led me away. "Good," he said. "Lila couldn't have done it better."

High praise, considering she had managed to rally the initial support for the Blackcoats from nothing but mild discontent. "Do you think they'll listen?" I said.

He pressed his lips together as we descended the stairs

toward a waiting Benjy, the crowd's screams ringing in my ears. "They'd better. We can't do this alone."

And if we didn't have the support of the people outside Elsewhere, too, then we were already dead.

II

SUPPLY AND DEMAND

The highest-ranking Blackcoats gathered in the living room of the luxurious Mercer Manor, a mansion that had been built inside Elsewhere to house Jonathan and Hannah Mercer. It served as our headquarters now, and most of the rebel leaders were hulking and scarred soldiers who appeared extremely out of place beside crystal vases filled with fake flowers and paintings of pastel landscapes. They looked as uncomfortable sitting on the fancy gilded sofa as I felt standing underneath a portrait of Daxton Hart. The way a few of the soldiers were eyeing it, I had a feeling it wouldn't be there long.

While we waited for Knox to finish up in his office, Benjy joined me and laced his fingers through mine. After my speech, he'd gotten swept up in a discussion with a handful of officers, and we hadn't had the chance to talk until now. As the others spoke in low voices, I squeezed his hand. "That was terrifying."

He ducked toward me, his lips brushing my ear. "I can't believe Knox finally let you tell everyone about Daxton."

I bristled. "He didn't *let* me do anything. We planned it together, and I was the one in front of the cameras."

Benjy hesitated, and I half expected him to drop my hand. Instead, to my surprise, he kissed my cheek before he straightened. "I didn't mean it like that."

I forced myself to unclench my teeth. It had been a long, stressful morning, and the last thing I wanted was to take my anxiety out on him. "I know. I'm sorry."

"Don't be."

Benjy, more than anyone else in that room, understood why Knox and I fought constantly. As much as Knox had helped me since I'd been Masked as Lila, he had also played fast and loose with my life, at times seeming as if he didn't care at all whether I made it out of this alive. And while I loved to blame him for it, I hadn't exactly been as careful as I could have been about my safety, either. But when I took risks, I did so willingly, knowing full well what the consequences might be. When Knox took risks, his own neck was never on the line. It was always mine. And he usually didn't bother to tell me what he was doing.

More often than not, Benjy was caught in the middle somehow. Knox had had no problem faking his death, sending him to Elsewhere, and putting him at risk time and time again as well, and no matter how often he insisted he did it for Benjy's safety, I had stopped believing him the moment he first put Benjy in the line of fire by hiring him as his assistant. I was the pawn in this game, not Benjy. I was the III who had no place in the world beyond the rebellion. Benjy was a VI—the highest rank a citizen could attain— and he had a future. A real future. I wouldn't let anyone, especially not Knox, take that away from him.

But no matter how bitter I was about everything that had happened since I had become Lila Hart, the fact remained that I believed in Knox. I believed he was doing the right thing, and even if I didn't always agree with his methods—or, more accurately, with how he didn't seem to trust me with his plans, even when I was a key part of so many—I still knew he wouldn't sacrifice my life unless he had to. And if my death was the difference between winning the war and losing, I would walk the plank willingly. He knew I would do anything to destroy Daxton Hart and help the people win freedom and equality and real opportunity.

So he used me. And no matter how much I complained, I let him.

We were both too stubborn and too convinced we were each in the right. It worked well when we were on the same page, but when we weren't, we both used our strengths against each other. And that had yet to turn out well for either of us.

Benjy and I stood in silence, our fingers still intertwined, until at last Knox appeared. He looked even worse than he had earlier, with deep shadows under his eyes and his hair sticking up as if he'd run his fingers through it one too many times. He stepped in front of the fireplace, with Benjy and me on one side, and his lieutenant, a fierce man called Strand, on the other. I hadn't liked Strand since he'd first arrested me and Hannah the day the Blackcoats attacked Elsewhere, but Knox trusted him, so I grudgingly tolerated him for now. He had, after all, just been doing his job.

"Now that the country knows Daxton's real identity, we have to be prepared for a backlash," said Knox without pre-

amble. "It could go either way. We could gain support—
I'm sure we *will* gain support, after Kitty's speech. But the
government has supporters, too. Powerful supporters who
won't be so willing to lose their Vs or VIs and find themselves on equal ground with the IIs and IIIs. That's what
we're working against. The brightest and most privileged in
the country aren't interested in equality, and while they're
a small percentage, they have enough power and smarts
between them to come up with a countermove to anything we try."

"So we just have to be smarter than they are," said Benjy,
releasing my hand. "For every move we make, we'll have
to anticipate their countermoves and come up with our
own solutions before they realize what they're going to
do. We have to be three steps ahead of them at all times."

"We're already two steps behind," said Strand. "They've
choked off several of our main supply lines. The few we
have left are sporadic at best, and half the time it's too risky
to even attempt deliveries. We may have enough bullets to
storm D.C., but without food and medical supplies, there
won't be enough of us left to do it."

"The citizens of Elsewhere are days away from rioting,"
said a fierce-looking woman with a scar running down the
side of her face. I recognized her from the Blackcoat bunker in D.C. "If we don't find a way to feed them, we'll be
dead before the battle even begins."

She was right. There were thousands upon thousands
of former prisoners in Elsewhere who had chosen to stay
and fight for the Blackcoats. We had an army at our disposal, but it was an army that could turn on us at any moment if we didn't give them what we'd promised: a better

life than the Mercers and the Harts ever had. So far, we weren't delivering.

"Is there another way to get supplies here?" I said. Several pairs of eyes turned toward me, and I crossed my arms. I had no military experience and no gift for strategizing, not like Benjy did. But I was excellent at asking stupid questions.

"Such as?" said Strand, barely masking his impatience. He liked me about as much as I liked him.

"Isn't Elsewhere almost completely surrounded by lakes? Can't we come in from a direction they won't expect?" I said.

"That's an idea," said Benjy suddenly, and he met my eyes and flashed a smile. It was the same smile he had given me back in the group home every time I'd bothered to help him with my homework, and no amount of applause could warm me from the inside out the way that smile did. "We have a strong defense here, and we know that any strike they mount will come from the south, over land. But the lakes surrounding the rest of the state—we have enough ships under our control to bring in something. It won't be enough to give anyone a life of luxury, but we'll have the basics, at least."

"They'll be expecting it," said Strand. "That's why we haven't tried it."

"So we create a distraction. Set up another supply line—make ourselves look desperate. Divert their attention from the water." Benjy glanced at Knox. "What do we have to lose?"

"Lives, that's what," said Strand. "Human lives."

"People are going to start dying anyway if we don't do

something," I said. "We'll ask for volunteers. No one goes who isn't willing. But we're *all* prepared to die for this, or else we wouldn't be here right now. And I, for one, don't plan on dying of starvation."

All eyes turned to Knox. He stared down at the carpet, his arms crossed as he worried his lower lip between his teeth. He was only in his twenties, but in the few months I'd known him, he seemed to have aged a decade.

"If we do nothing, nothing changes," he said, his gaze not wavering from the ground. "We do what we have to do to feed our soldiers. Benjy, you're in charge of setting up the new supply line and the diversion. Strand, you assist." He called out several other names, assigning them to find volunteers for the mission, as well as to round up whatever supplies we had left. By the time he fell silent and the meeting ended, everyone had a job.

Except me.

Benjy turned toward me, his eyes alight with purpose. I hadn't seen him look so determined since before we'd been sent to Elsewhere, and with as much as Knox and I fought, I was relieved he wasn't taking his frustration with me out on Benjy. "Do you want to brainstorm with me and Strand?"

"If feeding everyone in Elsewhere depends on Strand and I working together, we're all going to starve," I said, only half joking. "I'll be around when you get back."

Benjy hesitated and glanced at Strand, who tapped his foot impatiently near the entrance to the kitchen. "You're sure?"

"I'm sure. Now go before he tries to shoot me or something."

Benjy gave me a quick kiss and hurried to join Strand,

leaving Knox and I alone in the living room. As much as I wanted to be useful, elbowing my way into Benjy's assignment wouldn't help anything. He would spend the entire brainstorming session trying to explain something to me or backing me up whenever Strand tried to tear me down, and now that we both had a chance at a future beyond whatever the Harts dictated to us, I refused to hold Benjy back. I'd done enough of that already.

"So." I turned to Knox. "What do you want me to do?"

Knox moved to one of the abandoned couches and sat down heavily, settling his head in his hands. He had been slowly breaking down over the past couple weeks, and as hard as that alone was to watch, it was even more difficult seeing him struggle to hold it together in front of everyone else. Why he was letting his guard down with me, I didn't know, but somewhere in the back of my mind, I figured it was some form of a compliment. Or maybe he just didn't care what I thought of him anymore.

"I want you to explain to me why you thought pardoning Lila in front of the entire nation was a good idea," he muttered.

I blinked. "Out of all the things I said, that's what you're upset about?"

"She's going to get countless numbers of my men and women killed."

"So will you. He's blackmailing her, Knox. She doesn't have a *choice*—"

"Of course she does." At last he looked at me, his eyes narrowed. The dark smudges underneath them seemed even more pronounced than usual. "We all have a choice, Kitty. Every last one of us, and she's made hers. She'd rather see everyone inside Elsewhere die instead of face whatever consequences Daxton has in store for her."

"And what if it's a choice between us or killing Celia? Or Greyson?" I said. "You can't tell me you'd refuse."

A muscle in his jaw twitched. "It wouldn't be easy, but—"

"Right. You're the one who isn't afraid to sacrifice a pawn or two if it means winning the game." I glared at him. "The people love her. You can't condemn her as a war criminal, no matter what she does. The best way to get around what she's saying is to do exactly what I did—acknowledge her. Acknowledge the fact that she's really on our side, but is being blackmailed. It discredits anything that comes out of her mouth."

"If they choose to believe us. They could easily turn the tables."

"Our story's believable," I said firmly. "Theirs isn't."

Silence lingered between us. He stared at me, and pinned by his unwavering gaze, I felt more exposed than I had in front of the camera that broadcast my face to millions. "Do you understand how perception works?" he said at last.

"I'm not an idiot," I said, though I regretted the words the moment they left my mouth. Predictably, Knox's eyebrow shot up, and he smirked humorlessly.

"Depends on who you ask, which is exactly my point. To us, the truth is obvious. Lila is being blackmailed. She doesn't believe a word of what she's saying. But to others, especially those who don't want a war—who are content with their place in society and refuse to acknowledge the cruelty committed against the lower ranks—they see what they want to see, and they'll eat up anything that affirms their beliefs. Daxton knows that. He may not be a VI, but he knows how to manipulate the public—something he learned from Augusta, possibly, or perhaps it's an innate talent that made her choose him in the first place. And while we know how, too, he got there first. It's harder to disprove a lie than it is to tell people the truth from the beginning."

"Then we stick to our story," I said. "We don't pander or tell the country what they want to hear. We tell them the truth, over and over if we have to. Daxton will slip up eventually, or Lila will find a way out. Whatever he's holding against her—"

"She'll still be responsible for the deaths of countless people."

"And so will you." I crossed my arms tightly. "We're all going to be responsible for whatever happens next, so we better make sure things go our way. Lila isn't the enemy. She's never been the enemy. And if that's how you decide to start treating her, then we will lose every inch of support from the people that we've gained since the battle, and we will eventually lose the entire rebellion. Sacrifice a pawn to win the war, remember?" I shot. "The pawn isn't always a person. Sometimes it's your damn pride."

Knox stared at me, his jaw clenched and his fingers digging into the arm of the couch. For a moment I thought he might lash out at me, but if he had any desire to do so, he managed to swallow it. Instead he said in a shaky but measured voice, "If you want to protect someone who's trying to get us all killed, then you better make sure she doesn't succeed. Whatever happens as a result of her words and actions—that's now on you, is that understood?"

"Just add it to the list," I said. "I didn't kill Victor when I could have—that's on me. I told the Blackcoats the truth about him being Masked—that's on me, too. Lila's just another drop in the bucket."

"Until millions of people are dead because you have no idea what you're doing," he said. "Must be a hell of a bucket."

"You know what would be great?" I snapped. "If you could stop treating me like a problem for five minutes. I'm not completely useless, you know. You never would've taken over Elsewhere if I hadn't helped."

"Debatable," he said coolly.

"Seriously doubtful. Either way, doing it your way has gotten us here—with the supply lines cut off, and with thousands of people on the verge of anarchy, ready to hang you by the neck and flay you alive because you can't feed them. And I just bought you a few extra days."

"What do you want, a medal?" he said. "If they come after me, they'll come after you, too."

"Probably. But now we have a little more time to make sure that doesn't happen, don't we?" I headed toward the archway. "If you could give those speeches yourself, you would. But we both know you can't, so that's why I'm here. To give a voice to the rebellion now that Victor controls your first pick. Like it or not, you need me, Knox, and the sooner you realize it, the easier this'll be for the both of us."

He was on his feet in an instant, and he crossed the room faster than I'd seen him move since the battle. Grabbing my arm, he stared down at me, his skin hot against mine. I couldn't remember the last time he'd willingly touched me, as if he were trying to deny that I really existed, and I told myself that was why I didn't immediately pull away from him. Because it was nice to be acknowledged.

"You want to be more than a pawn?" he said. "Then be useful. Start figuring out how to keep the promises you're making to the people. If you were still one of them, what would you want on the other side of this? What does this ideal world of yours really look like?"

I glared at him. "If you don't know how to give the people their freedom, then why are we doing this in the first place?"

"Because people like you do," he said. "I can win us this war, if you'll let me. That's my place in all of this. Yours could be so much more if you stopped fighting me all the time and started thinking of solutions."

"Then stop pretending I'm incompetent and give me that chance," I snapped.

"Stop acting incompetent, and I will."

Yanking my arm from his grip, I muttered a curse under my breath and stormed out of the room, making my way out the front door and into the frigid winter air. The days when Knox and I saw eye to eye were clearly over, and never in my life had I been more aware of how easy it was to believe in the same principles, yet not be on the same team. I wanted to be on Knox's team. I wanted to be on his team more than anything in the world right now, but he refused to let me.

Maybe Knox felt the same way about me. As I marched down the muddy main street of Elsewhere, past men and women dressed in orange and red jumpsuits, my gut twisted, rejecting the thought. I wasn't completely unjustified, and after all, despite his many good qualities, Knox had never been the understanding or forgiving type. But from where he stood, I knew damn well I'd been a problem. Although Lila had copped an attitude, she had always done what he and Celia had told her to do, nearly losing her life as a reward for her cooperation. I was the one always questioning him. I was the one refusing to do what he told me to, because I was sure I had a better way, and he wouldn't tell me why it wasn't acceptable.

And though I'd listened to him upon occasion, I usually did what I wanted to do, never mind what he thought. Time and time again, throughout the months we'd known one another, I'd gone against his wishes. Most of the time, things had turned out all right, though he'd often had to scramble to fix whatever problems I'd caused in the process. But that was what our relationship was like: I caused problems, and he fixed them.

I paused in front of a burned-out shell of a building that used to be a bunk, the ruins black and charred. In all fairness, the *problems* I'd caused had paved the way for the progress the Blackcoats had made so far. I may not have been terribly obedient, but Knox always found a way to make the best of it, opening doors and finding opportunities we wouldn't have had otherwise. Sending me to Elsewhere for my insubordination, as much as I still loathed him for it, had given him a reason to come here and spy for the rebellion without raising suspicion.

We were already a team, I realized. A messed-up, dysfunctional team, but a team nonetheless. And that, ultimately, was why I couldn't leave Elsewhere. If I joined Hannah in some cottage in the woods like Knox wanted me to, he would have no one to blame when things went to hell. And blaming someone instead of taking responsibility for his own weak plans—that was how Knox kept his ego functioning. And without the belief that he alone could make this revolution happen, I was sure he would have stepped aside and let someone else handle it a long time ago.

I shook my head. It was ridiculous, but if he wanted me to try to do more, then I would. I had no idea how to form a government, or how to make good on the promises I'd made the people, but I would do my best. That was all any of us could do anyway.

"Hey, you. Hart."

I began to turn, but someone shoved me from behind, and I stumbled into a pile of blackened wood. "It's Kitty Doe, actually," I said as I righted myself and brushed the charcoal off my trousers. I turned, facing the woman and three men who had me cornered. Perfect. I tightened my hands into fists, but that wouldn't do me much good against all of them.

"Doesn't matter what you call yourself. You're still as much of a Hart as the rest of them." One man, squat and with a ragged mustache, stood in the front, his lips pulled back to expose several gaps in his smile where his teeth must have fallen out. That wasn't uncommon here. No use in the government paying for trivial things like dental work when the citizens of Elsewhere would probably die soon anyway.

"I'm an Extra," I said. "I didn't know who my parents were until—"

"You think we care about that, either?" The man stepped closer, his dark eyes narrowing. "Doesn't matter who you were. Just matters who you are now. And you're a Hart."

A second man cracked his knuckles, and inwardly I groaned. This couldn't be happening.

"The Blackcoats are on your side," I said. "*I'm* on your side."

"Then why do you sit up there in the manor all pretty and comfortable while the rest of us wallow in the mud like pigs?"

"You're welcome to leave anytime you'd like," I said.

"Yeah, that's a great idea," said the woman. "Let's walk out into the wilderness in the dead of winter with nothing but the clothes on our backs."

I gritted my teeth. She had a point. It was hard enough walking away from the life you knew when you had the ease of doing so without risking your life. "I'm trying my best. We're all trying our best," I said.

"How about a little incentive?" said the first man, and he grabbed my hair and shoved me to my knees. I yelped, and a heavy boot connected with my stomach, forcing the air from my lungs.

"Let go of her immediately," demanded a deep, familiar voice, and the former prisoner hesitated.

"Make me."

I tightened my abdominal muscles, preparing myself for another blow, but it never came. Instead I heard the click of a gun, and my attacker went still.

"Fine," he growled, releasing me. "Worthless bitch."

I fell to my hands and knees, wheezing as my hair fell into my face, forming a curtain around me. If I'd had the breath to reply, I would have, but instead they all slunk away without another word, their boots crunching against the frozen ground. It was probably for the best. I didn't want anyone else to die because of me.

"You're never going to be one of them, you know." A gloved hand appeared in front of me, and I took it, letting my defender help me up.

"It's not my fault my biological father was a Hart," I muttered, wincing as I touched my ribs. Rivers, one of the former prisoners who had been lucky enough to be picked as a low-level guard, touched my chin and inspected my face. His blue eyes were the same shade as mine, and I stared back. I'd been beaten up enough in the past month that another set of bruised ribs wouldn't be the end of the world, but it was the way they were talking, the things they were saying—that was what made a hollow form in the pit of my stomach. Was this what they all believed?

"It's not your fault you're a product of Daxton Hart, but it is your fault you're up there instead of down here," he said, glancing nervously over his shoulder. "Come on, let's get you to the doctor before they come back with friends."

"I don't need a doctor," I muttered. "I need something to *do*."

"You mean getting yourself beaten to a pulp isn't enough?" said Rivers.

"I've been doing that for weeks. I want to help."

"You just did this morning." Instead of leading me back up the hill, he guided me into the maze of narrow alleyways behind the buildings, away from the main streets.

"That wasn't helping. That was just—talking."

"It did more to help than anything the Blackcoats have done since the battle," said Rivers, and I huffed.

"Where are we going?"

"You'll see."

Had it been almost anyone else, I would have turned right around and returned to the relative safety of the main road. But Rivers had protected me time and time again, and if he was going to kill me, he would have done it ages ago. Besides, though we'd never voiced it aloud, we both suspected the unique color of our eyes wasn't by chance. If Daxton Hart had fathered me with a prisoner in Elsewhere, then it was possible he'd had other affairs. If I couldn't trust my potential half brother, then I couldn't trust anyone, and I wasn't that far gone yet.

We passed a few lone citizens in the darker alleyways, and though they all stared, none bothered to approach us or offer help. It was clear Rivers was right. I wasn't one of them, and I never would be.

But I wasn't a Hart, either, and I was barely a member of the Blackcoats as it was. I didn't belong down here, but I also didn't belong in the manor. And that was far scarier than anything Daxton could throw at me—the realization that no matter what rank I'd earned or whose face I wore, I had no idea where I really belonged.

III

CRACK

We wound through the alleyways in the heart of Elsewhere until, at last, Rivers opened a door and gestured for me to enter. It led into a building I'd never been inside before, and the smell of stale chemicals burned my nostrils.

"Do I even want to know what this place is?" I said, scowling as Rivers led me into a dank storage room filled with what looked like old towels.

"Better if you don't. Then you might have a chance of sleeping tonight," he said as he tugged on a rusted metal shelf. With a loud creak of protest, it swung aside as if it were on a pair of hinges, revealing a door. "I found this when I was still doing a work order here as a prisoner. It's an entrance into a network of tunnels."

I blinked in surprise. I'd thought the tunnel under Mercer Manor—the same that had protected any number of citizens during the Battle of Elsewhere—had been the only one. A last resort for the Mercers, if the prisoners ever started an uprising the guards couldn't handle. Hannah had shown it to me when she'd discovered that her husband planned to kill me on sight, and she'd insisted it let out somewhere safe beyond his reach. It had never occurred to me that there could be others. Mercer Manor had been protected—no citizen could have accidentally stumbled upon the entrance to the tunnel in their cellar. But this was right here, staring me in the face, where anyone could've found it. Where Rivers *had* found it.

"How far does it go?" I said, stunned. Suddenly the ache in my side from where steel-toed boots had connected with my ribs didn't seem to hurt as badly.

Rivers scratched his head, his blond hair falling into his eyes. "Not sure. I know some of the tunnels lead into the other sections, at the very least. For all I know, it spreads throughout Elsewhere."

I took a hesitant step into the darkness, and Rivers produced a flashlight, illuminating the narrow passageway. The ground was hardened from countless footsteps, but clumps of dirt hung from the ceiling, giving me the sickening sensation that it could collapse at any moment. "Have you told Knox?"

"Yeah. Even gave Strand a tour. They didn't seem interested." Taking my elbow, Rivers led me inside, swinging the shelf and door into place behind us. The tunnel sloped steeply, descending far belowground.

"Why not? This could solve the supply lines issue, if one of the tunnels leads out of Elsewhere," I said. "Not even Knox is that shortsighted."

"Couldn't tell you. Asking questions isn't my job," said Rivers, giving me a significant look as we approached a fork.

I hesitated. "But you think it's mine?"

Rivers shrugged and headed down the left branch.

"Maybe they have a good reason for not using it, but like you said, it could solve all our supply line problems. What's going on between the two of you, anyway?"

"Who? Me and Strand?"

He snorted. "I know exactly what's going on between you and Strand. You both hate each other so much that it's a miracle the walls don't ice over when you two are in the same room."

I made a face. "Is it that obvious?"

"I've seen machine guns that are more subtle. I mean you and Knox, you goof. What's going on there?"

"Nothing," I said, maybe a little too quickly. Rivers raised an eyebrow, and I raised one right back. "I mean it. Nothing's going on there. He was my fake fiancé, and now he's the head of the Blackcoats and wants to send me off to join my mother in hiding instead of letting me fight, but he knows he'll lose support if he doesn't have a mouthpiece who can string a sentence together, so here we are."

"Yes, I know all of that, thank you. I mean what is it you two aren't telling the rest of us?"

I eyed him. "I have no idea what you're talking about."

I expected some kind of quip in return, but instead Rivers studied me. Even in the dim light, I could see the blue in his eyes. He must have been able to see it in mine, too. "You know he's crazy about you, right?" he said.

"If you mean I make him crazy, then yes, I know," I said carefully.

"That, too," he agreed with a grin. "But we both know what I'm talking about."

Except I didn't. All I could see when I looked at Knox was the way he viewed me as nothing more than an annoyance. Our so-called friendship had been going steadily downhill since Augusta's death, and now we could barely say a word to each other without bickering. That wasn't him being crazy about me. That was us driving each other insane.

"I'm with Benjy," I said resolutely. "I love him."

"Doesn't stop Knox from wanting you."

"Knox is better than that," I snapped, and as soon as I realized what I'd said, I clamped my mouth shut. It was too late, though, and Rivers grinned.

"Is he? Wouldn't have thought it from the way you talk about him."

I gritted my teeth. There was no winning with Rivers, not when he seemed to be so damn sure and I had no way of defending myself. I had no idea how Knox really felt, but it didn't matter. My loyalty to Benjy would never waver, and the insinuation that I would happily betray my best friend for someone who barely seemed to like me made me bristle.

"You think you're being funny, but you're not. This isn't some sideshow to entertain you. This is my life. Benjy has been there for me in a way no one else ever has. He's my family, and you don't just push family aside for some itch you want to scratch. That's not how real love works. Real love is support, even when you're fighting. Real love is honesty, even when the truth hurts like hell. Real love is being there through every miserable minute and every infinite moment. Real love is—it's sitting in that cage together with a gun pointed at your head, knowing all you have to do to save your life is kill him, and instead you hold each other because living without him isn't living at all."

I sucked in a deep breath and blinked hard, an unnamed part of me twisting sharply. "Knox would have killed me if it meant winning the war. I'm nothing more than a pawn to him. But Benjy would have died for me."

Rivers was quiet for several seconds, until at last he slipped an arm around my shoulders. "Maybe you're right. Maybe the things I see when you aren't looking are just my imagination. But for what it's worth, I don't think you're a pawn to him. You're even more than the most important piece on the board. To Knox, there is no game without you."

"Then he's going to be bitterly disappointed when it ends." Pain radiated down my side, and I winced. "I'm with Benjy. I love Benjy. Nothing will ever change that."

"I don't doubt it," said Rivers, and at least he had the decency to sound slightly abashed. "Just—don't forget that there's more than one kind of love."

I scowled, shrugging out of his embrace despite the ache it caused. "What the hell is that supposed to mean?"

"Whatever you need it to," he said, holding up his hands in surrender. "Come on—this fork will take us as close to Mercer Manor as we're going to get."

I took a deep breath, willing the snarling, angry monster in the pit of my stomach to retreat. Rivers wasn't in charge of my life. Just because he had an opinion didn't give him any power over me. Who I chose to love was entirely up to me, and I'd made my decision long ago.

As we wound through the tunnel, I tried to map it in my head. It wasn't unlike the way I'd memorized the sewer tunnels back in the Heights, where I'd grown up, and if I was right, the tunnel would let out in—

"Clothing storage," said Rivers as he pushed open a piece of the wall. It, too, swung on hinges, but unlike the entrance we'd used, this closet was filled with racks and racks of boots. Most were worn and falling to pieces, and even those in the best condition were too far gone for anyone still in society to wear. Even IIs.

It was yet another reminder that despite being liberated by the Blackcoats, the prisoners were still exactly where they'd been before. But now we may have found a way to fix it.

"I want to map the entire tunnel system," I blurted. "And I want you to help me."

"I'd be happy to," said Rivers grandly, as if he'd expected this all along. But unlike when Knox blatantly used me to further his own goals, I didn't really mind. At least Rivers had had the forethought to let me think it was my idea.

We stepped out into a dingy hallway inside what must have been the garments building, where the clothing for the prisoners was made and stored. It was one of the nicer buildings in Section X, no doubt thanks to its proximity to Mercer Manor. To my surprise, we passed a few former prisoners still working, and in the distance, I heard the faint whirring of sewing machines.

"Don't they know they don't have to do this anymore?" I said as we reached the exit.

"We can't all sit around and think all day. This needs to be a functioning community," said Rivers. "Don't worry— they're here because they want to be, not because anyone is pointing a gun at their heads."

"They're here to avoid having someone point a gun at

their heads," I pointed out. "There's no safe place for them outside Elsewhere."

"That'll change," said Rivers with such offhanded assuredness that, had he been able to bottle it, I would have given anything I owned for just a taste. "We'll start mapping out the tunnels tomorrow, once you've had a chance to rest."

"We'll start on it after dinner," I corrected. "Once I've had time to take some painkillers."

We argued all the way back to Mercer Manor, where Rivers reluctantly agreed to meet me that evening—but *only* to draw a guide to the tunnels he was already familiar with. It wasn't the exploration I'd had in mind, but at least we were doing something.

I refused to let the doctor examine me, instead choosing to lie down upstairs in the bedroom Benjy and I now shared. We'd spent three days trapped together in that room while the Battle of Elsewhere raged outside, but I didn't see it as a prison. Not anymore. Instead, it was a refuge from whatever storm Knox and the Blackcoats were brewing downstairs, the one place I could be me without having to worry about being silenced or ignored. Or mistaken for someone I wasn't—though now that the entire country knew who I was, with any luck, those instances would become few and far between.

I turned on the radio and listened to the soft music, trying to lose myself in it and forget the rest of the world for a little while. But as soon as I closed my eyes, someone knocked softly on the door.

"This better be good," I called, turning my face from

the pillow enough to watch the door. Benjy slipped inside and offered me a smile.

"Heard what happened," he said. "Rivers said you wouldn't see a doctor."

"I'm fine," I muttered. "Breathing hurts, that's all."

"Oh, that's all?" He rubbed his hands together, warming them up. "If you won't let them take a look at you, then at least let me check to see if anything's broken. You could puncture a lung and die, and then where would we be?"

"You'd be fine," I said. "Knox would be adrift. He just wouldn't realize it for a while."

He smiled, but it resembled a grimace far too closely for it to be genuine. "I'm sure Knox will be pleased to know you're so concerned about him, but I wouldn't be fine without you, either. Let me take a look."

I immediately regretted bringing Knox up at all, but there was nothing I could do about it now. Reluctantly I tugged up my shirt and let him take a look at the angry purple bruise already forming on my side. Benjy gently began to examine my ribs.

"You shouldn't go down there alone anymore," he said. I frowned.

"Why are we doing any of this if we're too scared to talk to them? They have a point, you know. We're up here, getting the best food and the best medical care—"

"We eat the same things they eat," he said. "And they have constant access to doctors and nurses."

"We still live in this house while they live in bunks," I said. "That kind of difference might not seem like much, but to them, we might as well be poking them in the eye with our superiority."

"We need space to meet and plan."

"We could use the dining hall for space," I countered. "This manor is where the Mercers lived for years. Staying here, while nothing's changed for the rest of them—it isn't doing us any good."

"What would you prefer we do? Let everyone crowd in here?" said Benjy. His fingers pressed against a particularly tender spot, and I hissed. "No matter what kind of equality we want, there will always be leaders, and those leaders will always have some kind of marginal privilege."

"Then what's the difference between us and the Harts?" I said. "What makes us any better?"

"We won't abuse our privileges. We won't take and take and take and give nothing in return." He pulled my shirt back down and gently draped a blanket over me. "We're doing everything we can to make them as comfortable and happy as possible. The bunks aren't bad at all. They have heat. We're giving them fresh mattresses and clothes. We can't do it all immediately, Kitty, not when we're barely keeping our heads above water. But the sacrifices they're making right now—if we win, they'll be worth it. They know that. It's just a little hard to remember right now."

"It's a little hard to remember a lot of things," I mumbled, and he sat down on the bed beside me, running his fingers through my hair.

"Like what?"

I gave him a look. "You're patronizing me."

"No, I'm serious," he said. "Talk to me, Kitty. Let me help."

There was nothing he could do, not really—but he'd always been a salve to the terrible circumstances of our lives before. Taking a deep breath, I finally said, "I think I've forgotten what I really look like."

His hand stilled. "I haven't."

"How? I've looked like this—like Lila—for months," I said. "How could you possibly still look at me and see Kitty Doe?"

Benjy shifted so we were face-to-face, and he touched the curve of my jaw. Lila's jaw. "It isn't about what you look like. It never has been. It's about what's underneath, and that hasn't changed."

He was trying to be kind—he *was* being kind, like always. But I could see the way he looked at me sometimes, especially when he thought I wasn't paying attention. I tried to imagine what it would be like if Benjy were Masked into someone else—Knox, or Greyson, or Strand—and part of me knew that no matter how hard I tried, I wouldn't be able to separate them completely. He would always be somewhat changed. Maybe Benjy was better at this than I would be—maybe he still saw the real me underneath. But I wasn't the same anymore. The past four months had changed me irrevocably, and sometimes I wondered if he knew that. Or if he wanted to pretend as badly as I did.

"Yeah, but—" I hesitated, not knowing how to put the knot of frustration in my throat into words. "It's not just that. I don't know where I belong anymore. I'm a Hart. I'm a former prisoner. I'm a Blackcoat. But I'm not really any of those things, either. And I'm not who I look like. I'm not anything except that speech. And even that wasn't good enough for Knox, not really."

Benjy's hand resumed running through my hair, and he toyed with the ends. "Forget Knox. He's under so much pressure right now that nothing is going to make him happy, so you might as well focus on making yourself happy instead."

I frowned. Happy had become such a foreign concept to me that I wasn't sure I remembered what it felt like. "I don't know how to do that anymore."

"Sure you do." He smiled, but it faded quickly. "This isn't forever, Kitty. And when we've won, there will be a place for you in our new world, and a place for everyone who doesn't feel like they belong."

I wanted to believe him, but there was no good place in the world for me after the war was over. I would never be me anymore. I would always be Lila's double. And while others—smarter than me, most likely—would know how to use that to give them the life they wanted, I didn't.

At the rate I was going, as lost and confused as I was, I would always be someone else's idea of who I should be. And I hated that thought nearly as much as I hated the man known as Daxton Hart.

The radio crackled, the music replaced by white noise. I muttered a curse and reached over to turn it off.

"Wait, keep it on," said Benjy, and I frowned. But before I could ask when he'd gained an appreciation for static, a voice began to speak—one as familiar to me as my own.

"My apologies for interrupting your evening," said Lila Hart, though she didn't sound very sorry at all. "This will be brief. Earlier today, a girl by the name of Kitty Doe, who was hired to impersonate me at public events for my own safety, made several claims against my uncle, Prime Minister Daxton Hart. I am here of my own free will to tell you all that every word out of her mouth is a profound, grievous, and traitorous lie. The man who is your Prime Minister is and always has been my biological uncle, and the United States government will take every measure not only to prove this, but also to show you how deep into the well of lies the entire Blackcoat rhetoric goes."

I stared at Benjy, my stomach constricting painfully. He shook his head in resignation. "We knew this was coming," he murmured. "There was never any question how they were going to counter."

"But—" My mouth went dry. No matter how stupid it was, part of me had thought offering Lila a lifeline would change something. But of course it hadn't. She was still under Daxton's thumb, and she would be until one of them was dead.

I almost couldn't bear to listen to the rest of it as, one by one, Lila recounted my claims and insisted they were false. No matter how many holes she alleged were in my full story, she returned to Daxton's true identity over and over again. But while I dug my nails so deep into my palms I was sure they'd start bleeding, Benjy smirked.

"Do you hear that?" he said, and I shook my head. "'The lady doth protest too much.'"

"I have no idea what that means," I said miserably. "Can we please turn it off?"

Benjy switched off the radio, and merciful silence filled the room. Or mostly silence, anyway—from somewhere in the manor, I could hear Lila's voice filtering up toward us, her words muffled. But that was infinitely better than having her blasted in my ear.

"It means there's a very thin line between rightfully protesting, and protesting so much that it becomes clear you're trying to hide something," said Benjy. "Anyone with half a brain can tell she took a flying leap over the line."

I was quiet for a moment. "Do you think she's doing it on purpose?"

"Maybe, if her speech isn't scripted," he said. "If it is, clearly someone's panicking, and that someone is probably Daxton."

So there was a chance Lila was fighting back after all. I forced myself into a sitting position, wincing as my ribs protested. "I need to talk to Knox."

"No, you need to rest," said Benjy, reaching for my shoulder. "You may not have any broken bones, but that doesn't mean you're not injured."

I shrugged off his hand. "Benjy, I love you, but Knox was furious that I pardoned Lila for her crimes, and he's going to use any excuse he can get to undo that. She just handed him one on a silver platter." I swung my feet around carefully and stood. Though walking back to the manor through the tunnels hadn't been difficult, now that my body had had time to rest and the adrenaline had worn off, every little wrong move sent aching pain through me. "He won't listen to me with the other Blackcoats backing him up, so I need to talk to him before he calls a meeting to figure out a rebuttal."

"I'll be there to support you," he pointed out.

"And a dozen other Blackcoats will be there to support him," I said.

Benjy didn't look convinced, but rather than fight me on it, he stood as well and offered me a hand. "At least let me help you down the steps."

I gave him a long, searching look, but at last I accepted.

Together we made our way through the hallway and down the staircase, his grip on me strong and steady, the sort that never made me question whether he'd catch me if I fell. I didn't know how I'd lucked out, having Benjy in my life, but it was one of the few things I wouldn't trade for anything.

I was positive he would try to weasel his way into my talk with Knox, but to my surprise, once we reached the foyer, he let me go. "I'll be helping with dinner. Shout if you need anything."

"Thanks," I said, watching him head into the kitchen. As soon as he disappeared, leaving me alone in the marble entranceway with an ornate H decorating the floor, I crossed to the office that had once belonged to Jonathan Mercer, Hannah's husband. Even now, two weeks after she had killed him, I still felt a shiver run through me every time I approached the white double doors.

I cracked them open, my mouth open and a greeting on the tip of my tongue. Before I could say anything, however, Knox's voice shot through the room like a whip. *"No."*

"I need—" I began, but the words died on my lips. Knox wasn't talking to me. Instead he paced in front of his desk, and on the monitor I saw a feed of Celia Hart. The real Lila's mother.

Knox shot me a vicious look over his shoulder, but rather than forcing me to leave, he gestured for me to come in, sparing us both that fight.

I slipped inside and closed the doors, sticking to a corner where Celia wouldn't be able to see me. On the monitor, she leaned forward until her face took up the entire screen. She was beautiful, with long dark hair and the Hart eyes, but there was a fierceness to her that no one in their right mind would challenge.

Except Knox.

"I don't care whether you approve or not, Creed. I am just as much a founder of the Blackcoats as you are, and the D.C. team is under my command. This is not up for discussion."

"If you raid Somerset, everything we've worked for will be destroyed. We will once again be the enemy—do you understand?" said Knox, his hands tightening into fists.

My jaw dropped. Somerset was the traditional home of the Hart family, nestled in the heart of D.C., far away from the slums I'd grown up in. I knew eventually the Blackcoats would have to seize control of it to cement their power, but we weren't ready for an invasion yet. The majority of the Blackcoat army was trapped in Elsewhere, slowly starving to death. Celia might have a few hundred people at her command, but Somerset was undoubtedly crawling with guards and Shields. It was suicide.

"I don't care about raiding the manor," said Celia. "I care about separating the impostor's head from his body."

"If you kill Daxton—"

"He isn't Daxton." Her voice rang out through the speakers, as clear as if she were standing right next to Knox. "How long have you known, Creed?"

Knox stiffened. "Lila told me late in the summer. She found out when Daxton tried to assault her."

For a long moment, silence filled the office, and my heart pounded. "You've known for nearly six months, and you never said a word to me?" said Celia at last, her voice dangerously soft. "He tried to kill my daughter. He tried to kill me. All this time, all I had to do was tell the public who he really was—"

"And what good would that have done?" said Knox. "At best, Daxton—"

"Stop calling him Daxton."

Knox took a deep breath and released it. "At best, Victor Mercer would have done exactly what he's doing now—deny it and use your family to discredit the claim. Augusta would have backed him up, and you would have come out of it looking like a lunatic."

"I could have leaked it to the press without my name attached."

"No newspaper in the country would have printed it. They're completely under the government's control. At best, Victor would have forced the most trustworthy and liked members of the Hart family into backing his claims. At worst, we would have been at war before we were ready. Victor would have pulled no stops to protect his secret, and the Blackcoats would be nothing more than a footnote in the history books, if that. I knew if I told you the truth before we were ready, everything we worked for would be ruined. And that is why I kept it from you."

Celia stared at him, her blue eyes wide and full of shock—or shame, maybe. Or sadness. Anger. Betrayal. All of it combined into something I couldn't name. When she spoke, her voice trembled, as if it took every ounce of willpower she possessed to stop herself from bursting into flames. "How dare you."

"How dare *you* try to destroy everything we've worked for," said Knox. "You're blinded by anger and revenge. You've lost sight of the objective. This isn't about vengeance or payback for what Victor's done to you. This is about the country and its half a *billion* people counting on us succeeding. If you kill Victor now, you'll only turn him into a martyr, and no one will ever know who he really was. No one will *care*, because to them, he *is* Daxton Hart. Is that what you want? For that monster to go down in history as your brother?"

"Stick a gun in your mouth and pull the trigger," snarled Celia, and a moment later, the screen went black.

IV

BURN

Knox stood in the middle of the office, his shoulders slumped and his head down, taking one deep breath after another. I couldn't tell if it was because he was trying not to lash out or break down or both.

"That—" I began. Knox snapped around to look at me, his dark eyes already accusing. I dropped my folded arms and let them hang loosely at my side. As often as we bickered and fought, we were still on the same side. "That was pretty badass of you, you know. Standing up to her like that."

"It doesn't matter." His voice was tight and his words were clipped, and he lumbered over to the couch and dropped down gracelessly. "She's going to raid Somerset and try to kill Daxton anyway."

"Can't really blame her," I said slowly, not wanting to upset him more than he already was. "Lila's the only family she has left. Maybe she'll get her out of there and spare Daxton."

Knox shook his head, his fingers tangling in his hair. "If she has a shot, she'll take it. She isn't thinking rationally."

"Maybe he won't be there."

"We can play the maybe game all day, Kitty. In the end, we won't know until it's over."

I was quiet for a moment, my gaze drifting over to the black screen. There had to be something we could do. "Have you tried contacting Sampson? He could put a stop to this."

"She'll anticipate that. Sampson knows he ought to stop her anyway. He's the one who helped me come up with this playbook. If he has any say at all, he's already trying."

"Then maybe he'll succeed."

Knox sighed wearily. "Maybe. What do you want, Kitty?"

"I—" A pang of pity needled my side as I took in the circles under his eyes and the lines in his face that seemed to grow deeper every day. Now wasn't exactly the time, but there would never be a good time for this. "Did you hear Lila's speech?"

"Yes. I take it you did, too."

I nodded. "Most of it. You know she's saying those things under duress."

"It doesn't matter. She's still saying them."

"But—Benjy noticed something." I took a step closer to the sofa. He watched me, his dark gaze unwavering. "She's shoving it down our throats, that Daxton isn't Victor. She said it at least a dozen times. Benjy said she's pushing too hard—that any idiot with half a brain can tell she's protesting too much."

"Only those who are willing to hear it," he said. "Perception, remember?"

I frowned. "Still. Don't take this out on her."

"You've already pardoned her," he said. "I'm not going to undermine you, not when the public needs to trust you. But you will do and say exactly what I tell you to from now on, understood?"

Relief flooded through me, and I shrugged. "I could say yes right now, but we both know that would be a lie. But I do promise to talk to you about what I want to say ahead of time, if it comes to me. If something's impromptu—"

"Try to do as little of that as possible," said Knox.

"I'll do my best." I glanced at the door. "Dinner's almost ready. Are we calling a meeting?"

Knox sighed and straightened, his hair sticking up. "Nothing we can do here to stop it. Whatever happens is going to happen, whether the rest of the Blackcoats are worrying about it or not. And the last thing we need is half of them agreeing with Celia while the other half agrees with me."

"So...that's a no?"

"That's a no," he confirmed, and I furrowed my brow. I couldn't remember any issue within the past two weeks that the Blackcoats hadn't discussed and dissected ad nauseam. The idea of Knox hiding something this big from them was practically unfathomable.

"If Celia and the D.C. Blackcoats go through with it, you're going to upset everyone here when they find out you knew ahead of time."

"I have no intention of letting them find out," said Knox, and he leveled his gaze at me. "Can I trust you?"

It was the first time in weeks that he had even asked, let alone offered me the chance to prove it, and I nodded. "I'll grab some dinner for us."

"For us?" he said.

"I'm staying in here until we know what happened," I said. Knox started to protest, but I cut him off. "Don't pretend you're not going to sit in this room all night, scouring the news for any sign of the raid. I'm watching with you."

He rubbed his face with his hands. "It won't change what happens. If Somerset falls, there's nothing we can do but watch it burn. And if it does—"

"We're screwed. I know." I opened the door. "Chicken or tuna?"

"Chicken," he said, and as I stepped out of the room, he added, "Kitty?"

"Yeah?"

"Thank you."

There was a note of warmth in his voice that hadn't been there before, and I offered him a small, but genuine smile. "You're welcome."

In the kitchen, Benjy helped two other Blackcoats prepare enough plates to feed everyone staying in the manor, and before I stepped into his view, I watched him chat with the woman with the scar running down her face. He smiled broadly, his eager voice filtering over the clatter of dishes, and for a moment I let myself be carried back to the countless evenings we'd spent in the kitchen of our group home, helping Nina with dinner or washing up after. The cold marble of Mercer Manor fell away, replaced with wood and brick and heat from the fireplace. I would have given anything to go back there, even for just a day, and have Benjy look at me like I was me again. Maybe I was imagining it, but now that I saw him like this—with someone else, when he didn't know I was watching—it was clear that there was something missing from the way he talked when we were around each other. An easiness to our banter, jokes that made us both laugh, the way we used to tease each other without wondering if it was the last conversation we would ever have—even though I couldn't name it, I knew it wasn't there anymore. Maybe he was the one who felt he couldn't wholly be himself now that I wasn't completely me.

After I'd been Masked, we hadn't had much time at Somerset to be together, and any time we did have was spent worrying that someone would catch us. In Elsewhere, before the battle, we'd been separated—and, for several days, I'd thought he was dead. That all-encompassing grief had turned into unbridled joy and relief when Knox had revealed Benjy was, in fact, alive—and the weeks we'd spent together since had been comfortable and more like a taste of home than I'd thought I would ever have again. But maybe that was an illusion. Because we weren't home; we would never go home again. Benjy was the closest thing I would ever have to home again, but as I watched him turn to ladle gravy onto a plate, I couldn't help but wonder if I was, yet again, holding him back.

He caught my eye, and something in his expression changed. Once upon a time, seeing me would have sparked joy, and to some extent, it still did. But it was tainted with something else now, and I couldn't blame him for it. As much as I knew he loved me, I was also tied to the worst memories of his life, and I didn't know how many more he could stand before he cracked. I'd lost count of the number of times he'd nearly died because of me, and each one was another lifetime of guilt looming over me, knowing I'd never be able to make any of this up to him. We'd been here before, with me holding him back—when I'd achieved only a III on my test, and he was bound to get a VI. I would never be good enough for him, and the more I tried to hold on to him, the harder his life would be. The more his smile would fade every time he looked at me.

"Kitty—are you hungry?" He quickly finished preparing the current plate before grabbing another. "Chicken, right?"

"Two. One for Knox, too," I said, moving forward to help him. The portions were meager at best, but they were exactly what the former prisoners ate, too, and after today, I had no complaints. "How did everything go with Strand?"

"We've brainstormed a few ideas that we can implement starting almost immediately. It won't be easy, but nothing worth doing ever is, right?" He grinned. "Rivers told me about the tunnels. If they really do extend as far as he thinks they do, that will make our jobs infinitely easier."

"Yeah, well, let's hope he's right," I said. It was hard to say when he'd never tried to explore them, but then again, with the guards keeping such a close eye on the prisoners, I wasn't sure how he ever could have slipped away long enough to do so.

"He said you're going to start mapping it tonight—do you mind if I join you?" added Benjy, and I blinked. With the news of Celia's plan to attack Somerset, I'd completely forgotten.

"Actually, do you mind taking my place? I—" I hesitated. "I'm going to spend the evening with Knox."

Internally I winced, knowing how it must have sounded to Benjy, and sure enough, his hand stilled in the middle of placing a piece of chicken on a plate. "Oh. I thought we could spend some time together tonight."

Guilt twisted in the pit of my stomach. I couldn't tell Benjy the truth about why I wanted to stay with Knox, not without revealing Celia's call, but I owed him some kind of explanation. "I need to talk to him about everything going on with Lila," I said as steadily as I could. "If we don't come up with a counterattack soon, we'll lose any ground we gained this morning."

Benjy eyed me, and I could sense his uncertainty. I gave him a questioning look.

"What?"

"Nothing," he said, and he finished preparing our plates. "If you finish early, come find me."

"I will," I promised, and taking the plates, I forced a smile before heading back to the office, feeling worse with each step I took. I hated keeping secrets from him, but the more time I spent as Lila, the more of a habit it became.

As I walked away, able to feel his gaze burning into the back of my skull, I made myself a promise, too. After this war was over, there would be no more secrets between me and Benjy. Even if it meant telling the whole ugly truth, at least we would be honest with one another.

Knox and I settled in on the sofa, him sitting rigidly while I propped my feet up on a footstool. Every screen in his office displayed a different news channel, and together we watched as the anchors droned on and on about acts of terrorism that hadn't happened and shortages that didn't exist. Whatever Daxton's game was, it involved feeding the public lie after lie about our campaign. With communication between cities nearly nonexistent, few had any way of disproving the news channels' claims. Or any reason not to believe them.

"How can you stand watching this?" I said as I ate the last bite of hard biscuit. "It's all lies. Everything they say is just a bunch of propaganda for Daxton and the Ministers."

"I remind myself that out of all the crimes the government commits, lying to the public is pretty low on the list. Every government does it, no matter how good their intentions are or how much they care about their people." He glanced at me. "We're doing it right now, to our little part of the world."

I scowled. "That's not what I—"

"I know what you meant, Kitty. And I gave you my answer." He leaned back, his posture still stiff. "Once you accept that everything that comes out of a news anchor's mouth is propaganda, it gets easier to read between the lines. And that's what I'm listening for. The things they aren't telling us."

I fell silent for several minutes, listening to a man drone on about how the Hart family was holding together during this difficult time, in the midst of such terrible and hurtful accusations from someone they had treated like family. It was easy to sniff out the real story when I already knew it, and I waited for another to come on.

"How did you get started with the Blackcoats, anyway?" I said. "I know you knew Celia through Lila, but—what, did the three of you have dinner one day and decide to start a revolution? How did that happen?"

"Something like that," he muttered. "Celia's never been particularly subtle about her political ideology. I sought her out, and the rest fell into place."

"Wait—was your relationship with Lila an arrangement, then?" I said as a piece of the puzzle clicked into place. It made sense—Lila and Knox had never seemed to get along. "Was it a way to spend time together without being discovered?"

"Yes," said Knox, his tone growing shorter. "If it's all the same to you, I'm not in the mood for conversation right now."

It wasn't all the same to me. I still had a million questions to ask, ones I'd gathered every minute of every day we'd been forced to play pretend. But tensions were high enough right now, and I didn't want to give him any reason to try to kick me out.

So for the rest of the night, as the hours dragged by, I kept quiet. Sometimes Knox would make a comment about a story, and I would chime in with a response, but he never elaborated further than that. Those occasional remarks grew less and less frequent as midnight came and went, and sometime around one in the morning, I said hopefully, "Maybe Sampson talked her out of it."

Knox's jaw tightened. I set my hand over his clenched fist, and only then did he relax marginally. "If we haven't heard anything by dawn, I'll believe it."

Sometime around two, I fell asleep. I didn't mean to—I'd promised I'd stay up with Knox, and I wanted to. But my ribs ached, the couch was warm, and the lull of voices was too much to resist. I rested my head against the armrest, promising myself I'd only close my eyes. Within seconds, I was fast asleep.

The sound of sirens jolted me awake, and I sat up, my head spinning. "What—?"

Beside me, Knox's expression was impassive, but his fingers were digging into his thighs. The sirens weren't coming from Elsewhere. They were coming from the televisions.

Every news network had a different view of the same scene: an image of the front gate of Somerset. Lights from emergency vehicles flashed across the brick wall, and a camera zoomed in on a team of Shields climbing over onto the property.

My heart sank. "They raided Somerset after all. Is Daxton…?"

"I don't know," said Knox. "If Celia had the chance, she took it. I guarantee you."

Wide-awake now, I leaned forward and watched the images unfolding on the screens. It was the middle of the night in D.C., too, but light flooded Somerset like it was midday. Gunshots sounded in the distance, and I briefly closed my eyes, trying not to imagine where those bullets might wind up. I may not have known the other Blackcoats well, but we were still on the same side.

Someone knocked on the door, and I jumped. Strand poked his head inside, first glancing at Knox and me, then the televisions. "You're watching this?"

Knox nodded. "Call a meeting for dawn. However this turns out, we should know by then."

Thirty seconds after Strand left, one of the feeds cut to a reporter whose face was mostly obscured by a thick scarf. She didn't seem to care, however, as she excitedly rambled into the microphone. "We are receiving reports now that Prime Minister Daxton Hart's body has been spotted near the front of the Hart family home. Do we have visu—"

Suddenly an image of Somerset appeared. Normally it was a beautiful sight, and no matter how many times I'd been down the drive heading toward it, I'd always been captivated by the high windows into the atrium, the opulent balconies, the shining white exterior that reflected a shimmer of rainbow in the sunlight. But this time, I had to swallow a gag.

Daxton's body hung from the front door, held up by a chain wrapped around his neck. A hunting knife was buried to the hilt above his heart, and a big red X glistened across his chest. I doubted it was paint.

"Oh my God," I whispered, clasping my hand over my mouth. Beside me, Knox remained silent, but out of the corner of my eye, I watched his expression go from painfully neutral to barely suppressed rage.

"That's it," he said tightly. "It's over. We've lost the war."

V

THE AMERICAN DREAM

The camera lingered on Daxton's body for far longer than anyone decent ever would have looked. I turned away after I inspected the portion of his face I could see for any sign it wasn't him, but every detail matched. Even his dark eyes, which stared blankly out into the night.

Knox buried his face in his hands and didn't move for nearly an hour. I didn't know what to say to him—there was nothing *to* say, nothing that would make any of this any better. I couldn't apologize for revealing Daxton's real identity that morning, but that was the root of it. It was my fault Celia had done this, and it was my fault Daxton was dead. I didn't mourn him, but I did mourn our chances at a fair fight. Already the news networks were showing highlights from the late Prime Minister's life—mostly from before Victor Mercer had been Masked, which was almost amusing, considering the real Daxton Hart had died over a year ago. Better late than never, I supposed.

None of them even hinted toward the atrocities Daxton had committed in his lifetime. There wasn't a single word about the facts I'd laid bare in my speech. Just as Knox had predicted, Daxton was celebrated as a hero and a martyr who had died protecting his family and his country from a violent fringe group bent on terrorizing honest and decent American citizens. Any ground we might have gained that morning had disappeared beneath our feet, and already we'd begun to fall.

"We need to tell the others," said Knox roughly, once he finally came up for air. It was nearly dawn by now, and through the window I could see a pink stain on the edge of the horizon. "We need to prepare them for—"

He stopped, but he didn't need to finish. They needed to prepare to either spend the rest of their lives on the run as traitors, or they needed to prepare to be executed. *We* needed to prepare.

Benjy. Knox. Me. We weren't just enemies of the state anymore—we were enemies of the entire country. And no speech could change that now.

I stood. "I need to find Benjy." We needed to figure out what we were going to do, and fast. Benjy would be able to hide in plain sight, but everyone in the country knew my face. I would have to spend the rest of my life underground.

I was halfway to the door when the networks all crackled at once—the same sound I'd heard on the radio the night before. But this time it wasn't Lila's voice on the other end.

"I see you have once again tried to murder me, and once again, you have failed."

I whirled around, my heart in my throat. Seated behind a desk in a room I didn't recognize was Daxton Hart. "What—?"

Knox leaped to his feet and hushed me, his eyes glued to the screen.

"A knife to the heart and a chain around the neck. Not terribly symbolic, dear sister, but I suppose it gets the job done." Daxton leered at the camera, a hint of amusement dancing in his eyes. Like this was a game to him, and he'd just outsmarted us. "Only problem is, it wasn't me."

At this, he seemed to sober up. He folded his hands and furrowed his brow in his best impression of someone deeply troubled, but I knew him well enough to see the grin desperate to emerge.

"You and your band of terrorists didn't kill me, Celia. You killed a father of two who bravely volunteered to serve as my double at Somerset while I took refuge in a safe place far from your guns and threats." He stared into the camera, and the glint in his eyes never faded. "My son, Greyson, and my dear niece, Lila, are both safe with me, and they will remain so for the duration of this fight. And I promise you, citizens of the United States, I will stop at nothing to see these so-called Blackcoats brought to justice. The entire weight of the United States Army is coming for you, and the people will not protect a bunch of murderous traitors. And I promise you, sister, by the end of this—" He leaned in close enough for me to see a popped vein in his eye. "You will be the one in chains."

The broadcast cut out, and the stunned reporters and anchors all scrambled for something to say. Rather than listen, however, Knox turned the screens off, and silence permeated the room for several long seconds before he let out a victorious holler.

"That *idiot*. That egomaniacal *fool*." Knox whooped and hit the desk so hard that a paperweight toppled to the floor. "He'd won the war. He had it wrapped in a bow and delivered straight to his doorstep. All he had to do was keep quiet and let his generals do his dirty work, and he would have *had* us."

"And now he doesn't?" I said, confused. Knox turned to me, grinning for the first time since—I couldn't remember ever seeing him grin like that, actually.

"Because he couldn't stand giving Celia even the impression of a victory." Knox punched his fist into the air. "Now the whole country knows doubles of Daxton exist. First they'll question whether he's really who he claims to be—if he isn't a double himself, and the real Daxton's dangling by his neck on that door."

"He's the real Daxton. Or Victor, I guess," I said quietly. No one could fake that sadistic stare.

"I know," said Knox. "But they don't. They'll question it, and before long, that conversation will lead to them wondering if you were telling the truth after all. He just blew his entire defense. The sympathy, the martyrdom, his legacy—all because of his stupid pride and need to make sure everyone knows he's still in control." He shook his head, still beaming. "We have a chance, Kitty. We actually have a chance."

"We have more than a chance," I said firmly. "We're going to win this."

Knox and I walked into the noisy living room side by side, and instantly everyone fell silent. Several members of the Blackcoats paced, their expressions twisted with anger, while others slumped over with disappointment. No one, not even Benjy, looked happy.

"Why are you smiling?" demanded Strand as we headed to the front of the room. Knox stopped underneath the portrait of Daxton, and I stood beside him, for once not feeling like a burden or a nuisance. I hadn't done anything, but even if I had, Knox was too happy to care.

"Because we just went from losing this war to having a real chance at winning it," said Knox. As he launched into an explanation, Benjy joined me, his brow furrowed.

"Where have you been?" he whispered, taking my hand in his.

"I was watching the news with Knox," I whispered in return.

"All night?"

I nodded and gave him a strange look. "What else would I be doing with him?"

Benjy opened his mouth to say something, but wisely shut it. His grip on my hand tightened, however, and he didn't let go.

"Though Celia's plan backfired, it's also offered us an unparalleled opportunity to gain the country's support," said Knox to the other Blackcoats. "We must seize this chance and prove our allegations are true."

"How? By tying Daxton down and forcing him to admit it?" said Strand. But before Knox could answer, I knew exactly what he was going to say.

"The file."

Everyone in the room looked at me. I cleared my throat. It wasn't the first time I'd blurted out something ridiculous, but this time, I was absolutely sure I was right.

"There's a file full of evidence that Daxton is really Victor Mercer," I said. "I stole it a few weeks ago. It's part of the reason Daxton had me arrested and thrown into Elsewhere. I hid it," I added. "In Somerset."

"We'll send word to the D.C. team at once," said Strand. "We can have it in our possession in minutes and out to the public by noon."

Knox shook his head. "I'm not trusting anyone else with something this important. There could be spies among us, and this folder is the only chance we have to prove Daxton is Victor Mercer."

The rest of the room grumbled their discontent, but I understood Knox perfectly. We both knew the real reason for his hesitation was Celia. After the stunt she'd pulled the night before, I didn't blame him for not trusting her. He couldn't very well throw Celia's loyalty and rationality into question in front of her army, however, not when she was the one running the rebellion outside Elsewhere.

"So what are we supposed to do, then? Go get it ourselves?" said Strand.

"Yes," said Knox. "I'm going to assemble a team of volunteers willing to sneak into Somerset and steal the file back without ever alerting the other Blackcoats to our presence."

"We're not at war with ourselves," said Benjy. "Given the importance of this file, we could use all the help we can get."

"This is a need-to-know mission only," said Knox. "It does not leave this room, is that understood?"

The others nodded, though several cast wary looks at Knox. I squeezed Benjy's hand.

"I'm going with you," I said. Knox scowled, but I cut him off before he could protest. "I'm the only one who knows where the file is, and even if I tell you how to get there, it's possible you won't be able to reach it. Besides, I'm the one who hid it. I should be the one to recover it."

A deep line formed in his forehead. "If something happens to you, our campaign will never recover."

"Then I guess you'll have to make sure it doesn't," I said. "I know exactly where to find it. We'll be in and out, no problem."

"Don't jinx it," muttered Knox, but he nodded stiffly. Beside me, Benjy shifted.

"Kitty—"

"I'm the only one who can get to it," I said quietly, looking up at him. "It'll be fine."

He stared at me, doubt clear in his gaze, but there was no talking me out of this. I didn't just owe it to Knox and myself—I owed it to the entire country to do this. I was the reason Daxton wasn't dead in the first place, and countless people would suffer—had already suffered, and would continue to suffer—because of it. This was mine to make right; no one else's.

"We'll only have a short time frame before the Shields launch a counterattack," said Knox. "But if we can get in before sunset, we should be fine."

"And how do you propose we do that?" said Strand. Knox and I glanced at one another.

"I'm afraid that's classified," said Knox. "I'll need half a dozen volunteers. We'll take a jet out in exactly one hour."

What he needed half a dozen other people for, I couldn't fathom, but I didn't question it, either. It would only take two of us to get into Somerset—hell, I could do it on my own, but I knew Knox wouldn't let me go in without him. The more people who came with us, the worse our chances of going undetected were, and ultimately they would only get in our way.

When the meeting disbanded shortly after, I headed upstairs with Benjy at my heels. Neither of us said a word until we reached our bedroom, and he closed the door firmly behind him. "Kitty, you don't have to do this."

"Yes, I do," I said, searching for a clean set of clothes. "I know why you don't want me to go—"

"Do you? Because it doesn't seem like you do." He raked his fingers through his short red hair, exasperated. "How many times have we almost lost each other?"

"Benjy…" I paused long enough to study him. His face was stricken, and I softened my tone. "Too many. We've nearly lost each other too many times, and if this war keeps going on like this, eventually we will."

"If you keep taking risks like this—"

"Sometimes the risk is worth it. And some things—some things are more important."

"More important than what? Protecting the people you love?"

"Isn't that exactly what we're doing by fighting this rebellion in the first place?" I dug out a pair of black pants and a black top. Perfect for sneaking around. "I need to take a shower. I'll be home by dinnertime."

"Kitty—"

"We'll talk about this then, okay?" I said, but he grabbed the bathroom door before I could open it.

"No, we're talking about this now, because there might not be a *then*."

I let my hand fall from the knob and stared up at him defiantly. "You're not talking me out of this."

"Then we have a problem, because I don't know how many more times I can do this."

My mouth went dry. "You don't have to do this, Benjy. It would be safer for you if you weren't here anyway."

"Do you really think being away from you would help? I'd still worry constantly—"

"I don't want you to worry," I said, exasperated. "You should be focusing on your own life, not mine. And it feels like the deeper we go into this war, the more I distract you."

"You're *part* of my life, Kitty. The most important part." He reached out to touch me, but I shifted back, and he dropped his hand. "Yes, I worry about you. I worry about what this is doing to you—being Lila, fighting for people you didn't even know four months ago. I can tell it's slowly chipping away at you, one day at a time, and I hate myself for not being able to protect you from all of this."

"It isn't your job to protect me."

"But you'll let Knox try."

The ground felt as if it had dropped out from under me, and I opened and shut my mouth in shock. "Is that it, then? Is that what all of this is about? You're mad I stayed with Knox last night?"

"Well, I'm not exactly happy about it," he said, with more sarcasm than I'd thought he had in him. "You're hurt. I wanted to be there for you—to give you a relaxing night where you could rest. Instead, you spent it with him. And sometimes—" He stopped.

"Sometimes what?" I pressed, an edge in my voice. "Whatever it is, let it out, Benjy. Because there might not be a *then*, remember?"

The moment I said it, guilt washed over me. He'd done nothing to deserve this fight, and I was being a complete jerk about something I knew was quickly becoming a problem for us. Rivers pointing out Knox's supposed feelings had been bad enough; Benjy bringing it up made me want to claw the walls with frustration and anger. And if he really thought I would ever do anything with Knox when he was waiting for me just a room or two away, then he didn't know me at all.

Or maybe he knew me better than I knew myself. At this point, it wouldn't exactly have been difficult.

I pushed the traitorous thought aside. I knew myself well enough to know I wasn't torn between them. I'd chosen Benjy long ago, and I would continue to choose him for as long as he let me.

"Sometimes I feel like a third wheel in my own relationship," he said at last. "Sometimes I feel like we're both holding on to each other because we're familiar, and because we're used to it, and because it's something we had from before all of this that makes us both happy."

He was saying everything I'd worried about since that stupid conversation with Rivers, and my stomach twisted into knots. "That's not a bad thing. Something familiar—something that feels like home—"

"It is when it's holding you back." He leaned toward me, his stare unwavering, and even though all I wanted was to duck into the bathroom and drown out the rest of the world, I couldn't look away. He pinned me there with his eyes alone, looking at me in a way he hadn't in months. As if he could see beneath the layers of my body to parts of me I didn't even know existed. "Sometimes I feel like I lost you a long time ago, and no matter how hard we try, we're never going to find each other again."

"What the hell are you talking about?" My voice cracked, and to my horror, my face began to burn. "I'm right here. I've *been* right here. I'm sorry things are hard right now. I'm sorry I spent the night with Knox instead of you. But I am *right here*, Benjy, and I'm not going anywhere."

"Yes, you are," he said sadly, and he brushed a stray lock of hair from my eyes. "You're going to D.C., where you're going to break into Somerset with the most important person in your life, once again leaving me behind."

I swallowed hard. "*You're* the most important person in my life."

"Not right now, I'm not. And I'm not sure I have been since you were Masked."

I shook my head, hot tears burning in my eyes. "That's not fair."

"None of this is fair, Kitty. It is what it is. It doesn't mean I love you any less, and it doesn't mean you're not still my best friend. But it does mean things aren't great right now, and I'm not sure we can get back there again. Not when we're both thinking about a time and a place that doesn't exist anymore."

"It exists for me," I mumbled. "A place where we can go when this is all over—just you and me. No ranks, no Blackcoats, no Harts to worry about. Just us."

"What if this is never over? What happens to us then?"

"It will be," I said firmly, my frustration turning to anger. "If you want to give up on it, fine—but I'm not."

He gave me a watery smile. "I wish you were right." Stepping aside, he opened the bathroom door for me and said gently, "This is the last time, Kitty. After this, either you stop risking your life, or I stop depending on your heart to fuel mine."

I didn't trust myself to speak. Instead I slipped into the bathroom and closed the door behind me, leaning against the painted wood as I struggled to breathe without breaking down into sobs. I couldn't do this now. I *wouldn't* do this now. He was wrong—there would be a *then*. And when I got back, we would figure this out. Because even though he was right—even though right now, Knox and the Blackcoats and the hundreds of millions of people depending on us were the most important people in my life—I refused to live without Benjy.

He wasn't there to see me off. I knew I shouldn't have been surprised; that was the worst fight we'd had in recent memory, and both of us needed the chance to breathe away from each other and gain the perspective everyone seemed so crazy about lately. But it still hurt enough that, when Knox greeted me in front of the military plane waiting for us near the edge of Sector X, I didn't feel the least bit guilty about flashing him a small smile. And why should I have felt guilty for being kind to him, anyway? We were friends.

Theoretically. When he wasn't being a jerk.

We boarded last, behind the six volunteers who were risking their lives to give us the chance to sneak into Somerset and steal the file on Victor Mercer. As I passed them in their uniforms and winter military gear, part of me was terrified Benjy would be among them. But Knox wouldn't do that to me. *Benjy* wouldn't do that to me. Or the mission.

Thankfully, while a few of the faces were familiar, none of them were his. Still, after the plane took off, leaving the

muddy gray of Elsewhere behind for the muddy gray of
D.C., I joined Knox toward the front of the plane, where
he sat in a jumper seat. The others lingered near the back,
laughing and playing a card game as they ignored the
bumps and rattles of the plane.

"We should be doing this alone," I said to Knox, sitting
down in the seat across from him.

"Who says we aren't?" He flashed me a ghost of a smirk,
but it was hard to believe it when I could see the weight of
the entire war resting on his shoulders.

"So what's the plan?" I said. "We're using the tunnel,
right?"

"Unless you know of another way inside without the
Shields finding us."

"But Celia knows about it."

"She's probably using it, too," he said. "If we do run into
trouble, we'll tell them we're there to meet with Celia."

The plane rattled unexpectedly, and I gripped the arm-
rests. "So we probably won't get in and out undetected?"

He shook his head. "But we're still Blackcoats. We're
still on the same side."

"Didn't seem like it from your performance this morning," I said, and he shrugged.

"Celia brought that on herself. If she can't play nice, then
we don't include her. Plain and simple."

"But she runs the other half of the army."

"I know," he said, but he didn't elaborate. It seemed like
a dangerous proposition to me, cutting them off from our
plans, but maybe he would be more lenient once we had
the file in our hands.

We sat in silence for a few minutes. Knox stared out the

window, and I listened to the men and women in the back. They didn't invite us to play their game, and I realized, with somewhat of an epiphany, that I didn't expect them to. Knox was their commander, and while I might have had little to no real power over the Blackcoat army, I was still a figurehead. We were separate from them the same way VIs were separate from IIs, and something about that thought made me squirm.

Benjy was right. There would always be leaders, and those leaders would always be set apart somehow, even if it was only as trivial as not being invited to play a card game. I had no doubt that if I asked to be dealt in, they wouldn't argue, but I would be unwanted. A threat, in some small way, to their fun. Different, no matter what I did or where I was raised. It was one more thing to look forward to after the war ended, I considered bitterly—a lifetime of exclusion for no other reason than who and what I was.

"Why are you doing this?"

Knox's gaze drifted back toward me, and he raised an eyebrow. "Didn't you just ask me that earlier?"

"You didn't give me a straight answer," I said. "And I don't mean why are you doing this *now*. That's obvious. I mean—" I gestured toward him. "Why did you start? What made you wake up one morning and decide to try to take down the United States government?"

"It wasn't that easy," he said, but the hint of a smirk returned. "Is that how it was for you?"

"I woke up in a body that wasn't my own, looking like the mouthpiece for the revolution," I said. "Didn't exactly have much of a choice."

"Sure you did," he said, leaning back in his seat. "You had plenty of choices, just like the rest of us."

It hadn't felt like it at the time, but I didn't regret it. And truth be told, if I'd known then what I did now, I would've done the same thing. No—not the *exact* same thing. I would've done some things differently, like all my arguments with Knox. The recklessness that had landed me in Elsewhere. I could've been a better team player, and I was working on that, slowly. But I didn't regret the risks I'd taken and would continue to take as a member of the Blackcoats.

"You're still dodging my question," I said, crossing my arms. They'd given me a leather bomber jacket for the mission, and it was the warmest thing I'd worn in weeks. "I agreed because I believe in the same things Lila was talking about. Because I believe in what the Blackcoats are trying to do. I've lived at the bottom, and I know how awful it is—I know how unfair society can be. But you were raised with a silver spoon in your mouth, and even if you weren't, you didn't have the Blackcoats back then to voice what was already going on in your head. So—what made you speak up? What made you risk your life and your family's legacy for a bunch of people that, if you wanted, you'd never have to acknowledge? You could've been a Minister, like your father. You could've been living a cushy life in your own little bubble. And that's what I don't get—why aren't you?"

Knox closed his eyes and leaned his head back, and several seconds passed in silence. I thought he wasn't going to answer. *He* probably thought he wasn't going to answer. But in a low voice, barely audible over the hum of the engine, he finally spoke.

"I had a brother."

"You did?" Never, not once, had Knox mentioned a brother to me. I couldn't remember him bringing up his family at all, really, except his father.

He nodded, opening his eyes once more. He refused to look at me, however, focusing on his hands instead. "A twin brother, actually. Fraternal. Everything was fine for the first couple years, but then he started acting—strange. Or maybe he had always been acting strange, and it was only because I was different that my mother noticed as early as she did."

"What kind of strange?" I said, confused.

"Quiet. Stared at his blocks for hours instead of playing with them. Didn't speak like I did. Always seemed a little behind." Knox shrugged. "I don't remember the details much, and my mother rarely talked about it."

"What happened to him?" I said, almost afraid of Knox's answer. But maybe that was the point.

"Most of the time, when there are—moderate deficits in a child, they're given a chance to take the test at seventeen anyway," said Knox. "But because my father was concerned about the family's image, and because my brother eventually stopped communicating altogether, the process was—sped up." He cleared his throat, his expression growing pinched. "When we were six years old, they declared that by keeping him within our society, we were only delaying the inevitable, and—the sooner he was declared a I, the easier it would be on me. So they took him away."

I stared at him in horror. I had never met a I before I'd arrived in Elsewhere. Somewhere in my mind, I'd expected vegetables—faceless, comatose people who had no sense of self or place. Not real people with real lives. Not a little boy who was too quiet for his father's liking and didn't play with blocks the way he was supposed to.

"I'm so sorry, Knox," I said softly, because there wasn't anything else to say. I couldn't imagine that level of pain, either for Knox or his mother. And selfishly, I didn't want to. "Did you— Have you looked up his records in Elsewhere? Maybe he's still—"

"He's not," said Knox. "I wouldn't be surprised if he never made it to Elsewhere to begin with. A young child like that...his organs would have been valuable and needed."

A wave of nausea hit me, and my grip on the armrest tightened. "But—he was your brother—your father's a Minister—"

"Not even Ministers' children are immune to genetic or developmental anomalies," said Knox. "I didn't fully understand what was going on. I still remember my confusion the day they took him away and I was told he would never be coming back. My mother was a wreck. She never recovered, and she—" He cleared his throat again. "Anyway. She's the reason I got to this point. My father never said my brother's name again after they took him away. All the pictures of him disappeared, and if you'd met my family after, you would never have known there should've been one more of us. I think he was hoping I would forget about my brother.

"But my mother made sure I didn't," he continued. "She used to tell me stories about how we played together when we were young. That was one of the few times I ever saw her happy after that. And once I was old enough, she used to tell me about what the country was like before the Harts took over. I began to see injustice everywhere I looked, and once you see it, you can't unsee it. And I couldn't ignore it, regardless of the privileges and advantages I would have had if I did. She's the reason I do this. My brother is the reason I do this." Finally Knox looked at me. "Is that what you wanted to hear?"

"I wanted to hear the truth, that's all," I said, at a loss. Something inside me felt hollow, and instinctively I started to reach across the space between us, needing to offer him some form of comfort. But he shifted awkwardly and crossed his arms, hiding his hands. I dropped mine back in my lap. "I just—I never understood how you and Celia and Lila could risk it all when you had everything to lose. It wasn't like that for me."

"Yes, it was," he said quietly. "It was almost exactly the same. The only difference between us was the fact that you knew what it was like, having nothing. You knew the value of what you were betting, and yet you did it anyway."

I didn't know what to say to that. He must have known what he had to lose, too. We all did, and yet we all chose to do this. "Thank you."

"For what?"

"For trusting me. I know I've given you every reason not to."

"Yeah, well. We're in this together," he said with a sigh. "And since you've decided to stick around, it's the least I can do until you prove I can't anymore."

"That's not going to happen. Not this time," I said, and that ghost of a smile returned.

"Don't make promises you can't keep, Kitty. We both

know eventually you're going to directly disobey me and do something monumentally stupid, and once again, I'll be the one cleaning up the mess."

"I'll try my best not to, then," I said. He nodded.

"That's more like it."

A moment passed, and we could have easily slid into comfortable silence. Instead, I watched him, and he held my gaze, and in that moment, I felt as if I could ask him anything and he wouldn't say no.

"What was your brother's name?" I said, before I even realized I was speaking. But I didn't regret it, unlike most things I blurted out, and while his eyebrows twitched upward, he didn't shut me out like he could have.

"Maddox," he said. "I called him Max, because I couldn't pronounce Maddox. He couldn't say Lennox, either."

"And that's where Knox came from?" I said, and he flashed me a tight smile.

"Exactly."

Despite the pain in his eyes as we spoke about his brother, there was also a warmth that emanated from him, unlike anything I'd ever seen from him before. He told me about some of his favorite memories with his brother who barely spoke—only to him, he admitted, and even then, those instances were rare—and as he went on, answering my steady stream of questions openly, I realized what was different.

I'd never seen him talk about someone he loved before.

This was the Knox who was my friend. The one I trusted, the one I believed in. And there, in the middle of the sky, with nothing but air between us and the rest of the world, I was grateful to have a glimpse of him again.

Eventually our conversation died down, but I sat across

from Knox for the rest of the flight, staying away from the others. Occasionally one of us would say something, spurring a short exchange, but we always reverted back to companionable silence. It was nice, in a way. But it didn't do much to quell the anxiety forming in the pit of my stomach over what we were about to do.

As we began our descent outside D.C., I couldn't help but wonder how many of us would make it back alive. Because if there was one thing I'd learned working with Knox, it was that nothing ever went completely according to plan.

"Soldiers," said Knox as soon as we'd landed in the middle of a snowy field. "Your job is simple. Protect the plane."

Several of them gaped at him. "Excuse me?" said one man with a blond goatee.

"You heard me. Protect the plane," said Knox. "It's our ticket back to Elsewhere. If the government spots it, we're on our own, and believe me, it's a very long walk back to safety."

He led me down the ramp and across the snowy field, toward a waiting black car. I glanced over my shoulder to see the soldiers circling the plane with their weapons at the ready, as if there were battalions of government agents waiting for us to land in this very spot. At least they were taking their mission seriously.

"They thought they were going to come with us into the city," I said as I climbed in on the passenger side. Knox sat in the driver's seat and turned the key hanging in the ignition.

"Strand and Benjy and the entire lot of them would never have let us come if they knew it was only the two of us," said Knox as the engine purred to life. "We're both too im-portant to go anywhere without a security detail tailing us."

"But that's exactly what we're doing." I wasn't afraid, not exactly, but the more guns we had, the better our chances were. If someone took Knox out, I would have no idea what to do or where to go. And if someone took me out—Knox didn't know where to find the file. Our mis-sion would be a failure.

"What they don't know won't hurt them, and the only way to get this done quickly and efficiently is if it's essen-tial personnel only," said Knox.

"Us," I said, and he nodded.

"Us."

I examined the screen on the dashboard. The radio was muted, but red arrows pointed along the road, no doubt heading straight for Somerset. "Did this car appear out of nowhere?"

"I made a call before we left. Celia restored communica-tions after she took over Somerset, and Sampson dropped it off for us. No one knows we're coming but him." Knox pressed the accelerator, and we took off down the dirt road. "Where did you hide the file, Kitty? Are you going to have to go into the vents to get it?"

I nodded. "It won't take me long."

"Are you going to tell me where it is, or am I going to be surprised?"

I shifted in my seat to face him. "Remember when you pretended to kill Benjy in front of me and let me believe he was dead for days?"

Knox's grip tightened on the steering wheel. "Surprise, then. Never been a fan."

"Like I said back in the manor, even if you knew where it was, you probably wouldn't be able to get to it anyway."

"Fair enough," he said with a sigh, and I knew the hardened, exasperated Knox had returned, burying the vulnerability so deep inside him I doubted he even remembered it existed.

I settled back and gazed out the window as we drove toward D.C. We weren't far—an hour at the most—and part of me was eager to see my home again. I hadn't grown up in Somerset or anywhere near it; I'd grown up in the Heights, the poorest part of D.C. But the city was still my home.

"Is that your go-to plan?" I said after a minute. "Faking a death?"

He glanced over at me, his gaze lingering for longer than it should have, considering how fast he was driving. "What are you talking about?"

"I mean—that's what you did for Lila. You helped her fake her death. You faked Benjy's death. I'm never going to be able to fully believe you're dead, you know. Part of me will always be absolutely positive you've faked your own."

"Oh? And who says I'm dying before you?"

I shrugged. "You're the one who left our security detail behind."

"True," he allowed with a smirk. "Maybe you've got a point after all."

When D.C. finally came into view, the knot in my stomach grew into full-on nausea. It was one thing to sneak into an office to steal a file or overhear a crucial conversation. It was another thing entirely to walk in right under our allies' noses, knowing full well we were keeping secrets that could win or lose the war.

Driving through the streets and seeing the gradual shift from poverty-stricken and hungry to rich and well fed was even more striking now that I'd spent so much time in Elsewhere. Knox and I were both silent as we took it all in, and at last he pulled up to the side of the street in one of the most affluent areas of D.C., only blocks from Somerset.

"Here." He handed me a black knit hat and sunglasses. "It isn't the best disguise, but we only need to get into that alleyway."

"Your face is just as familiar as mine is," I pointed out as I put them on. He shrugged.

"I'll pull my hood up. We'll be fine."

That was about as ominous as he could get, but the entrance into the tunnel that led underneath Somerset wasn't far. Fifty feet at the most, buried in the alleyway behind a rusted door no self-respecting V or VI would have ever touched. As far as I knew, there were no cameras in the alleyway—there couldn't possibly be, not when that tunnel had gone undiscovered for so long.

We piled out of the car into a misting rain, and when he offered me his elbow, I took it. This wasn't entirely unlike the first time we'd wandered the city together, shortly after a bombing had put the Hart family into lockdown. Rather than behave, we'd snuck out for a night at a club—or at least that was what I'd thought. Instead, Knox had tried to negotiate a weapons acquisition, and that had been the first time I'd noticed there was much more to him than the facade of a spoiled Minister's son he showed the world.

We made it to the door without incident. Knox pulled the rusting handle, and I could sense his relief when it opened to reveal a dark descending stairway. "Ladies first."

"You just want me to take the bullet for you," I said, but I ducked inside anyway. I remembered exactly how many steps it took to reach the bottom, and I counted in my head as Knox pulled the door shut, leaving us in complete darkness.

"Someone took the flashlight," he said, his heavy footsteps following mine.

"We don't need it. It's a straight shot." Once we reached Somerset, there would be enough ambient light for us to make it through to Knox's old suite, where a trapdoor opened up into his closet. In the meantime, I ran my hand along the dirt wall, smooth from I didn't know how many years of use. Someone had built this tunnel at some point, but until Knox had revealed it to me, he and Lila had been the only two living people to know about it. Not so much anymore.

"I can't believe they left this unguarded," I said a few hundred feet later. It was eerie, walking through pitch blackness, not knowing for sure where it would end. Against my better judgment, I reached back and grabbed the first part of Knox I could find: his sleeve.

"We'll find out once we reach Somerset," he muttered, prying my grip from his jacket and taking my hand instead. His skin was warm and rough, and despite the tension in his voice, he wrapped his fingers around mine gently. "If they're smart, they'll have guards stationed at that entrance, and they'll know we're coming. If the Shields tried to infiltrate this way, it would be like shooting fish in a barrel."

"Why would you want to shoot fish in a barrel?" I said. "That metaphor makes no sense."

"It makes perfect sense," he argued. "It's not about *why* you'd do it. It's about how easy it would be if you did—"

He stopped suddenly, tugging me back when I tried to keep going. "Did you hear that?"

"Hear what?" I said. "If there's someone at the end of the tunnel, we'll tell them who we are, and—"

"No need, Kitty." A woman's voice sounded only a foot away from me, and I heard the click of a gun behind me. "I know exactly who you are."

VI

SACRIFICE

It had been months since I'd seen her face-to-face, but I would have recognized Celia Hart's voice anywhere. Even underground in a black tunnel, with my heart pounding and adrenaline rushing through my body like I was in a race, I could picture her in my mind, clear as anything. Dark hair so unlike her daughter's, blue eyes, the porcelain Hart skin; tall and athletic, with a strong jaw, a beauty mark below her left eye, and a look of disdain for anyone who dared to get in her way.

"Is this really necessary?" said Knox calmly.

"Yes, it is. And get your hand off your weapon," she said. "There's another soldier behind you, ready to pull the trigger if you so much as unholster it."

She must have been wearing night vision goggles, I realized. No wonder she'd been able to sneak up on us without either of us figuring it out. Now that I knew she was here, I could smell her shampoo and sense the heat of her body in the cool air.

"We're not the enemy, Celia," said Knox. "There's no reason for this."

"There's every reason for it when I've gone to the trouble of stabbing my fake brother in the heart and hanging him up by his neck, only to discover it wasn't my fake brother after all." She nudged the small of my back with her gun. "Start walking, Kitty."

I stumbled forward in the darkness, not letting go of Knox's hand. "You think we're Masked?"

"If you really are who you say you are, you didn't tell me you were coming," she said. "You gave no indication you had any desire to visit D.C. And considering we have a strong family tradition of forcing other people to look like us for money, rank, or so-called patriotism, yes, I think it's a strong possibility that the impostor would have gone to this sort of trouble."

There were a thousand things I could have said to prove to her I was who I claimed to be—we'd had enough private conversations that it wouldn't have been hard to pull up some small scrap of memory only the two of us would have. But Knox would have been able to do the same, and yet he didn't. So for now, I stayed silent.

"How do we know you're really who *you* claim to be?" said Knox. "The Celia I know would never point a gun at my head."

"I'm not pointing my gun at you. I'm pointing my gun at Kitty," she said. "Goulding is pointing his gun at you."

"Ah. Morning, Goulding," said Knox. "Or afternoon now, I suppose. It's been a while. How's Jessica?"

"Good," grunted a low voice behind us. "Due any day now."

"And you're still making the poor man work, Celia?" There was an easygoing quality to his tone, the sort that was supposed to relax everyone. I'd heard it before, when he'd been trying to calm me down or get on my good side, and I'd thought I was immune to it by now. But even with Celia digging the barrel of her gun into my jacket, I couldn't help but breathe a little easier. Whatever this was about, we would get it sorted out soon enough.

The tunnel was long—nearly a mile, if I had estimated correctly, but in the darkness, it felt three times that. Finally, Celia warned me about the upcoming staircase, and I took the steps two at a time, eager to get my vision back.

As Knox had predicted, a pair of guards stood waiting at the secret entrance—or not so secret anymore, I supposed—to Somerset. I only saw them when one pushed open the door, and light flooded the tunnel at last. Even though it was barely brighter than candlelight, I squinted.

"Kitty, Goulding will take you to Knox's old room," said Celia, and I frowned.

"Don't you want to make sure it's me first?"

"I can tell it's you," she said. "You're not nearly as mysterious as you think. Knox, you're coming with me."

"I would rather not be separated from Kitty, if you don't mind," he said. "It's been a rough night and day for both of us."

"Too bad. Once I debrief you, you'll have plenty of opportunity to relax," she said. "I assume that's why you came, after all. To discuss the ground my team gained last night."

"We're all part of the same team," he grumbled, then glanced at me. "All right with this?"

"I don't need a babysitter, Knox," I said testily. Besides, that would give me plenty of time to retrieve the file while

Celia was distracted. It wasn't exactly what we'd planned, but it wasn't the first time we'd had to wing it, either.

"I see Elsewhere didn't starve the feistiness out of you," said Celia. "Come on, Lennox. I don't have all day."

Reluctantly Knox followed Celia through another passageway, one I'd never gotten around to exploring. I'd had my own way around Somerset, and any passage Knox knew about, at the time, had been practically worthless to me. But it must have been useful to the Blackcoats; on our way up the stairs and through the creaking attic, we ran into four more members of the rebellion, and each offered me a flash of a smile and a greeting.

"Down you go," said Goulding as he opened the trapdoor for me. I lowered myself into Knox's old closet, wrinkling my nose at the scent of dirty clothes. In the living room of his suite, I plopped down on the leather couch, toeing off my boots and stretching my legs as if I had every intention of staying put for a nice, long nap. Goulding, however, lingered near the door, his stance square like a trained soldier's. Apparently I wasn't the only one settling in for the afternoon.

"Is this your first baby?" I said, and he nodded.

"Just got married last year."

"Do you know if it's a boy or girl?" I said. He didn't look much older than me, and the thought of having a kid sometime in the next five years was terrifying. If I even survived that long.

"We're hoping to be surprised," he said gruffly.

"Congratulations," I said with a smile I genuinely meant. It was jarring to hear other people's lives were continuing almost exactly as they had been before the rebellion—

even for other Blackcoats—but of course they were. The entire world hadn't stopped just because I'd been Masked and thrown into Elsewhere. And at least it wasn't all death and darkness. Goulding's expression didn't change, however, and I lay down, too afraid of falling asleep to actually close my eyes. If he was going to stay, then I had to come up with a way out of here, and fast.

There were no vents large enough for me to crawl through in the bathroom or the bedroom—I'd looked months ago, just in case. The only vent I could get through was the one directly above Knox's desk, a few feet away from where Goulding stood. And I highly doubted Goulding would be willing to let me leave right in front of him.

"Do you know how long Celia's going to talk to Knox?" I said idly, and Goulding shook his head. "Am I allowed to walk around, or do I need to stick to this suite?"

He managed an apologetic look, at least. "Celia's orders."

"Knox runs the Blackcoats, too, you know," I muttered.

"You report to Knox, I report to Celia."

I made a face and sat up. "I do not report to Knox. I don't report to anyone."

"My mistake, Miss Hart."

Collapsing back on the couch, I huffed. "Doe. My last name's Doe." It was the same last name given to all the Extras and orphans in my group home, though now that I knew who my biological parents were, I supposed my last name really *was* Hart. Or would be, if I decided to take it.

That was a decision best left for another time, when the entire war wasn't riding on me bypassing Goulding and retrieving the file. I eventually curled up on my side, facing away from him, and forced my breathing to remain steady, hoping if he thought I was asleep, he would slip away. No such luck. He couldn't stand guard over me indefinitely, though. Eventually he would have to use the bathroom, or his shift would end, and he would go home to his wife and unborn baby. Nothing lasted forever, although by the time he finally did move, it felt like hours had passed.

"What?" A crackle of static burst through the silence of the room, and I twisted around. Goulding pressed his earpiece and ducked his head, as if that would stop me from hearing everything he said. "In broad daylight? How long do we have?"

Suddenly an earsplitting siren began to wail, and I jumped off the sofa and pulled my boots back on, fear coursing through me. "What the hell's going on?"

"You need to come with me," said Goulding, and he crossed the room before I could tie my laces. Taking my elbow, he half guided, half dragged me to the door and shoved it open.

"*You* need to tell me exactly what's going on," I said, trying to yank my arm from him. His grip tightened, and we darted down the hallway toward the stairwell.

"Somerset is under attack. The government is retaliat—"

Suddenly a deafening blast ripped through the manor, and the ceiling gave way, raining fiery debris over us. A block of cement landed squarely on my foot, and I yelped as I felt the bones snap. Goulding shoved me back toward Knox's suite, and I took off running as fast as I could, doing my best to ignore the pain.

I shouted Goulding's name as I ran, but if I had any voice, the ringing in my ears drowned it out. When I reached Knox's door, I pushed it open and whirled around, ready to grab Goulding and pull him in.

But he wasn't there. He wasn't anywhere, and the ceiling in the hallway had caved in completely, leaving a mountain of burning rubble exactly where Goulding had stood.

My stomach lurched with shock and fear and grief for his poor wife and baby, but there was no time to be sick. Instead I burst into Knox's suite and climbed into the vent, my pulse racing, my hands sweaty, and my foot throbbing. Any second, another bomb could drop and kill me instantly, and no one would know until they found my body days or weeks or even months later. But I had to get that file. The outcome of the entire war depended on it.

Time seemed to alternate between standing still and jumping forward, leaving me with holes in my memory. One moment, I was crawling through the vents, and the next, I stood on a bookcase in the drawing room, rooting around the vent for the loose sheet of metal that had cut me four times before I'd learned to avoid it. I wasn't sure what had caused it, exactly, but it allowed for a thin space between the vent and the ceiling, perfect for stashing the file.

At last my fingers brushed the edges of the folder and, with effort, I managed to coax it out from its hiding place. I flipped it open and hastily skimmed through it. I couldn't read the official documents, but they all seemed to be there, along with the single picture of Victor Mercer. No one had found it. No one had stolen the crucial information we would need to expose him, and we finally had a shot at winning this war.

Shouts rose from the atrium just outside the drawing room, and I ducked, clutching the folder to my chest. My hearing was still iffy at best, but I could make out the words over the hum.

"Fan out!" barked a man. "The Prime Minister wants his sister and the leaders alive, but kill any other rebel on sight."

Terrific. I hauled myself back into the vents and scrambled back to the residential wing, my injured foot protesting with every shake and jolt. If I could make it to Knox's room, I could reach the passageway that connected to the tunnel. It was my only chance of getting out of here.

Silently I hoped that Knox had somehow managed to escape. Fighting was useless. It would only get more people killed, but Celia was undoubtedly too stubborn to give in. She'd fight to the death, I was sure of it. I could only pray she didn't take Knox down with her.

Time did that funny jump thing again. Maybe it was the adrenaline and fear, or maybe I'd hit my head and hadn't noticed. Either way, before I knew it, I dropped into Knox's room, landing hard on his desk. Another bone in my foot snapped, and I cried out, balancing on the other one instead.

Somehow, miracle of all miracles, Knox was there, and he wrapped his arms firmly around me and helped me to the ground. Dust streaked his face, and there was a shallow cut below his eye, but he was there. He was okay. "What happened, Kitty?"

"Goulding—Goulding is dead, and there are armed soldiers heading our way," I said through gritted teeth. I could feel a sharp edge of bone tearing at my skin, trying to slide out. "I have the file."

"Figured that was where you were," said Knox, but he

couldn't hide the naked relief on his face. "I'm getting you out of here."

I tried to put pressure on my broken foot, and excruciating pain shot through me like a thousand volts of electricity. "I can't—I can't walk."

Shouts echoed down the hallway. The soldiers were getting closer. "I'll carry you," said Knox, but before he could pick me up, I shoved the file toward him.

"You can't carry me and run all the way back to the car."

"Yes, I can. I'm not having this argument with you right now, Kitty."

The shouts grew louder, and anger pulsed through me. "They are *seconds* away from bursting in here. If you were the one who couldn't walk, you'd make me do the exact same thing. You need to get this file out of here. The entire rebellion is counting on it."

At last his fingers closed around the folder, and his face contorted into a look I'd never seen from him before. "Here—" He fumbled with his holster. "Take my gun. It'll give you a fighting chance."

"They'll kill me for sure if I'm armed. Unarmed, there's a chance they won't." Someone banged on Lila's door, and I winced. "I can only buy you so much time, Knox. *Go.*"

He touched my cheek wordlessly, his eyes shining as he held my gaze for an infinite second. "You're one of a kind, Kitty," he said thickly. "Wherever they take you, I'll find you."

I managed a short nod, my throat constricting too tightly for me to speak. But it didn't matter—he didn't give me time to reply. One moment he was there, and the next he was gone. And for three quiet seconds, I was alone.

The door burst open in a shower of splinters and chunks of wood, and four armed men carrying shields and automatic weapons spilled inside. Their shouts melded together into a wall of noise I couldn't comprehend, but I held up my hands and made sure they could see my face.

One of the men stormed toward me. "The double is here," he said into his sleeve before grabbing my hands and forcing them behind my back. Metal cuffs tightened around my wrists, and I winced.

"My foot—my foot's broken. I can't walk."

"Won't need to," he said, and I felt the sharp stab of a needle in the back of my neck, right over the scarred X. My vision blurred, and as my knees gave out, the world went black.

VII

DÉJÀ VU

Beep. Beep. Beep.

In the hazy edge of consciousness, I was sure I was still dreaming. I heard those beeps sometimes—on quiet mornings where, for a split second, I forgot who I was now. They were the same beeps I'd woken up to in the Stronghold four months ago, when I'd discovered Daxton had Masked me into Lila Hart. Those were the last things I'd heard before everything had changed, and they were almost comforting, in a way. A reminder of who I used to be.

"Kitty?"

A familiar voice drifted toward me. I didn't want to move. Everything felt heavy and sluggish, and I would have given anything to fall back asleep and never have to worry about anything ever again.

"Kitty—come on, wake up. I know you can hear me."

Annoyed, I cracked open my eyes. White walls and crown molding. The smell of antiseptic. Sunlight streaming in through a window behind me as I lay in a bed that was far too comfortable to ever be in a hospital.

The Stronghold.

This was the exact same room I'd woken up in before.

Everything that had happened at Somerset rushed into my mind, as if it had all been waiting for me to come crashing back to reality. So the soldiers had kept me alive after all. And now I was here, in the Stronghold, the most fiercely protected safe house the Harts had. It was somewhere in the Rocky Mountains, surrounded on all sides by snowy peaks. I knew because I'd tried to leave once, and I'd discovered the only way out of here was by air. There was no way the Blackcoats could launch an attack here and win, not when the Stronghold was so well fortified.

"There you are. Kitty, it's me—it's Greyson."

At last I turned my head. Greyson Hart, only living son of Daxton Hart, lingered at my bedside. His blond hair fell into his face, and he raked it back, offering me a small smile.

"Hey. How do you feel?"

"Like shit, probably," said another voice—Lila. I raised my head. She stood nearby, her arms crossed and her expression sour. "That's what happens when you take the drugs away."

"I cut off your sedatives and painkillers," he said apologetically, but I couldn't find it in me to care. "I can start them again, if you want."

I shook my head. Now that he'd mentioned it, my foot was beginning to throb, but it was hardly noticeable. "What's going on?" I croaked. My throat was raw. "Why am I not dead?"

"You might as well be," said Lila sharply. "Welcome to hell."

She had no idea what hell really was, but I held my

tongue. They were the only two allies I would find here, and I couldn't afford to alienate them.

Greyson glared at her. "We don't know what he plans to do with her yet. He wouldn't have let the doctors near her if he only planned on killing her once she woke up."

"You *have* met this asshole, right?" said Lila. "Dark hair, roughly six feet tall, twisted lump of coal where his humanity ought to be?"

"Now, Lila. Is that any way to talk about your only uncle?"

I closed my eyes again in the futile hope that if I couldn't see him, he would disappear. It was pointless, however, and I could hear his footsteps on the carpet as he moved closer to my bed.

"You're not my uncle," she snarled. "My uncle's dead."

Daxton made a noncommittal sound. "And yet here we are, with nearly the whole country on my side. Good morning, Kitty."

With effort, I forced myself to sit up. A wave of dizziness washed over me, and I reassured myself that it was likely due to whatever they'd used to knock me out rather than any serious head injury. My foot ached, and my vision blurred at the edges, but other than that, I was fine. It was a far cry from the last time I'd woken up in that bed, when I'd discovered they'd put me through countless surgeries to make me look exactly like Lila. "Why did you keep me alive?"

"Are you complaining?" He raised an eyebrow, and I shook my head minutely. "I kept you alive out of the goodness of my heart."

"You don't have a heart," said Lila. "You kept her alive

because if you'd killed her, you would have turned her into a martyr."

So it was the same reason why Knox hadn't wanted Celia to kill Victor. It was staggering, the thought that my death could have had that level of impact—might still, if the bleak future I pictured panned out. But, selfishly, I preferred staying alive.

"I could still kill her." Daxton stared at me, his dark eyes running up and down my body. I glared back. "No one would ever have to know."

"We would," said Lila. "And the next time you put me on air, I would tell the entire country."

"And see Greyson die in front of you? My dear, don't be silly." Daxton smiled and tore his stare from me, and I felt as if a fist had loosened around my insides. That was how he was doing it, then. That's how he had bought Lila's cooperation. And I didn't doubt for a second that he was mad enough to really kill Greyson just to prove a point to Lila.

"We have the file," I blurted, hoping I wasn't wrong. "The Blackcoats will trade us for it. Lila, Greyson, me—if you release us, you'll never have to worry about the contents being made public."

Daxton considered me for a long moment, his gaze once again locking on mine. A single look from him was enough to make my skin crawl; his leering stare made me feel like I needed to shower for the rest of my life, however long or short it may be.

"Well, you certainly have the upper hand, don't you?" He grinned, but there was nothing good or humorous in it. "Let them release the file. Their campaign has already failed. My team can easily disprove their lies and slander, and the only public outcry they'll gain is from malcontents already on the fringes of society. Everyone else is rather happy with their places in all this, and I daresay they value a full belly over your particular brand of righteousness."

I gaped at him, dumbfounded. He had been willing to do anything—*anything* to stop that file from becoming public knowledge only a few weeks ago. Something must have changed. Something big.

"I'll leave you three to it, then," he said. "Lunch should be served shortly. Do yourself a favor and eat, Kitty. You look far too thin."

He waltzed out the door, leaving Lila, Greyson, and me to stare at one another. The Blackcoats' ace in the hole—the thing Knox and I had been so willing to die to protect—couldn't possibly be worthless.

"He's bluffing," I said. "There's something else going on."

"I don't think there is," said Greyson quietly, and he perched on the bed beside me. "He's three steps ahead of us at all times. I don't know how, but no matter what we try, he's always there."

"We'll figure something out," I said, swallowing hard. My mouth was dry, and all the water in the world couldn't help it. "Do you know—do you know if they captured Knox, too?"

Lila shook her head and gestured toward the muted television playing in the background. A reel of footage from inside Somerset played as Shields shot down Blackcoats, and for a brief second, I thought I saw my blond hair hanging limply over one soldier's shoulder. "It's just you. Mom escaped, too. There's a list of dead they've been reading on the news—Blackcoats. More than twenty of them. They're trying to shame the families into compliance in case any of them are sympathetic, too."

"Shame doesn't cause sympathy. They're just fanning the flames and turning more people against them." So would the contents of the file. "Whatever Daxton says, don't believe him. He's losing support. The media—they're just spouting the lies he wants you to hear. They're unreliable."

"We know," said Greyson. "The problem is, most of the country doesn't."

"They'll figure it out," I said. "The more the Blackcoats reveal, the more they'll have to listen."

"The ones who want to hear it, anyway," muttered Lila.

"People need hope," I said. "More than you think."

"Don't lecture me on hope. I'm the one who gave up years of my life to deliver speeches—"

"Lila." Greyson's sharp voice cut through hers, and she stopped. Instead of reaming her out, however, he nodded to the television, where a burst of static had interrupted the anchor. "Turn it up."

She turned on the volume just in time for Knox's face to appear. Someone had stitched up the cut underneath his eye, and he looked exhausted, but judging by the background, he had made it back to his office in Elsewhere. He was safe.

"As I'm sure you've heard by now," he began, "yesterday morning, Celia Hart, one of the few living members left of the Hart family, reclaimed her familial home at Somerset from the impostor, Victor Mercer."

"He's wooden," said Lila immediately. "He always has been. Can't give a speech to save his life."

"Quiet," said Greyson, and she huffed.

"We expected the government to fight back," continued Knox. Lila was right. He *was* wooden, and he continued to drone on as if he'd never felt a single emotion in his life. "Instead, they chose to bomb the residential sections of Somerset and invade with an order to kill everyone on sight, knowing full well there were innocent civilians inside, including members of the staff who were never given a choice to leave or surrender. The media has released a list of the Blackcoats who died in the fight. But we can now confirm there is a list twice as long of the servants and staff members who were also killed. I will read them now."

As he read off the names, several of which I recognized from my stay in Somerset, Lila looked at me. "They're screwed without us."

"Benjy can give a speech," I said, my fingers laced tightly together. "I don't know why he isn't the one on camera."

"Because the people know Knox's face," said Greyson.

"What good does that do if a dead body emotes more?" said Lila, shaking her head. "He's killing us."

"He's telling the truth," I said. "He doesn't need to embellish it to get the point across. Every single name he's reading—he's made rebels of their families now. Families that probably would have never gone against the Harts otherwise. Daxton killed twenty rebels, sure, but he just created a hundred more."

Lila fell silent, for once, and the three of us turned back to the television. Once Knox finished reading the list, he said quietly, "To the friends and families of the ones lost in the Battle of Somerset—I'm truly sorry. Their sacrifice will not be forgotten, and their names will not be lost to time. They will be remembered."

He cleared his throat and averted his eyes for a split second before raising them toward the camera once more. "I'm also deeply sorry to say that, in the midst of the fight, a key member of the Blackcoat Rebellion, Kitty Doe, disappeared. We have not yet received word on whether her body was recovered or if she has been taken by the opposition, but we will do everything humanly possible to find her."

Knox paused and stared into the camera, and despite the fact that he had no way of knowing I was watching, it felt as if he was looking directly at me. Something inside me twisted, and I took a deep breath, releasing it slowly.

"Her sacrifice and the sacrifices of those lost in the battle weren't for nothing," said Knox, and he straightened again, regaining the little composure he'd lost. "The Blackcoats now have in our possession proof of the impostor Victor Mercer's identity, including medical records, photographs, and interview transcripts from the selection process, which was ordered by Augusta Hart. Unfortunately," he added, "we have learned that every doctor who helped perform the Masking procedure on Victor died within three months after the surgeries, including the head of his team, renowned medical expert Patrick Hastings. Victor's secret did not die with them, however, and I will now present as many pieces of evidence as this time allows."

The three of us sat glued to our seats as Knox went through each piece of evidence, starting with the picture of Victor Mercer I had found. There was no smoking gun— no pictures of Victor immediately post-surgery, no official certificate of any sort. But there was a mountain of smaller pieces of evidence that added up to an undeniable truth. Victor Mercer had replaced Daxton Hart almost a year and a half ago, and he had been running the country ever since.

The broadcast ended abruptly in another burst of static. As soon as the news anchor returned, Lila turned the television off, and we sat in silence for the better part of a minute.

"This is my fault," said Greyson at last. "Grandmother would have never bothered to Mask a replacement if I'd been willing to be Prime Minister."

"Don't be an idiot," said Lila. "Grandmother did whatever she wanted, the rest of us be damned."

"But if I'd just cooperated—"

"Then what?" I said wearily, because for once, I agreed with Lila. "Would the country have been a better place?"

Greyson blinked. "I could have made things better."

"Would you have introduced democracy?" I said. "Gotten rid of the test? Given everyone equal rights and an equal say?"

"I—" Greyson swallowed hard. "I want to say yes, but I don't know."

"I do." I gave him a small smile. "Augusta would have had you under her thumb for so long that by the time she finally died, you wouldn't have known better anymore. This is the way it had to happen. It was put into motion long before Victor Mercer was Masked as Daxton. If you were running the country instead of him, you would have been the one with a target on your back."

Lila's mouth fell open. "The Blackcoats would have *never* hurt Greyson—"

"You would have gone after Augusta," I agreed. "And

I'm sure Greyson would have been much more willing to compromise. But there's a reason we can't just assassinate Daxton and be done with it. The army, the Shields, the Ministers of the Union—the key components of the country as it stands would still exist without him, and *that* is the problem."

"So how are we supposed to win this war?" she spat, and I shrugged.

"By turning the rebellion into a revolution. And we can do that with the people on our side. But we have to come up with a plan. I know Daxton is using Greyson against you, so we need to find a way around that. We need to get Greyson to safety, or—"

"I'm not leaving Lila," he said firmly. "And I'm not leaving you, either. You're my sister."

His words brought me up short. This, I realized, was the first time we'd been face-to-face since I'd discovered the real Daxton Hart had been my biological father. Greyson must have heard my speech. I searched his expression for any sign of disgust or sarcasm, but I found only fierce determination. He believed me. Just like that, without any real proof, other than the color of my eyes, he trusted me enough to accept me as his own flesh and blood.

"Then we'll all find a way out of here together," I said, a smile flickering across my face. It was brief, but it was genuine. "There are three of us and only one of him, and he isn't half as smart as he thinks he is. There must be something we aren't thinking of."

"When the hell did you become the brains of this operation?" said Lila, eyeing me warily.

"The day you gave up," I said without malice. I should

have been offended, but it was a legitimate question. Greyson was a genius who invented things I couldn't even dream of, and Lila was the one with the silver tongue and the zinger for every situation. I couldn't even read. My only worthwhile quality was the fact that my eyes matched hers.

Her expression soured, but before she could retaliate, the bedroom door opened, and a pair of guards entered. "You need to come with us," one of them announced.

"Where are we going?" said Greyson as he stood and reached for a pair of crutches in the corner. I carefully swung my legs around. Someone had dressed me in flannel pajamas, and my foot was in a brace.

"The Ministers of the Union have called a meeting, and they would like for the three of you to be present for it," said the second guard. I took the crutches from Greyson and stood, wobbling as I leaned on them. I'd used them before for an ankle sprain, but that had been years ago.

"What's the meeting about?" I said as the three of us traipsed toward the door. Greyson remained at my side, his arm held out as if he intended to catch me if I fell. Some long-buried part of me swelled with an emotion I couldn't name. Pride? Relief? Gratitude? Acceptance? Despite our differences, and despite all I'd done to work against his family, he still welcomed me as his sister, unconditionally. I didn't deserve him. None of us did. He was too damn good for the world he'd been born into.

"Follow us," said the first guard, leaving my question unanswered. I hobbled as fast as I could down the long hallway that led through the heart of the Stronghold, stopping only when we reached the elevator that could take us up to the open sky.

Instead of hitting the top button, however, the guard hit a lower floor, and the elevator glided downward. As I struggled to keep my balance on my crutches, I caught sight of myself in the mirrored walls. Daxton hadn't just let the doctors treat my foot—I was cleaned up, too, with all traces of my stay in Elsewhere completely gone. The cuts and bruises I'd accumulated, the freckles that had appeared under the cold sunlight—someone had even dyed my roots to match. I glanced at my nails. My manicure was back.

Daxton wanted me for something. He had kept me alive for a reason, and whatever that reason was, he wanted me to look like the best version of myself—or what passed for myself—as possible. I suppose it hadn't gained him much favor, having Lila's double look like a mess on national television. It showed ill treatment on the government's part, and when sympathies for Lila were still so strong, it made sense that he would want me looking like I hadn't just spent weeks in the worst place in the country.

The guards led us through a maze of hallways, and by the time we reached the meeting room, my arms trembled with exertion. Greyson quickly found a chair for me along the edge of the spartan room, and I sank into it gratefully while taking in the faces of the twelve Ministers of the Union.

I had met most of them at one party or another during my tenure as Lila, and I tried to remember their names. Minister Bradley was a given; he'd cropped up too many times in my life as of late for me to ever forget his wandering eyes or handlebar mustache. I'd seen Minister Creed, Knox's father, from a distance, but had never officially met him—which, in retrospect, seemed odd, considering I was supposed to be his son's fiancée. I remembered what Knox had told me about his twin brother, and any connection I might have felt toward the senior Creed vanished.

Daxton burst into the room, flanked by a pair of guards. He wore a well-cut dark suit, and his hair was slicked back the way Victor Mercer had worn it in the single photograph I'd seen. I glanced at Greyson to see if he'd noticed, too. He stared at the man posing as his father with more hate in his eyes than I'd thought he was capable of.

"Sorry, am I late?" said Daxton breezily, taking a seat at the head of the table. His guards stood beside him, both with their hands on their weapons. "My deepest apologies, gentlemen. I had a few calls to make. Now, what seems to be the trouble?"

Minister Creed stood. He sat at the opposite end of the table from Daxton, and he squared his shoulders as if readying himself for battle. I doubted he'd ever seen the wrong end of a gun before, but to his credit, he spoke without any hint of apprehension in his voice. "With all due respect, you know exactly what we asked you here for. The evidence the rebels have uncovered—"

"Is completely unsubstantiated," said Daxton with a dismissive gesture. "Anyone could falsify those documents, and it's rather convenient that everyone they claim to be connected to the procedure is dead."

"Very convenient," agreed Creed, his brow furrowing. "Though far more convenient for you, I'd say."

Daxton chuckled, and the sound of it sent an icy dread running down my spine. "If we're going to talk convenience, let's discuss the fact that your son is the one behind all of this Blackcoats nonsense. If our suspicions must fall on one of our own, you seem far more likely a candidate than me, Minister Creed."

Creed reddened, and I could tell from his clenched jaw and deadened stare that this wasn't the first time he'd faced that kind of accusation. "I have proven my loyalty time and time again. If Lennox were in front of me right now, I would not hesitate to execute him like the traitor he is."

"Well, then. Let's make that a priority." Daxton turned his attention toward the others seated at the table. "Gentlemen, tell me you don't really believe their conspiracy theories. They're simply trying to sway the public against us."

"Against *you*," corrected Creed. Daxton narrowed his eyes, and one of the guards shifted.

"Believe me, if they take me out, they will make sure you come crumbling down with me," he said. "If you want to continue to enjoy your current lifestyle, I would highly recommend ignoring their fiction and supporting me."

"There's a simple way to get this sorted once and for all, isn't there?" said Minister Bradley, not bothering to stand as he stroked his mustache. "The girl said she felt a V on the back of your neck. One of you, yes?" He eyed me and Lila.

"The one with the crutches," said Daxton with a sniff, answering Bradley's silent question. "Is that what this has come to? Feeling the back of my neck like I'm a common criminal?"

"It would be the easiest way to solve this—dispute," said Bradley with a shrug, as if it didn't matter to him one way or the other. As long as he got to keep his job, I supposed it probably didn't.

"And what will you do if you find I am in fact this Victor Mercer character, as they claim?" he said.

"Well—" Bradley looked at Creed helplessly, and Creed cleared his throat, casting a fleeting look at the armed guards.

"We have all agreed that, should you prove not to be a member of the Hart family, you will be relieved as Prime Minister and indicted for treason. Should you decide not to show us your neck, we must assume the worst, and the results will be the same."

All twelve Ministers stared at Daxton. They may not have been as influential as he was individually, but together, they formed the most powerful body in our country. I furrowed my brow. It couldn't be this easy. After all the Blackcoats had risked—it couldn't possibly be as simple as the Ministers of the Union stripping him of power. I glanced at Greyson. He was next in line for the title of Prime Minister. If he was the one they appointed in Daxton's place, this war would be over by sunset.

"Very well, then," said Daxton slowly. "I suppose you've left me with no choice." He rose and walked around the side of the table. "Creed, if you'd like to do the honors."

Something about this wasn't right—there was too much of a bounce in Daxton's step, and his tone was lighter than someone facing charges of treason would ever sound. I watched him closely, my nails digging into my thighs. The Blackcoats had played their ace. Now he was about to play his.

Daxton stopped an arm's length away. "Go on, then," he said, and Creed lifted his hand, his chin jutting out and his mouth tugging into a frown. Apparently he hadn't expected to do this himself.

Bang.

The instant his fingertips brushed against the back of Daxton's neck, a shot rang out, and Creed doubled over. I dropped to the ground, pure fear coursing through me and taking over every instinct and desire I had. Lila shrieked, and as Greyson threw himself over her, the other Ministers shouted, half of them ducking underneath the table.

Bang. Bang.

Creed collapsed, and even from a distance, I could see the pool of blood spreading from his head and torso. Several of the other Ministers stumbled out of their seats and toward the door, but a dozen more guards entered the room, blocking their way and drawing their weapons.

"Now, does anyone else object to me retaining my position as Prime Minister?" said Daxton. The Ministers fell silent. He crossed his arms, tapping the barrel of his gun against his biceps. "Good. I'm sorry to say your services are no longer needed by your country. I've taken the liberty of drawing up an amendment granting the Prime Minister— me—full power over the government, and your last act as Ministers of this great union will be to sign it."

From the inside of his jacket, he pulled out a rolled-up piece of paper. A few speckles of Creed's blood had managed to stain the edge, and Daxton sighed. "Ah, well. Can't have a revolution without shedding a few drops of blood, can you?"

He tipped me an enormous wink, and I clutched one of my crutches. Knox had said nearly the exact same thing to me only a few weeks before.

"A few of you may stay on as my advisers if I so choose," he continued, addressing the Ministers, "but the rest of you will make your homes down here for the foreseeable future, until it is safe for men of your rank to return to Washington."

"Down here?" gasped another Minister—Minister Ferras, whom I had only met once before. "But—"

Bang. Bang.

The second Minister collapsed only a few feet from me, and my stomach heaved. It took everything I had not to be sick.

"Does anyone else feel like rejecting my most gracious offer to protect you from the Blackcoats until the end of this war?" said Daxton.

No one else said a word.

Daxton sniffed. "I do hope this isn't the end of our good relations, Ministers. It's been a true honor."

He unrolled the paper and set a heavy pen directly in the middle. One by one, the Ministers approached and, with trembling hands, signed the amendment granting Daxton complete power over the country. There would be no Ministers of the Union to check him now; no one to tell him no, no one to stop him from doing whatever he wanted, consequences be damned.

He waited until every one of the ten remaining Ministers had signed the paper. Then, reaching down, he dipped Creed's lifeless finger in the pool of blood, pressing it against the document, as well. Once he had repeated the process with Ferras, he squared his shoulders and smiled like a cat assessing its prey. "There we are. I'm so pleased we're in full agreement." Rolling it back up, he tucked it into his pocket. "Now come, Greyson, Lila, Kitty—it's nearly time for lunch. I'm famished."

The idea of going anywhere with that murderous monster made me lose any appetite I might have otherwise had, but Greyson and Lila stood, and I reluctantly followed. A dozen guards remained in the room—to wrangle the Ministers, I assumed—while the original pair positioned themselves firmly between us and Daxton. To act as human shields, maybe, but I was having a hard enough time keeping up, and Greyson and Lila clung to one another in fear.

"You do enjoy duck, don't you, Kitty?" Daxton called over his shoulder as he headed toward the elevator. Another pair of guards joined him, this time leading the way. "I couldn't remember. If you'd like, I can have the staff make you anything you'd like."

"Duck is fine," I said shortly, purposely slowing down. Daxton and the guards didn't seem to notice, but Greyson did. He let go of Lila and met my slow hobble, his brow furrowed with concern.

"Your arms have to be sore. When we get back, I'll make sure to find you a wheelchair or—"

"A wheelchair would be nice," I said, even though I had no intention of giving up my crutches. I took a few more painful hops before stopping completely.

Greyson and Lila did, too. "Here, let me help," he said, taking my crutches. "They might be too short for you."

"You're next in line," I whispered. "And the Prime Minister has complete power now."

His frown returned, and though he fiddled with my crutches, he nodded slowly. I reached out to steady myself against the wall.

"The first chance we get, we're going to kill him."

Both he and Lila looked at me sharply, but neither had the chance to reply. "Do keep up," called Daxton from in

front of the elevator, and Greyson handed me my crutches.
I tested them gingerly. They were taller now, and they did
fit a bit better.

The guards circled back around to escort us to the waiting elevator, and as we all piled inside, I used the mirrors
to meet Greyson's and Lila's eyes. It was up to us now. All
we had to do was find a way to kill the most powerful
man in the country, and we would win this war for good.

VIII

OASIS OF SAND

Lunch was an uncomfortably awkward affair. Daxton insisted on sitting next to me, and he continued to fill my plate with duck, potatoes, salad—every time I took so much as a single bite, he would replace it with another serving.

"You really are too thin, my darling," he said. "I would hate for anyone to think you've been mistreated."

So I'd been right; that was the reason he'd had me fixed up and made over after all. "What are you going to have me do?" I said, pushing a piece of potato around my plate. I would have taken the rotting food in Elsewhere over this any day if it meant I didn't have to sit next to him.

"Oh, you know. Nothing too strenuous. You have, after all, had a difficult few days." He served himself another piece of duck. "You'll be addressing the people after dinner tonight. Showing them that you're alive and safe—you know, the usual."

He wanted me to negate any sympathy Knox's announcement had created. It was the first smart move he'd made in ages. "What do I get in return?"

"What would you like?" he said jovially. I glanced at

Greyson and Lila across the table. Neither had said a word to me, but they had whispered back and forth to one another a few times. Apparently this wasn't unusual, because Daxton didn't seem to mind.

"You only need one mouthpiece, right?" I said. "And the people might love Lila, but I'm the one who's been working with the Blackcoats. With all these—*claims* about who you are, Lila's word won't mean much. But mine, since I'm the one who accused you to begin with—mine is gold."

"You want me to release Lila," he said, taking a bite and chewing slowly as he watched me.

"I want you to release Lila *and* Greyson," I corrected. "Do that, and I'll say anything you want."

"No," said Greyson, his voice barely above a whisper, but his tone unshakable. He set his fork down. "Lila and I will continue to cooperate if and only if you release Kitty. She's injured, she'll have no chance to make it back to Elsewhere, and the Blackcoats are on the brink of starvation. She'll pose no threat to you."

I gaped at him. "Greyson—"

"This isn't a negotiation," he said to me, and then he looked back at Daxton. "What will it be?"

I stared at the pair of them, my gut twisting with the need to inform them just how important it was that they escape as soon as possible. Daxton wouldn't let me go, not when I would undoubtedly return to the Blackcoats the first chance I got and report to the world what I had witnessed in the meeting room with the Ministers of the Union. Greyson's and Lila's silence could be bought. Greyson had never been much of a fighter, and Lila would never return to the Blackcoats. I didn't blame her. She'd already risked her life enough.

But my life—my purpose—was tied to this war. And I was determined to keep my word; the first chance I had, I would kill Daxton. I couldn't do that while they were in the Stronghold with me, not when my failure would inevitably mean their deaths. But as soon as I was alone with him, he wouldn't be able to use Greyson and Lila against me. And as much as I wanted to survive to see the end of this war and the Blackcoats' success, that would never happen while he lived.

It was a risk I was willing to take.

They had to know that. They had to understand. But rather than meet my eyes, Greyson stared steadily at Daxton, and in an instant I knew he understood what I was trying to do. And that was why he was making his bargain.

"Interesting." Daxton looked back and forth between us, the tines of his fork tapping against his plate. "You want to protect them, and they want to protect you. It's sweet, in a way. We really are one big happy family, aren't we?"

Lila's mouth twisted with barely disguised disgust. "She can give your speech tonight, but we want her on a helicopter to D.C. by midnight. You want to prove to the public that you're really sympathetic and mean us no harm. What better way to do that than to release her? And not only that, but you'll be sending a clear message to the Blackcoats. You're not afraid of them. Especially not a seventeen-year-old III."

"You make a good case, but that isn't surprising. You could sell sand in the desert, my dear Lila," he said with a smile that, from anyone else, would have been warm.

"Both offers are enticing, and both have their merits. But you forget, I could just as well keep you all."

"You could," I said coolly. "But where's the fun in that?"

He barked with laughter, throwing his head back in an undignified manner that would have made the prim and proper Augusta curl her upper lip. "Indeed. I'll tell you what. I will accept one of your offers—*after* Kitty's broadcast, provided she follows my script."

"Which offer?" said Lila, and he shrugged.

"That's the fun of it, isn't it? You'll just have to wait and see."

Neither Lila nor Greyson seemed to think it was any more *fun* than I did, but we kept our collective mouths shut, and after lunch ended, I returned to my room. Each of them had a suite down the same hallway, it turned out, but they didn't invite me into theirs, and I didn't ask. I wanted to get out of the Stronghold and out from under Daxton's thumb more than anything, but I couldn't do it at the expense of their freedom. I wouldn't.

It was entirely possible I wouldn't have much of a choice, however, and I spent the rest of the afternoon icing my foot and scanning the news channels, searching for any new messages from Knox or the Blackcoats. I tried to sleep, but the anxiety churning in my stomach kept me from dozing off.

I couldn't go off script, not if I wanted to have a chance to get Greyson and Lila out of here. In my mind, at least, mine was the better deal. If Daxton let me go, he would have gained nothing from keeping me alive to begin with; but if he released Lila and Greyson, he would have me as a prisoner at his beck and call.

Despite my cautious optimism, I knew the most likely scenario would be Daxton refusing to honor either deal, and all three of us remaining in the Stronghold for the rest of the war. Maybe we would find a way out eventually, but not in time to do much to help the current efforts. For now, I could only hope Daxton's stupidity in revealing Celia's mistake bought us the support we needed, the way Knox seemed to think it would.

A knock sounded on my door shortly before dinner. I'd managed to dress myself in something other than flannel pajamas, choosing from the half dozen outfits hanging in the closet. "Come in."

I wasn't sure who I was expecting—no one in the Stronghold would listen to me, anyway, if I'd tried to deny them entry—but relief coursed through me at the sight of Greyson. "You look nice," he said, nodding toward the cocktail dress I wore.

"Getting my foot through pants hurts too much to try right now," I said, tugging awkwardly at the waist. I'd worn plenty of fancy dresses as Lila, but I'd never gotten the hang of them completely. "Is it almost time for dinner?"

"In a few minutes," he said, closing the door behind him and turning the lock with a click. I looked up, frowning.

"What—"

"I have something for you." He held up a small velvet box, the kind that usually held a ring or a fancy pair of earrings. Lila had had dozens of them in Somerset. "An early Christmas present."

I had no idea what day it was anymore, let alone how close it was to Christmas. A week, maybe, but I couldn't be sure. "What is it?" I said, taking the box and weighing it in my hand.

"Open it and see."

I untied the ribbon. He'd given me two gifts before: the first, a necklace that had doubled as several different kinds of lock picks, had been meant for Lila. The second had been a picture frame that, when the right button was pushed, revealed a photograph of me—the real me—and Benjy on the last Christmas we'd spent together as ourselves. Both were exactly what I'd needed at the time, even if I hadn't known it then.

I cracked open the box to reveal a tiny silver cuff that matched my necklace. It was simple—the kind of thing that blended in as an accessory rather than standing out. Nothing that would capture notice, even if Daxton was looking right at it.

"It's beautiful," I said, and it was. It was a fine piece of jewelry, with silver vines wrapping around to form the cuff. "How am I supposed to, uh—wear it?"

"Here, allow me." Greyson plucked it from the velvet box and scooted closer to me. "Look at the television."

Obediently I turned my head, and Greyson slid the cuff onto the cartilage of my ear, sliding it down until it rested just above the lobe. He gave it a gentle tug, and it stayed on firmly, no piercing required. I touched it, running my fingertips over the metal. "Thank you."

"You're welcome." He inched away to give us both a little more room and folded his hands in his lap. "It's one part of a three-piece set."

"Where are the other pieces?" I said, and he held up his wrist. A plain silver cuff link caught the light.

"Like it?"

I smirked. "I'll like it better once I know what it does."

"They're communicators. As soon as I activate it, all three pieces will connect, no matter how far apart they are. You could be on the other side of the country, and I would still hear you."

"How? That's on your wrist," I said. "Unless you have some weird ear anatomy going on—"

He chuckled, and after the day we'd both had, it was a welcome sound. "The cuff links are a little different. They come with a piece that slides on the inner part of the ear, right on the cartilage." He turned to show me, tapping on the part of his ear that stuck out. "It's in there, and it won't fall off until I decide to remove it."

I tried to spot whatever it was he was talking about, but to no avail. "Who has the third piece? Lila?"

He shook his head. "I'll make one for her eventually, if she wants. But I had one smuggled out to Knox. He should be receiving it in the next couple days."

"You—what? Knox?" My mouth dropped open. "How did you—"

"The less you know, the better," he said. "Just trust me on this, Kitty. They'll work. And whether you leave or Lila and I leave, we'll all have a way to communicate."

I threw my arms around him, my heart swelling with gratitude and that same acceptance I'd felt earlier, when he'd done nothing more than help me with my crutches. This was what family really was. "You are a *genius*."

"I'm not. I just see things differently, that's all." He awkwardly hugged me back, and a moment passed before he

said, "I'm sorry we didn't get to know each other growing up."

"Yeah, me, too," I said, still holding on to him. He relaxed a little in my embrace. "We'll make up for it when
the war's over. We'll go on vacation somewhere, talk about
stuff, figure each other out—"

"Is that what siblings do?" he joked. "My brother—our
brother, I guess—he mostly ignored me."

Jameson, Greyson's older brother and the original heir
to the title of Prime Minister, had been killed in the same
bombing that had taken the lives of the real Daxton Hart
and his wife. Greyson had only been spared thanks to that
marvelous brain of his, when he'd skipped the outing to
tinker on his inventions instead, and I couldn't have been
more grateful for it. "I won't ignore you," I said, as I let
him go and tapped my cuff. "I won't even ask how to turn
this thing off in case you get too chatty."

"There's a gemstone on the side," he said with a smile.
"All you have to do is slide it down. Slide it back up to turn
it on. Obviously you'll want to keep it on as much as possible, just in case, but if you absolutely need your privacy—
well, I didn't want to give you any reason to take it off."

"I won't," I promised, and I pressed my lips together.
"I'll miss you, Greyson. Stay safe, all right? Whether I'm
the one who goes, or you and Lila are."

"You too," he said, all traces of humor evaporating. "If
he lets you leave, this way you'll be able to tell Knox where
to find you. You'll be able to rejoin them."

A second chance with the Blackcoats. It seemed almost
too good to be true. I nudged his arm. "Don't jinx it. Daxton could decide not to let any of us go."

"It's possible," he allowed, and for a moment, a shadow passed over his face. "A lot of things are possible. But you and Lila both made very good points. He might have won a few battles, but he'll figure out soon enough that he's losing the war. If he backs out, we'll renegotiate in the near future. Either way, we're all smarter than him individually, and he knows it. He'd be an idiot to keep all three of us here indefinitely and give us a chance to work together."

"He *is* an idiot," I said. "One who thinks he's a genius. They're the most dangerous kind."

"No, the most dangerous kind are the ones with power," he said.

"And Daxton now single-handedly rules over the entire country."

Greyson covered my hand with his and squeezed. The weight of the amendment's implications settled on my shoulders, and I took a deep, calming breath. The crazier and more desperate Daxton grew, the more enemies he would make. The situation seemed impossible right now, but he was slowly digging his own grave. We just had to be patient.

"Was the real Daxton anything like this?" I said. All my life, I'd been fed the public image of Daxton Hart—an upstanding family man who cared about the people and wanted us all to succeed. It was nothing more than propaganda, of course, but after meeting Victor Mercer's version of Daxton, curiosity snaked through me, leaving me with more questions than would likely ever have answers.

"He was—smarter," said Greyson after a moment. "He was still ruthless, and up until now, I think he would have mostly done the same things. But he was much cleverer about achieving his goals. You wouldn't even know he'd entrapped you until it was over, and he had his metaphorical hands around your neck."

That was something I could picture all too easily. "Was he violent?"

"He used violence as a tool. That's what Victor does wrong," said Greyson. "He uses violence for pleasure. It's not the same. It's never been the same, and Grandmother must have known. I think that's why she kept such a tight leash on him."

I exhaled. Victor's Daxton seemed to have an endless thirst for blood and sadism, but I thought I could live with being the real Daxton's daughter as long as I knew that piece of him wasn't real. "We'll get him. Or he'll get himself. One way or the other, he won't last much longer."

"I hope you're right," he said with a flicker of a smile, and I wrapped my fingers around his.

"I'll make sure I am."

At dinner, Daxton went on and on about how pleased he was by the public's reception of the news that he had dissolved the Ministers of the Union. It was true that the Ministers had taken the brunt of public disapproval for the various laws they had passed, but they were laws that, if Daxton hadn't come up with himself, he had certainly supported. I listened silently, letting him ramble. It would have been easy to mention the fact that he controlled the media, and therefore anything they reported was biased in his favor, but I didn't want to do or say anything to upset his good mood.

At last, once dinner was over, we moved down a level to

what must have been his office. It was guarded by two soldiers and an electronic lock, and behind the double doors
sat an exact replica of his office in Somerset. Bookcases
lined the walls, a large mahogany desk stretched across the
back of the room—there were even fountains at the entrance and the Hart family portrait hanging on the back
wall. The only difference I could see was the fact that there
was no air vent in the corner that would grant me access. As
far as I'd been able to determine, the vents in the Stronghold were too narrow for even a small child to fit through,
let alone an adult.

A small camera crew waited for us, and I took my seat on
a short couch in front of a bookcase. While a woman did
my makeup and hair, Daxton read the short speech aloud
for me twice, and he made me repeat it again and again
to make sure I had it memorized. I'd never been able to
read, but it wasn't until I'd been Masked as Lila that it had
become a real problem.

"Good luck," said Greyson, and Lila flashed me what
she must have thought was a supportive smile. Instead she
looked like she'd taken a sip of vinegar.

"Thanks," I said. The speech was simple: tell the world
who I was. Prove it by flashing the X on the back of my
neck that was hidden beneath my hair. And say in no un-
certain terms that my earlier accusations about Daxton's
identity were false. Daxton had written the speech himself,
and it was only forty-five seconds long at most.

Easy.

But when the lights came on and the producer counted
down, I glanced at Lila and Greyson standing in the corner
together, and part of me—the stupid part that was respon-

sible for every mess I'd made in the past four months—
screamed at me not to listen to Daxton. To say anything
that would help the rebellion. To do *something* to prove I
was worthy of being a Blackcoat.

The red light came on, and I held my breath. For the second time that week, I had the entire country's attention. I
could have been brave. I could have said anything. I could
have given the Blackcoats the push they needed to win this.

Instead, word for word, I recited exactly what Daxton
had told me to say.

My bravery wasn't worth his retaliation, and I knew
him well enough by now to know he wouldn't take it out
on me. He would kill Greyson. Or torture him in front
of me. Whichever he thought would hurt me more. And
whatever problems I was causing the Blackcoats by revealing myself to be alive, it was worth it for the small chance
that Daxton would let Greyson and Lila go.

I stared resolutely at the camera as I spoke, but I could
feel their eyes on me. Those forty-five seconds were the
longest of my life, and when at last the camera turned off
and the red light darkened, I dared a glance in their direction, only to find Lila staring at me as if I'd just gift
wrapped the Blackcoats and handed their surrender to Daxton. Despite all the times she'd done the exact same thing,
somehow she'd expected me to act differently, to take that
risk.

I couldn't. Not when their necks were on the line.

I'd done my best for the Blackcoats, telling the country
my entire story just a few days ago. It was up to them to
decide what they believed now. And if that wasn't good
enough for Lila, so be it. I was the one who had to live

with myself after this was all said and done, and I couldn't do that with Lila's or Greyson's blood on my hands.

"Very good," said Daxton, clapping delightedly. "You're a true star, Kitty. I never quite saw it before all of this unfortunate madness, but you, my darling—you're something special."

"Does that mean you're going to keep me and let Lila and Greyson go?" I said, and he stood, offering me his hand. Against my better judgment, I took it.

"Oh, no, no—I couldn't possibly force them to leave the safety of the Stronghold, not when there's a war raging out there," he said, his eyes widening innocently. "You, however, seem terribly eager to leave us."

"I—" I opened and shut my mouth. I couldn't tell him no, not when he would jump on the chance to keep all three of us. But I couldn't bring myself to say yes, either. "I'm worth my weight in gold, remember?"

"You are, and you just told the public everything I needed you to say," he murmured, tucking a lock of hair behind my ear. "I'm afraid my use for you has diminished dramatically, so really, it only makes sense that you be the one I release. Unless you've had a change of heart."

He was going to make me say it. Of course he was. I relaxed as much as I could and smiled. "Not at all. As fun as it's been here with you, I wouldn't want to distract you from all the important work you're doing."

"Oh, but what a delightful distraction you are." He brushed his knuckles up and down my jaw. "Your helicopter leaves at midnight. Don't be late. I will miss you terribly, Kitty."

"Maybe we'll meet again someday," I said sweetly. Plenty

of people deserved to watch him bleed to death, but self-ishly I wanted to be the one to slit his throat. He patted my cheek and finally walked away, leaving me to exhale sharply and fumble for my crutches.

So this was it. Whatever Daxton planned on doing to me—if he would keep to his word and drop me off in D.C., or if he would abandon me in the middle of nowhere and let the elements have me—I wouldn't be here to protect Greyson and Lila. It would be back to square one for them, and I could only hope everything that had transpired that day would give one of them the courage to do what had to be done. Greyson was smart. He could figure out a fool-proof plan to kill Daxton, or at least as foolproof as a plan like that could get. And Lila was braver than she thought she was. She would find the courage to carry it out.

Whatever happened to me, the game had changed now. The Ministers of the Union, the file—something monu-mental had shifted in this war, and none of us would be able to understand the true weight of it until we saw it in hindsight, but at least all of this hadn't been for nothing. There was no turning back now—not for the Blackcoats, not for Daxton, and definitely not for the people.

I was halfway back to my room when the click of heels echoed down the hallway to meet me. At my slow pace, it didn't take long for Lila to catch up. "I can't believe you," she snarled.

"If I went off script, Daxton would have hurt you or Greyson, and neither of you would've had any chance of getting out of here," I said. "I wasn't going to risk that."

"And look how that turned out," she spat. "We have to

stay here, while *you* get to go back to your little bunker and save the world."

"You think I want to be the one to go?" I said incredulously. "I'd give anything for you and Greyson to be the ones released. You've both been through enough, and Greyson especially—he doesn't deserve this."

"Oh, and I do?"

I scowled. "That's not what I meant."

"Then what did you mean?" she said furiously as she stormed down the hallway. "Because the more you talk, the less I understand."

I gritted my teeth. For someone who seemed to hate Daxton, she certainly seemed to trust his word. "You realize there is a distinct possibility that this is a trap, right?"

Lila blinked at me. "And?"

Did she really not get it? "And by this time tomorrow, it's entirely possible I'll be dead."

"He wouldn't kill you. It would give the Blackcoats the martyr they need to rally the country." She rolled her eyes. "Besides, you're the great Kitty Doe, with nine damn lives. You don't know how to die."

"No one's immortal. Not me, not you, not Daxton—no one." I ran my fingers through my hair, frustrated. She didn't get it, and I didn't know how to make her understand. "It doesn't matter if killing me would be stupid. He's long past the point of being rational. If that's what he wants to do, then you know he's damn well going to do it."

"It'd be worth it to get out of this hellhole." Lila shoved over a vase containing fresh roses. It crashed to the ground, shattering into a hundred pieces and spilling water and roses everywhere. I quickly hobbled out of the way.

"You think *this* is hell? You have a warm bed to sleep in, food to eat, clothes to wear, you don't have to handle human hearts every single day—"

"Will you just shut up already?" She whirled around to face me, and I fell silent, stunned to see tears in her eyes. "So I didn't spend a few weeks in Elsewhere. Sorry I'm not as stupid as you are, but that sure as hell doesn't make this place any easier to bear. Do you have any idea how long it's been since I've had even the *illusion* of freedom? Yet here you are, with a golden ticket out of here, and you look like you're heading to your own funeral. I would give *anything* to get out of this place, but you can't even bother to appreciate the fact that because of Greyson and me, you might actually have a future now."

"Of course I appreciate it," I said, gingerly picking my way around the vase shards. "That doesn't make this any safer for me, though. And if you wanted to go so badly, then you shouldn't have tried to make that deal in the first place. Daxton might've let you go if you hadn't—"

"It was Greyson's idea, not mine. Believe me, I would have been more than happy to take the first ride out of here and never look back." We reached my bedroom door, and Lila yanked it open for me. "When you get back, do me a favor, all right?"

"What?" I said cautiously, pausing in front of her.

"Don't waste it. Tell everyone what happened with Minister Creed and Minister Ferras. Tell them we're being held hostage and used against each other. Tell them what kind of monster Victor Mercer is, and don't pull any punches. If I can't rally them, then you have to. And whatever you do—" She leveled her gaze at me. "Don't you dare let Knox get in front of a camera again."

We stared at one another, and I took a shaky breath. "If I survive long enough, I will."

I limped through the doorway, collapsing on the chaise longue at the foot of the bed. Lila rolled her eyes at me. "Would you stop acting like he's going to kill you? He won't. You're his favorite toy."

"And he doesn't want to let anyone else play with me," I muttered.

Lila shut the door and locked it. "Fine. You know what? If you don't want to go, then I will."

I winced and slowly unwrapped my bad foot. "What the hell are you talking about?"

She sniffed and went to the freezer, wordlessly tossing me an ice pack. "You heard me. If you're too chicken to go, then I will."

"But—" I stared at her for so long that my palm began to grow numb, and I hastily pressed the ice pack against my foot instead. "Daxton will know we've switched. He'll use it as an excuse to kill both of us."

"Not if we're careful. And besides, we only have to fake it long enough to get me on the helicopter." Her blue eyes were bright with excitement, and she studied me closely. "We're still exact matches, and all it would take is five minutes at the most—that's all we'd have to pretend to be each other."

"*You'd* have to pretend to be *me* for five minutes," I corrected. "*I* would have to be *you* for the rest of the war, otherwise you know Daxton will take it out on Greyson."

She knelt beside the chaise, taking my cold hand in hers.

"Then pretend to be me. *Please*, Kitty. We can do this—I know we can. You fooled my own mother once. There's no way you won't be able to fool that megalomaniac, too."

My heart pounded, and my mouth went dry. "I can't do that. You know I can't do that. What if something happens to you? What if he drops you off in the middle of nowhere? What if it really is a trap?"

"Then at least I won't be here," she said fiercely. "And that's worth the risk to me, Kitty. Maybe it isn't to you, but to me—I would do anything to get out of here."

I blinked rapidly, a million thoughts running through my mind. Half of them were reasons why this couldn't possibly work, but the other half were reasons why it could. And reasons why it *should*. Everything she wanted me to tell the world—it would mean infinitely more coming from her. If the real Lila Hart were on live television, telling the truth about what had happened, then even the staunchest Daxton supporters would have no choice but to question everything. Or at least enough to break through to them, one by one, bit by bit. That was all we really needed. That extra push that could turn the tables on Daxton and give the Blackcoats the power they needed.

It was worth the risk. Especially if Lila was willing to take it. No, not willing—eager. She stared at me, practically begging, and the hope shining in her eyes was almost enough to make me agree.

"My foot is broken," I said at last, but even to my ears, I sounded pathetic. "And there's an X on the back of my neck, remember? My rank is gone. No one will believe I'm you."

"They don't have to, as long as they believe I'm you."

Lila stood and moved to the cupboards and cabinets that filled the white room, and I instantly knew what she was doing. It may have been my bedroom at the moment, but it was also more fully stocked than any hospital room in the country. "We can give me an X. And we'll give you pain medication for your foot so you'll be able to walk on it."

"What if it doesn't heal right? What if I have a limp for the rest of my life?" I said.

"So what? Add it to the list." She pulled out several items from the cabinets and tossed them on the bed. "We can work on the details."

I winced. "Lila—"

"What? Is a limp that big a deal to you? Daxton doesn't ask to see us much anyway, so you can just stay in here and let it heal."

I shook my head. "It isn't that. It's too risky. They might check my neck. They *will* check yours, and if they touch it, they'll feel your VII."

"They won't," said Lila firmly. "No one is crazy enough to X out a VII. No one."

"Except you."

"Yeah, well." She shrugged. "I don't want to be me anymore. You can be me—you're good at being me. But I'm done. I don't care about the risk involved. I don't care where I end up. I just want to be gone, Kitty. I want to be free. And if that means dying in the middle of nowhere, then fine. I'd rather die out there tomorrow than die in here a hundred years from now."

It was the feeling behind her words—deep, unshakable, and full of everything she wanted for herself in her own life—that struck a chord within me, and finally I had no choice but to relent. Because I knew that feeling. I'd lived that feeling every day of my life as Lila, and if one of us had the chance to escape and start over, it should have been her. She had been Lila Hart far longer than I had, after all. She deserved a break. "Okay. If you're sure this is what you really want."

Her shoulders relaxed, and she broke out into a wide grin. "I'm positive."

I bit the inside of my cheek so hard that the sickening copper taste of blood filled my mouth. This was crazy. Insane. A million things could go wrong, and it would only take one for Daxton to discover us. One wrong move. One wrong look. One wrong anything, and it was over. At best, we would both be stuck here; at worst, we would both be dead. "We can't tell anyone. Not even Greyson. Not until you're gone," I said, my voice trembling. He was going to kill me. And if Knox ever found out, he'd resurrect me and kill me again.

"I know," she said firmly, but it wasn't enough to settle my nerves. "This is just between you and me."

"And—and if anything does go wrong—"

"We'll figure it out." She exhaled sharply and focused on me again. "You need to protect him, all right? You need to do everything you can to make sure Greyson makes it out of this in one piece. As soon as Victor thinks he's about to lose, he'll go after Greyson. I know he will."

"I'll protect him," I said. "And I'll find a way to kill Victor. It won't be easy, but—"

"If anyone can, it's you." She pressed her lips together, and for a moment, guilt flashed across her face. "I shouldn't leave him."

"He'll understand," I said gently. "He knows how hard you've had it. And I think he'll be glad at least one of you got to be free."

Lila nodded, a jerky gesture that didn't look natural. "He's my best friend, and he's the only real family I have left. So please, just—make sure he's okay."

"I will," I promised. "No matter what. But, Lila—" I paused. "I know you've never liked me, but you and I are cousins, too. You'll always have me. And your mom loves you. And Knox. You have more people in your life than you realize, and once this war's over, we'll get to be a normal family. No backstabbing or plotting or murders. Just family."

She shook her head with a rueful smirk. "Maybe, but we'll never be normal."

"Probably not," I agreed. "Could be fun to try, though."

"You have a very strange definition of fun," she said, and I managed a smile. She wasn't wrong.

We spent the next several hours taking care of the details. The first thing we did was brand an X into the back of her neck with a small laser she'd found—the same kind Hannah had used on me my first day in Elsewhere. I was careful to match my X exactly, and though it was a punch to my gut, permanently marring Lila's perfect VII tattoo, she beamed as soon as she saw it.

A cream took care of the redness and swelling, and we did her nails to match mine. Once Lila had painstakingly duplicated my makeup from the interview, I scrubbed it off my face and let her replicate her usual look on me instead. We switched outfits, shoes, hairstyles—and finally the time came to figure out how to make this work with my broken foot.

"You need to be on the roof," she said as she gently inspected it. It was still swollen enough that wearing shoes would be difficult. "I'm going to pump you full of painkillers and give you a shot to make the swelling disappear. It won't be comfortable, but you'll be able to walk."

"Do you think this is enough to fool Greyson?" I said. I hated lying to him, but he couldn't know, not until Lila was safely gone.

"Just pretend to be mad at him for making the deal," she said. "If you can sell that, he won't notice any other differences. Not right away, at least."

I nodded. "And you can do my accent, right?"

"What, you mean sound like I grew up in the slums and never read a book in my life?" she said, in a perfect imitation of my voice and dialect.

"You're horrible," I said, and she shrugged, producing a needle from one of the cabinets.

"You've known that for months. Now hold still—this might pinch."

At fifteen minutes to midnight, we walked down the hallway together. She limped on my crutches, my brace on her foot and my grimace on her lips. Meanwhile, I walked beside her, my foot almost numb. I would pay for this as soon as the painkillers wore off, but for now, Lila's plan was working.

"Remember, you're pissed off at Greyson," she said as we stepped into the mirrored elevator. "Don't be nice to him. I know it's hard—he's like a baby animal sometimes.

It's impossible to be mean to him. But you have to sell this, got it?"

"Got it," I said, and I carefully adjusted my collar so the chain of my necklace wouldn't show. I couldn't bear to part with it, but I kept it hidden underneath my clothes most of the time anyway. Greyson would never notice. "You're sure you want to do this?"

"Positive," she said. "This is exactly what I want."

At least one of us was certain, and I took comfort in that. We were silent on the ride up to the roof, and when the doors opened, a blast of frigid wind hit us. I pulled up the hood of Lila's coat and shivered. She wore my bomber jacket, the one I'd worn while trying to sneak into Somerset, and I almost felt bad it wasn't heavier. But in her excitement, Lila didn't seem to notice the icy air.

The helicopter was already on the roof waiting for us, and the pilot stood nearby, along with several guards. I wasn't sure what they thought we were going to do—hop on the helicopter with Lila?—but Greyson stood toward the edge, his hands shoved in his pockets and a thick scarf wrapped around his neck.

I kept my distance and did my best to look as silently furious about the whole thing as possible. Lila, on the other hand, approached Greyson and caught him in a hug, dropping one of her crutches in the process. I held my breath, waiting for her to put her foot down and give us both away, but instead Greyson ducked down and got it for her.

She had the hard job, I figured—she was the one who had to convince Greyson she was me. But if he suspected anything, he didn't let on. As I wandered toward them, making sure not to limp, they hugged again, and I saw

Lila whisper *I love you* into his ear. It was true for both
of us, but from my vantage point, I could see the flash of
pain on her face when she said it, and I knew that was directly from her.

She approached me next and caught me in a hug as well,
this time holding on to her crutches. "Remember what
I said," she whispered, and I nodded. "Now glare at me
while I go."

I did exactly that, burning a hole in her head as she
hobbled toward the helicopter. One of the guards stopped
her and brushed her hair away from the back of her neck,
and my heart pounded as I waited for him to touch the
scarred X and feel the VII underneath, rather than the III
on mine. It was the only difference between us and the
only way to tell us apart for sure, but Lila was right; apparently the guard didn't think anyone would purposely
X out their VII like that, and he let her go without touching her skin.

Relieved, I watched as the pilot opened the door for
her, and she climbed in with effort, selling the whole broken foot thing. It was impressive, and if I hadn't known
any better, I would have thought she was me. I could only
hope the same held true for Greyson.

"Goodbyes are always difficult, aren't they?" said an oily
voice near my ear, and I set my jaw.

"Did you even think about sending us instead?" I spat,
exactly the way Lila would have. The pilot hopped inside, and the blades began to spin. I held on tightly to my
hood as it threatened to fly off. The last thing I needed
was Daxton discovering the switch before Lila was safely
off the mountain.

"Of course, but you made far too strong a point, darling. I delight in the thought of getting to show the Blackcoats my merciful side."

"You don't have a merciful side," I said as the helicopter rose in the air and turned, heading toward the horizon. A trickle of regret ran through me—that could have been me getting out of this place, heading back to Knox and Benjy and the Blackcoats. But Lila had lived her whole life under her family's rule one way or the other; she deserved to know what it was like to make her own choices for once.

"Don't I?" His voice grew thoughtful. "I suppose you're right, my dear Lila."

"Kitty?"

Greyson's voice crackled in my ear, and it took every bit of willpower I possessed not to react. The ear cuff, I realized. I'd forgotten to give Lila the ear cuff.

"Kitty, can you hear me?"

I saw Greyson moving his lips, his brow furrowed as he fiddled with his sleeve. He thought it didn't work. But then our eyes met, and a look of horror passed over his face.

He knew.

At that exact moment, a strange whistling sound echoed across the mountain range, and Greyson turned white. Confusion coursed through me, and I opened my mouth to ask if he was okay.

But then I saw it—a trail of light in the dark sky, whirling away from us at a horrifyingly fast pace.

And just as I put the pieces together, that trail of light reached the helicopter in the distance, and a fiery explosion lit the horizon.

"Mercy is terribly overrated," said Daxton calmly, and as he walked away, I watched in silent shock as the burning helicopter fell from the sky and crashed into the mountains below.

IX

GHOSTS

I didn't remember how I got back to Lila's bedroom. Someone was screaming—it might have been me, or it might have been Greyson—and I vaguely recalled strong arms around my torso, carrying me somewhere. But when I came to, I was once again lying in bed with no real memory of how I got there.

Lila was dead. If there was anything left of her, it was scattered on the side of a mountain now, and I was the only person who knew it was her. Everyone else thought it was me. It *should* have been me. I should never have traded places with her. I should have seen this coming. Daxton was never kind or generous—he was only cruel and sadistic, and of course he never intended to let any of us out of here alive. Of course he wanted to permanently silence the mouthpiece of the opposition, as soon as I'd told the country everything he'd wanted me to say. I should have known. I should have *known*.

Stupid, stupid, stupid. *Stupid*.

And Lila had been the one to pay the price.

"Was it her idea, or—or was it yours?"

I looked over at the couch, and my heart shattered into a million pieces. I was wrong. I wasn't the only one who knew it had been Lila.

Greyson sat on the sofa, his head in his hands and his shoulders shaking. His sleeves fell to his elbows, and I spotted red impressions of hands much larger than his own on his forearms. "I just want to know," he said thickly. "She was so angry at me. She knew it was the right thing to do, and she knew—she knew she had to play along, but she didn't want to. She wanted to leave. She wanted out of here so damn badly, and—"

"It doesn't matter. I went along with it. I let her take my place," I whispered. My throat was sore. Maybe I'd been the one screaming after all. "I didn't know—I had no idea Daxton would—"

Greyson let out a choking sob, and I sat up, not knowing what to do. I had no right to cry over Lila's death. She'd never liked me, not really. I couldn't blame her. I wouldn't have liked someone living my life, either. But Greyson loved her, and he'd already lost her once, when they'd had me Masked in the first place and we'd all thought Daxton's assassination plot had worked. And now he'd had to watch her die for real, right in front of him, and this time there was no possibility that she'd managed to sneak away. We'd both seen her get on that helicopter. Whether or not they ever bothered to find her body, there was no question she was gone.

Greyson stood at last and came to sit on my bed. He made no move to hug me, but he leaned against the headboard beside me and pulled his feet up next to mine, and we sat there together in silence for more seconds than I could count. I didn't dare say anything. There was nothing I *could* say to make this any easier for him, and if I hadn't already lost him completely, I didn't want to hurt him even more.

"Thank you," he said hoarsely, and he sniffed. I turned my head to look at him, my brow furrowed. "For—for giving her that chance. You didn't know it would end like this. And Lila—" His voice caught in his throat, and he cleared it. "She didn't feel any pain. It happened too fast. She probably didn't even realize..." He wiped his eyes. "All she wanted was to leave. She died happy."

I didn't know what to say to that, either, so instead I took his hand. He didn't pull away.

"You gave me a second chance with her," he said. "And the past few months...they've been a gift. I got to say everything I wanted to say. I got to tell her how much I loved her and how much she meant to me. But she stayed because of me. She let Daxton catch her because of me. I was always holding her down, and I'm glad—" Another sob escaped him, and it took him a moment to regain his composure. "I'm glad she finally had the courage to leave me. She deserved to be free."

"She didn't want to leave you," I said softly. "She loved you, and she made sure I knew how important protecting you was."

"She was always trying to protect me, but she should have been protecting herself." Greyson turned to me, his eyes red and puffy. "I don't care what promises you made her. Promise me you won't make the same mistake."

My throat tightened, and I swallowed hard. "I can't make you that promise. I'm sorry."

He closed his eyes wearily and leaned back against the

headboard. Another minute passed, and at last he whispered, "We're going to kill him."

"Yeah," I said. "We are."

I waited for the news of my death to hit the media, but it never did.

Part of me was glad. Even though Benjy and Knox knew better than to believe everything they heard on the news, I didn't want to give them any inkling that they might have lost me. Not before I could explain what had happened.

But the other part of me—the part that had given Daxton's speech and knew that if news broke that I'd mysteriously died only hours later, everything I'd said would be thrown into question—wished Daxton had crowed about it from the rooftops. He certainly did about everything else. The camera crew even had an interview with him and the former Minister Bradley the day after Lila's death, and Bradley was all too pleased to discuss how the Ministers of the Union had felt that, during this time of war, it would be best for the country if the Prime Minister could bypass the usual government channels. They left the lingering impression that the dissolution of the Ministers of the Union was temporary, but Greyson and I knew better.

Though we were nearly always in the same room, I gave Greyson as much space as he needed. Sometimes he sat in bed with me and read aloud, and sometimes he sequestered himself on the far side of the room, not saying a word for hours at a time. We watched the news together as much as we could stand, but try as I might, it was impossible for me to read between the lines the way Knox could.

Every morning I woke up with my stomach in knots,

certain Daxton would take one look at me and know I wasn't the real Lila, but over the course of the next several days, I didn't see him at all. Greyson and I discussed plan after whispered plan of how to take him out. While he slept, at dinner, bribing a guard for a gun—there were any number of ways we could do it, but nothing was a guarantee. And the more distance Daxton kept between us, the more impossible it became. As terrified as I was of having to once again step into Lila's shoes, I was more than willing to take that risk if it meant getting a clean shot at Daxton. But soon enough, it became painfully obvious that he might not give us that chance at all.

Four days after Lila's death, I woke up to a crackle in my ear. "Kitty?"

I blinked in the darkness. It was after midnight, and I could hear Greyson's soft snores from the sofa bed. So where had the voice come—

"Knox?" I gasped. Greyson's snoring stopped.

"It's good to hear your voice," he said, sounding relieved. Greyson sat up and turned on his reading lamp, giving me a questioning look.

"The earpiece," I said, tapping the cuff. "Knox is on the other end."

While Greyson fumbled with his, I hugged my pillow and tried not to grin too hard. It had worked. It had really worked.

"Are you okay? Is Benjy all right?" I said, the words tumbling out of me in a rush.

"We're fine," he said. "I don't want to give you too many details, just in case, but—we're fine. I've put Benjy in charge of another division, and he'll be moving out soon."

My enthusiasm deflated. "But—you're supposed to watch his back."

"I am," he said. "He'll be safe, I promise. Safer than the rest of us still in Elsewhere. But talk to me—tell me what's been going on."

Any lingering joy I had left over making contact with him dried up completely. He didn't know. Of course he didn't—how could he?—but in my excitement, I hadn't thought about being the one to deliver the news. I didn't think I could, and I hesitated, trying to force the words to come together.

"Lila's dead." Greyson's voice joined our conversation, and I looked at him in shock. He stared at his hands.

"Lila's—what?" stammered Knox, sounding as if all the air had left his lungs.

"Daxton thinks it's me," I said quietly. "He was—he said he was going to let me go, but Lila and I switched places. He blew up the helicopter. He thinks I was the one inside."

"But—it was—"

"Lila. Yeah," said Greyson. I hadn't seen him cry in days, but his voice tightened.

Knox was silent for so long that I thought we'd been disconnected. But at last he cleared his throat and said gruffly, "I'm sorry. If you would rather I not broadcast it—"

"No. Not yet," said Greyson, looking at me. "Kitty has to pretend to be Lila. If Daxton finds out we outsmarted him— He's coming undone as it is. I've never seen anyone grow more unraveled over such a short period of time. I don't know how long we have before he loses it completely."

"Where are you?" said Knox. "The Stronghold?"

"Yeah," I said. "He has all the Ministers of the Union here. He forced them to sign the amendment giving him absolute power."

"I figured as much," he grumbled, and then, as I remembered the cramped meeting room full of Ministers who were now as much prisoners as Greyson and I were, something awful occurred to me.

Knox had no idea his father was dead.

"Knox…" I trailed off and looked at Greyson, but he'd already done the hardest part. I couldn't make him say this, too. "Your father tried to stop him. He led the movement to have Daxton removed as Prime Minister, but before he could… Daxton—Victor—he killed your father."

Silence. I could hear Knox breathing on the other end, in and out, in and out, in and out. At last, in a voice hardened into steel, he said, "Good. One less Minister to get in our way."

I said nothing. As someone who had grown up without real parents, it seemed unfathomable to me that anyone could be so heartless about losing their own. But after what Minister Creed had done to Knox's brother—and Knox, and Knox's mother—I couldn't really blame him for it. Blood didn't always make a family.

"I'm going dark now," said Knox. "I have a meeting in the morning, and you two need to get some rest. Do whatever you have to do to stay safe, all right? Don't take any unnecessary risks, and for God's sake, Kitty, *behave*."

I shook my head, knowing full well he couldn't see me. The one time I hadn't followed the rules in this place, I had gotten Lila killed. I wasn't playing that game anymore. "Tell Benjy I love him."

"You can tell him yourself when we get you out of there. Good night. And Greyson—" He paused. "I'm sorry."

The cuff cut to static again, and the other end went dead. I sighed and collapsed back down on my pillows. Hearing Knox's voice hadn't solved all my problems, but it had made me feel a little better, knowing he was out there. Knowing I could talk to him now, if I needed to.

Greyson fiddled with something in his ear, and at last he said, "I'm going to take mine off."

"What?" I squinted at him. "Why?"

"I don't want to know what the Blackcoats are doing," he said. "I'll put it back on if you have to do a speech—I can feed you lines if we need to, so Daxton doesn't figure out you can't read—but otherwise, the less I know, the better."

I blinked. Lila and I hadn't even considered the possibility that I would have to make another speech as her. "But—"

"I'm not a Blackcoat," he said. "And while I admire and support you, I don't want to be one, and I have no business listening to you and Knox discuss your plans. I'm right here with you every day anyway," he added. "If Knox really wants to talk to me, you can let me know."

"All right," I finally said, hugging my pillow. "But you're an important part of this, okay? Maybe you aren't on the front lines of the war, but you'll be on the front lines of rebuilding the country once it's over, and they're going to need you. We're all going to need you."

He pressed his lips together. He'd said over and over again that he had no interest in being Prime Minister, but now I didn't see how he had much of a choice. We would need him. A Hart who was an ally of the Blackcoats, even if he wasn't actually a rebel. I couldn't run the country, after all. It would have to be him.

"Okay," he said at last. "When the time comes, I'll be there. Just—in the meantime… I'm not a soldier, and I'm not a battle strategist."

"Then come up with a way for us to rebuild," I said, remembering the task Knox had given me after my speech. It was far more suited to someone like Greyson, who had knowledge and experience to draw from. "Figure out how we're going to transition the country. You're smart, and you're inventive—if anyone can do it, it's you."

"I'll try," he said, and he settled back down into bed. "Good night, Kitty."

"Good night," I said, and for the first time since I'd arrived in the Stronghold, it *was* a good night. Or at least as good as it would ever get, with Lila gone and Daxton still alive. Knox was okay. Greyson had something to focus on other than the loss of his best friend. And now we had a direct line of communication to the rebellion. The Blackcoats' chances of winning the war had never been better, and though my guilt over Lila's death was a deep, constant ache that I knew would never leave me, as I drifted off to sleep, for the first time I let myself picture what my life could look like when this was all over.

Several weeks passed, and Greyson and I continued to be virtually imprisoned in Lila's room together. We had a small Christmas celebration that didn't include much more than a sip of champagne for us both, and we rang in the New Year by watching the news anchors report on a story about a bombing in New York that Knox assured us hadn't happened. Daxton continued to avoid us, and by the time mid-January rolled around, I had become certain we wouldn't see him until the war was over. The few times I tried to go see him, I was denied by guards I was sure would enjoy shooting me if I gave them an excuse, and no matter how hard I looked, I couldn't find a way to get to him inside the Stronghold. He was invulnerable.

But then, one evening, as Greyson and I sat across from one another on the sofa, each sketching the other, a guard burst into the room. I jumped, and my pencil made a dark line across the middle of Greyson's nose.

"The Prime Minister requests your presence at dinner," he said gruffly.

"Now?" I said.

"Immediately."

Together Greyson and I stood, and I pulled on a pair of Lila's most comfortable shoes. My foot had mostly healed by now—enough for me to walk without painkillers, at least—but I slipped my arm into Greyson's for extra support as we followed the guard.

Daxton already sat at the head of the dining room table, sipping a glass of wine. He stood as we entered and performed an exaggerated bow. "Greyson. My dear Lila. How I've missed you both."

"If only we could say the same," I said. Though it had been jarring before, now that I had known Lila—now that I had spoken with her and had meaningful interactions, now that I had come to care about her as more than just the girl I had to be—playing a dead girl made my skin crawl.

Greyson and I started toward Daxton's end of the long table, but two guards stopped us less than a third of the way down. "Your seats are over there, I'm afraid," said Daxton, gesturing past us. Two place settings sat at the very end of the table, dishes already served. "It isn't that I don't crave your company, of course—it's my guards, you see. Terribly overprotective."

So my suspicions were right; he must have had some idea that Greyson and I wanted nothing more than to kill him. At least we were all on the same playing field. I took my seat and eyed the juicy steak on the plate. Of course that was what Daxton had chosen to serve us—to serve Lila, who didn't eat red meat. It was possible he suspected me, but it had been a long time since I'd tried to eat something I knew full well Lila wouldn't touch. It was far more likely he was just trying to upset me. Upset Lila. And she would have risen to the bait.

"Are you trying to starve me on purpose?" I demanded, picking up the wine instead. Daxton's hand flew to his chest in a mock apology.

"Oh—oh, dear. Did they...? Of course they did." He motioned to one of the servers. "I've made Lila's dietary requirements crystal clear to you all. Why you can't follow a simple request, I've no idea."

Wordlessly the server picked up my plate, and within seconds he replaced it with a chicken stew. It smelled like something Nina, the matron of my group home, would have made, and if I'd had any appetite at all, I would have inhaled it. Annoyed, I picked up my utensils, wishing Greyson and I were taking dinner in Lila's room instead. At least he appeared to be content for now, cutting into his steak without complaint.

"There, much better," said Daxton, and he took a bite of

his meal. With his mouth full, he added, "Have you two been keeping up with the news?"

"Yes," I said. "Is that why you wanted us to come to dinner? To make sure we knew you're winning?"

"To make sure you knew *we* are winning, darling," he said. "After all, when we eradicate the rebels, you will both be at the forefront of the celebrations."

I took a bite of stew, trying to quell my nausea. Being in the same room as Daxton would have been enough to make me sick on a good day, but the thought of supporting him after the war made my stomach roll. "How long do you think it will be before you've—before *we've*—won?"

Though Knox didn't tell me much about what the Blackcoats were doing, he did tell me enough to reassure me that we were getting closer and closer to overtaking the government every day. In fact, hearing him tell it, Daxton was only a few key battles away from losing. I was much more willing to believe Knox than I was Daxton or the media, so when he casually lifted his wineglass and murmured, "Minutes, Lila," I nearly dropped my spoon.

"What?" I had to have misheard him. He was sitting at the other end of a dining room meant to seat fifty, after all.

"Minutes," he repeated, his mouth twisting into a gleeful smirk. "With all the trouble they've been causing, I thought to myself, why bother trying to reason with them? Clearly they aren't interested in civilized discussion, so I'll simply have to take care of Elsewhere myself."

The edges of my vision went dark, and I clutched my spoon. "How?" I choked out. "What are you going to do, Daxton?"

"Oh, it's been done," he said with a dismissive wave of

his hand. "I ordered the strike hours ago. The bombs should reach Elsewhere..." He checked his watch. "By dessert."

There was still time. I stood shakily, and the room around me spun. "I need—I need to lie down."

"You won't be staying for the show?" said Daxton, disappointment saturating his voice. "I promise you, Lila, you won't want to miss this."

I caught Greyson's eye, and he stood as well, hurrying around the table to help me. "She hasn't been feeling well for a few days," he said. "I'm sure the shock isn't helping."

"Shock? And here I was, thinking you'd be pleased to know you're almost free." Daxton sighed and threw his napkin down. "Fine. See if I try to do anything nice for you again. Go take your nap. I'll have my guards alert you when the Blackcoats are nothing more than a pile of charred remains."

Knox was in Elsewhere. Rivers. Strand. Thousands upon thousands of prisoners who had stayed to fight with us. It took a moment for my muddled mind to remember that Knox had moved Benjy, by some miracle—he was in another Blackcoat safe house, far away from Elsewhere and the massacre that was about to occur. No, not just a massacre—there was no word for the sadistic deaths of tens of thousands of people on the orders of a single madman.

I let Greyson lead me out into the hallway, and I leaned heavily on him. Two guards followed, and he glared at them. "I know how to get back to our room."

"Sir—"

"You're making it worse," he said, his grip tightening around my shoulders. "Go."

They exchanged a look and, reluctantly, they returned

to the dining room. If Daxton knew that we were now wandering around the Stronghold without a chaperone, he must not have cared, because they didn't return.

"Knox." A lump formed in my throat, and I fiddled with my ear cuff. "Knox—please, you have to be there. They're going to bomb you. Right now. It's happening now. You have to get out of there."

Silence. I looked at Greyson, desperate and panicked.

"It's not working. It's not *working*, Greyson—"

"We'll go back to the room and use mine," he said calmly, but I could hear the nervous edge to his voice. "Just take a deep breath and—"

"We don't have time to go back to the room." I looked around wildly. The elevator was only a few yards away. "The office. We'll be able to send them a message from Daxton's office."

"But—"

I slipped out of his grip and darted toward the elevators, hitting the down button over and over. It took ten infinite seconds for the doors to open, and I leaped inside. Greyson remained in the hallway, hesitating.

"You don't have to do this," I said, my heart pounding. If Daxton caught me, he would execute me for sure.

Muttering something that sounded suspiciously like a curse under his breath, Greyson jumped inside the elevator as the doors closed. "I know I don't have to, but I will."

Clenching my jaw, I nodded once, gratefully. It would be easier with someone who knew how to work the equipment.

Seconds seemed to stretch into minutes as the elevator descended, and at last the doors opened. Daxton's office was only a short walk away, and I raced down the hallway, ignoring my bad foot.

The door was locked, but I had my necklace off in an instant and passed it over the sensor. The red light flashed to green, and I turned the handle, my hands trembling. "I don't know how to work any of these things," I said as we both slipped into the office, and I closed the door firmly behind me.

Greyson marched up to the desk and hunched over the screen, his fingers dancing over the array of buttons. I hurried to his side as the screen went white, and a faint ringing sound echoed from the speakers.

"Pick up," whispered Greyson, and he grabbed my hand. I squeezed back, my heart in my throat. This couldn't be it. Maybe Daxton was lying. Maybe it was just another twisted game for his amusement. Maybe he'd wanted to see what we would do.

Or maybe it was real, and Knox, Elsewhere, and all its citizens were seconds away from turning into ash.

"Why isn't he picking up?" I said frantically, my voice hitching. "He's always in that stupid office. He never leaves. He eats in there, he sleeps in there—"

The screen turned black, and Greyson pressed a few more buttons. "Hold on, I'm trying again."

The white screen returned, along with the ringing. I bit my lip so hard I could taste blood, and every cell in my body was focused on that box, waiting for Knox's face to appear. He had to answer. He had to get out of there. I wouldn't accept anything else.

"It's pointless, you know."

I'd been so engrossed in the hope that Knox would pick

up that I hadn't heard the office door open, and as I looked up, I forgot how to breathe. Daxton stood between the two fountains at the entrance, four guards surrounding him—including the ones Greyson had dismissed.

"The drones are two minutes out," he said. "They're quicker than I expected, as it happens. But regardless, even if you were able to warn Lennox and the other Blackcoats, they would have no time to escape. All you would do is give them a few moments to ponder the pointlessness of their entire existence."

I blinked rapidly, and several tears rolled down my cheeks. I didn't bother wiping them away. Knox and the Blackcoats deserved them. "You're despicable."

"I'm a dictator, darling. It comes with the territory." He motioned to his guards. "Escort them to the couch. I have something I want them to see." Daxton winked at me. "You won't want to miss it."

I struggled as the first guard led me to the sofa and pushed me down. Daxton continued to keep his distance and two armed men between us at all times, and no matter how badly I wanted to rip his throat out, consequences be damned, I wouldn't have made it five feet.

Greyson sat down beside me, far more cooperative than I had been, while Daxton pressed a few buttons on his screen. "Ah, there we go. Straight from the drone," he said, and he angled it so we could see.

The image was dark, but a spotlight appeared, illuminating the ground. I couldn't pinpoint the section, exactly, but I did recognize the uniform gray buildings and straight roads of Elsewhere. I squeezed my eyes shut.

"Oh, Lila. You *will* watch," said Daxton, and I heard the

click of a gun. My eyes flew open. He was pointing the barrel directly at Greyson's head.

My chin trembled, but I forced myself to stare in the direction of the screen. I tried to look past it and focus on the bookshelves instead, but there was no ignoring the images. There was no pretending this wasn't happening.

I spotted Mercer Manor, and my stomach twisted as the few bites of dinner I'd taken threatened to come up. The lights were on. They were still there, and they had no idea that they were all about to die.

"And then...the magic," said Daxton gleefully. Silently the screen exploded into flashes of white and fire, and then everything went black.

That was it. No sound effects. No screams. No indication that tens of thousands of people had just died. Just silence and a blank screen.

Elsewhere was gone.

X

NOOSE

That night, I stared into the empty darkness, certain I would never be able to sleep again. Though Greyson had given me something to relax, it hadn't stopped the image of Elsewhere burning playing in a continuous loop in my mind.

It was only after I'd cried myself out and pretended to be asleep that Greyson had finally passed out on the sofa bed. As he snored, I quietly slipped out of bed and padded to the adjoining bathroom, where I shut the door and turned on the sink to drown out the sound of my voice. Taking a deep breath, I sank down in the empty bathtub and touched the silver cuff on my ear. I couldn't bring myself to take it off, no matter how useless it was now.

"Knox?" I whispered, hoping in vain to hear something—anything. Even just the slightest crackle would be enough. "Knox, if you aren't faking your death, if you didn't find a way to protect yourself from the bombs or get out of there, I'm going to find your corpse and kill you all over again. I hope you know that. I hope you know how mad I am at you right now, because—because until there's a body, I'm never going to be able to believe you're dead. Not after all the stunts you've pulled before. Because that's something you'd do, isn't it? Scare the shit out of me like this. Make me think you're dead. You don't have to, you know." My voice broke. "I can keep a secret. You know I can keep a secret. Whatever your stupid plan is, I won't tell anyone. Not even Greyson. Just—please be there. Please."

Silence. My throat tightened, and I rested my head against the tiled wall, blinking back tears. He couldn't be dead. I couldn't make myself believe it. But even if he was, I would never see a body. Not in whatever was left of Elsewhere. And if he was really gone, I would drive myself crazy for the rest of my life, always wondering. Always hoping.

"I'm sorry," I whispered. "I should have listened to you. I should have done things your way from the start. I had no idea what I was doing, and I thought you didn't, either, but—you did. And no matter how much of an idiot I was, you were always looking out for me. But when I finally had the chance to do the same for you, I failed."

I closed my eyes, picturing the last time I'd seen Knox's face. Standing together in his suite at Somerset while he touched my cheek, with all the gratitude and apologies that hung between us unsaid. I had to say them now, though. If Knox really was dead, he would never hear them, but I needed to say them for my own benefit. And if he had found some way to survive—if he was still out there somewhere, listening to every word I was saying, then it was worth the mortification. And the broken nose I would give him if I ever found out. Either way, I could never forgive myself for not warning him in time, but I had to

make sure the universe knew I'd tried. I had to make sure
I knew I'd tried.

"I know you were ready to sacrifice everything for the
Blackcoats. I know—I know you'd prepared. But you
weren't supposed to die." My voice caught, and it took me
a moment to clear my throat. "You were supposed to live
and see the end of it. You were supposed to make it happen. But it can't happen without you—I hope you know
that. If you're listening, I know you're probably itching to
say that I could do it, but I can't. There's no one left. Lila's
gone. You're gone. And even if Benjy manages to avoid
getting caught, I'm never going to see—" A soft sob bubbled out of me. "I can't do this on my own, Knox. Please."

"You're not alone." Greyson slipped into the bathroom
and climbed into the bathtub opposite me. I shifted to
give his long legs room. He looked about as exhausted as
I felt, but his eyes burned with determination. "We'll figure this out together, Kitty. That's what Knox would have
wanted us to do."

Wordlessly I nodded, not trusting myself to speak. Right
now, with the images of Elsewhere disintegrating still
etched into the back of my eyelids, it was hard to feel even
an inkling of hope. But Greyson offered me a pillow he'd
brought from the bedroom, and I tucked it behind my head
gratefully. I didn't plan on sleeping tonight, but lying on
the hard porcelain with Greyson right there—it was better than getting lost in the darkness. And right now, all I
wanted was to find something to hold on to and cling to
it with all my might.

We were both all the other had left. And if we were
going to make it through this, we had to do it together.

Over the next three days, the government made hundreds of arrests and even more kills as they cleaned out what remained of the Blackcoat safe houses. The stream of faces and names on the news never seemed to end, and Daxton delighted in regaling Greyson and I over dinner with the progress his army had made that day. I kept holding my breath, hoping Knox's name would crop up—better he be arrested than a pile of ash in the smoldering remains of Elsewhere. But it never did.

On the fourth day, once the government had rounded up every Blackcoat they could find, we gathered in Daxton's office for the executions. Once again my hair and makeup were done by professionals, and I was dressed in celebratory red with the American flag pinned to my dress. Greyson was forced into a blue suit, and Daxton wore white. It would have been comical if I could remember what funny felt like.

Minister Bradley was there as well, lingering to the side, but always a presence. I refused to acknowledge him, knowing what he must have been willing to do in order to remain one of Daxton's trusted advisers, and thankfully he didn't try to speak to me, either.

On a wider screen hung up in front of the Hart family portrait, Daxton, Greyson, and I watched as Blackcoat after Blackcoat was executed on live television in front of a crowd of onlookers in the middle of D.C. Some were mercifully shot in the back of the head. But the higher up the ranks they went, the less merciful they became.

"Ah, Lieutenant George Sampson. I believe you know him personally, Lila," said Daxton as cameras panned on us, recording every flinch, every wince. I couldn't hide my

grief for those who had risked their lives to bring about a
better country. I wouldn't. Those who had supported us
and survived—they had to know that they weren't alone.
"Would you like to say a few words?"

Sampson stared directly into the camera, his chin raised
defiantly. I shifted my gaze from the screen to the nearest lens. "Lieutenant Sampson is a brave man whose only
crime was to be on the losing side of a war," I said. "History may remember him as a traitor, but I will remember
him as an ally and a friend. Thank you for your guidance
and never-ending support, Lieutenant, and thank you for
your sacrifice."

I could feel Daxton glaring daggers into the side of my
head, but what was he going to do? He'd already destroyed
nearly everything I loved, and Greyson and I had done everything he'd told us to do. Now he would spend the rest
of his life parading us around as his pets. The war was over.
He had declared victory over the Blackcoats. Any retaliation against us now would only lose him what little public
support he still had. Daxton might have won through sheer
brute force, but that didn't mean it was what the public had
wanted. We were now an ideal without an army. But we
wouldn't be forever.

Sampson nodded once, confirming he had heard me.
The crowd was silent, and at last the ground beneath him
disappeared, leaving him to hang. The rope was too short
for him to break his neck in the fall, however, and he fought
and twitched for several minutes before he finally stilled.

I watched every terrible second of it, my eyes watering,
but I refused to break. Sampson had known the risks. We

all had. Every single Blackcoat had been willing to die for the cause, and I had to comfort myself with that knowledge.

I was positive that had to be the last of the executions for the day. Sampson was the biggest fish they'd caught, and there would be no more executions until they captured Celia. *If* they captured her, I told myself again and again. Even with most of her army arrested or dead, she was more than capable of disappearing completely, and I hoped against hope that she wouldn't try to rescue me. If I were Lila, that would be one thing, but I wasn't. And I wasn't worth the risk.

Instead of fading to black while they cut Sampson's body down, however, the hooded executioner escorted one more person onto the stage. He wore a black bag over his head, and his hands were handcuffed behind him, but I would have recognized him anywhere.

The edges of my vision darkened, and for one infinite, gut-wrenching moment, the world went silent.

No. Not him.

Not him.

"Benjamin Doe, coconspirator and assistant to Lennox Creed, leader of the Blackcoats," announced Daxton. My insides seized, and I forced myself to breathe steadily. Lila wouldn't care about Benjy, at least no more than she would have cared about the others who had died on that stage today. I wanted to scream and wrap my hands around Daxton's neck until he was dead, but we were surrounded by armed guards standing off camera. If I so much as twitched toward him, I would be restrained.

For a second, I considered it anyway. I didn't care that it would expose me. I didn't care that I would likely be dead before I was able to leave so much as a bruise on his neck. It would be worth it for the slimmest chance that maybe, just maybe, I would succeed before he could murder my best friend and one of the few people left in this world that I loved more than my own life.

But while my mind whirled with the desire to kill, my body didn't want to die. My feet remained frozen to the floor, my hands glued to my sides, and though everything inside me screamed to do something, to stop this before Benjy paid the price I should have—and would have—paid a thousand times over for him, I couldn't move. I couldn't speak. I could only stare at the screen and struggle not to scream.

The executioner pulled off Benjy's hood. His scruff was days old, his face was pale, and there were deep purple bruises underneath his eyes. But he didn't look defeated. Instead, there was a spark to him, and he looked out at the crowd. Maybe he didn't know he was about to die. Or maybe he welcomed it, after whatever torture they had put him through. My insides lurched at the thought of what Daxton must have done to Benjy just to spite me. Just to win yet another battle against me, even from beyond the grave.

I searched for any sign of injury, but whatever the Shields had done to him, they had been careful. There were no marks, no bruises, no obvious sign of abuse. Just my knowledge that out of everyone who had stood on the platform that day, Daxton would have relished Benjy's pain the most.

"You are charged with treason, conspiracy to commit treason, and war crimes too numerous to name," said Daxton as Benjy looked up at the screen that must have displayed our faces. "How do you plead?"

"Guilty." Benjy didn't so much as flinch as the crowd booed, and instead he kept his focus resolutely on us. I stared back. I couldn't watch this. Whatever Daxton was going to do to Benjy, it would be a million times worse because of who he was to me. Who he *had* been to me, as far as Daxton was concerned. But I couldn't look away, either. I couldn't let Daxton steal the last glimpse I would ever have of Benjy.

"That makes things much easier, doesn't it?" said Daxton, and though I refused to look at him, I could hear the grin on his face. "Benjamin Doe, you are hereby sentenced to death."

For the briefest of moments, I let my eyes flutter closed. All the things Benjy and I had survived together—all the times we'd been so sure we'd lost each other, only to find our way back to one another again. This was it. This was the end. And I would never get to say goodbye.

We'd fought the last time we'd seen each other. We'd both said things we didn't mean, and for some crazy reason, we'd both entertained the thought of being able to live without the other. Now he would never know how sorry I was and how much I needed him. Now I would never be able to tell him how much I really, truly loved him.

My fingers twitched toward Daxton, but Greyson immediately grabbed my hand and squeezed it. I had to bite my tongue to stop myself from saying something that would give Daxton the excuse he was waiting for to execute both me and Greyson, but I wanted to. More than anything in that moment, I wanted to destroy his world just like he was about to destroy mine.

I could have. I would have, consequences be damned. He could kill me. He could rip me apart limb from limb. He could cut me open and make my entrails dance while forcing me to watch. I didn't care.

But I was already about to lose Benjy, who stood on a platform a thousand miles away, far beyond my reach. There was nothing I could do to save his life. Even putting a knife through Daxton's gut wouldn't stop his execution now that he had been sentenced, and if I tried, it would only mean putting Greyson's life at risk, too. I couldn't lose them both today. Regardless of what Daxton did to me, I couldn't survive a world without either of them in it.

I was as powerless as I had been standing on top of the Stronghold, watching that missile head straight for Lila's helicopter. Only this time, I understood exactly what was about to happen.

The executioner prepared Benjy for hanging in the same gallows Sampson had died in only minutes earlier. As they tied the noose around his neck, he continued to stare into the camera, and I couldn't help but wonder if he was staring at me. The only time he hadn't been able to tell the difference between me and Lila was when he hadn't thought it was a possibility at all. But now, maybe—

Maybe Knox had told him. With that small comfort in mind, I watched him in return, not daring to smile or indicate I had any attachment to him. But I didn't look away, and neither did he.

"Any last words?" said Daxton, and Benjy smiled, his eyes watering.

"Find a little happiness. You'll be okay."

He did know. And though I couldn't give any indication that I knew he was talking to me, I took a deep breath
and exhaled slowly, pressing my lips together. Benjy was
everything good in my life, and without him, I wasn't
sure happiness could exist. But I would try.

Benjy continued to hold my stare as the executioner
walked around to the control panel that would make the
floor drop out from under him. Like Sampson's rope, it
was far too short to break his neck. Benjy's death would
be long, and it would be painful. And I could only hope
he was prepared, because I sure as hell wasn't.

"Wait."

Daxton's voice rang out just as the executioner's fingers
touched the switch. Greyson and I both looked at him, but
he focused on Minister Bradley instead, who nodded once
in encouragement.

"Out of the goodness of my heart, and because of your
potential to contribute to this world as a VI who was, I
believe, merely led down the wrong path—something we
have all fallen prey to at one time or another, I'm sure—
I hereby grant you, Benjamin Doe, a full pardon for your
crimes."

A murmur of shock rippled through the crowd, and
Greyson caught my eye. I couldn't smile, but everything
inside me shattered into a million shards of hope, each one
sharper than the next. They cut into me, and if I could
have bled to death from desperation alone, I would have.

"I want to make this country better than it has ever
been before, and I must acknowledge the mistakes of my
forefathers," continued Daxton, raising his chin. "I wish

to extend the hand of friendship and peace to those who have supported the rebels during this difficult time."

Minister Bradley cleared his throat softly, and he and Daxton exchanged a look. Whatever was going on, this wasn't completely Daxton's idea. But he spoke the words anyway, and the world around me began to spin.

"Because of this, Benjamin Doe, you will henceforth work for me as an adviser, and your principles and brilliant mind will help pave the way for peace between our two warring sides. I want nothing more than to help the people of this great nation, and in order to achieve true greatness, we must forgive old wounds and allow ourselves to heal."

My legs shook beneath me, and it was all I could do to remain standing. I didn't know why Daxton had chosen Benjy to pardon, and right now, I didn't care. All that mattered was that Benjy was still alive.

Daxton ended the broadcast, and as soon as the screen went dark, he clapped his hands together. "Well, that was fun, wasn't it?"

"Indeed," said Minister Bradley from the edge of the room, and he stepped closer to us. "You did a marvelous job, Your Grace. You showed true mercy to those who needed it most."

"Why him?" The question came from Greyson, not me. "You could have pardoned anyone."

"But not everyone was the beloved of the bitch who tried to kill me," said Daxton, practically preening. "What better revenge than to keep her boyfriend alive and make him work for me for the rest of his miserable life? Now, if you'll excuse me, I have to prepare for our return to D.C. I recommend you both do the same."

With an exaggerated bow, Daxton marched out of his office with Bradley at his heels, leaving Greyson and I alone with the camera crew. I didn't dare say anything as we headed back to the elevator, and even on our way up, I didn't speak. It was only when we reached our room that I collapsed on the sofa and buried my face in my hands.

"I don't know whether to be happy he's alive or—" Or buried in grief for the others who had died. Benjy might have meant the most to me, but all of those men and women had had families and loved ones, too. It felt wrong to be happy. It felt wrong to be anything but catatonic with heartache for all the lives we had lost in this war.

"You can be happy Benjy's alive and mourn the Blackcoat losses at the same time," said Greyson, sitting down next to me. "This is a good thing, and not just for the obvious reason. Daxton has no idea who you really are. If he did, he would have relished the chance to kill Benjy in front of you."

Maybe one day I would be able to use that against him. Maybe one day, as soon as he let his guard down while still believing I was Lila, who had faked her own death instead of trying to cause his, I would be able to get close enough to do it. For now, I stared at my freshly painted nails, elation and devastation swirling around me, slowly becoming one and the same. "Do you think it was all worth it?"

"The rebellion?" said Greyson, and I nodded.

"We wound up doing the opposite of what we wanted. We gave Daxton unlimited power instead of returning it to the people. And now we can't even get close enough to him to make sure that power is in the right hands instead."

"Fighting for what you believe in is always worth it,"

he said quietly. "It only takes one voice to give others the chance to see possibilities, and that's what Lila did. That's what you did, too. The Blackcoats fought for basic human rights. Nothing is more worth it than that. Sometimes—" He set his hand over mine. "Sometimes the answer is no, but that doesn't mean you shouldn't ask the question."

"Even when it costs countless people their lives?"

"Especially then." He took a deep breath and released it. "The people still love Lila, and as long as Lila is alive, they will still have hope. It might be a long time, but this isn't over. Even if we have to wait for Daxton to die of old age, we will see revolution in our lifetime."

I leaned my head against his shoulder, and he wrapped his arm around me. I still didn't know which way was up, or how I should feel in the midst of all that had happened, but I did know he was there for me the same way I would always be there for him. And that was worth more than words could say. "What are we supposed to do until then?" I said.

"The same thing we've always done." He rested his head against mine. "Keep hoping."

XI

ASHES

The next day, Daxton, Greyson, and I boarded a jet to D.C. Now that the war was over, Daxton no longer needed the protection of the Stronghold, but even so, he kept himself holed up in the back room of the jet, refusing to get anywhere near us. I didn't blame him, not really. He must have known that the instant he let either one of us close to him without armed guards pointing their weapons directly at us, his life would be forfeit.

Together Greyson and I played a card game on the table I had shared with Knox only a few months before. We couldn't talk about anything suspicious, not with the guards breathing down our necks, but we spoke quietly about the things we wanted to do when we returned to D.C. Greyson wanted to get back to inventing. I wanted to bury myself in work that was rewarding—charities, foundations for families of the soldiers on both sides, working toward bettering the education children from the less desirable neighborhoods received. Little things that were still within my power to do. Things that, over time, could make a real difference.

Daxton might have won the war, but he couldn't beat the hope out of me completely.

At least that was what I thought, until we began our descent. As we neared the ground, I pulled up the window shade, expecting to see Washington, D.C., sprawled out beneath us. Instead, all I saw were the charred remains of what used to be civilization.

"What...?" said Greyson, leaning in closer to get a better look, but I sat back against my seat, gulping in lungfuls of air. Of course he would take us here. Of course he would make sure to rub our noses in everything he was capable of.

"It's Elsewhere," I managed shakily. "Or what's left of it."

The destruction was endless. Miles and miles of nothing but the dead and blackened. The plane landed on what had once been the main street of Section X, and I couldn't stand the thought of what the wheels were running over.

"Wear these," said a guard, and he handed us masks to place over our noses and mouths. I pulled mine on, willing myself to hold it together.

There was nothing left. Everything was burned beyond recognition. And it had all been too fast for anyone to escape, but no one could have possibly survived long enough to suffer.

As Daxton exited the back room, the guard led Greyson and me off the plane and onto the ashy ground. Something crunched beneath my boot, and I tried not to think about what it might have been.

"Ah, Section X," said Daxton as he stepped down, two armed guards at his side. "What a delight it is to return to such a familiar place."

I knew exactly where I was: we stood in the spot where

the factory used to be. All that marked it now was a twisted lump of melted metal. And it was, in fact, the very section Victor Mercer had run with his brother, Jonathan. He had lived there much longer than I had, and if I could picture what the street used to be, he undoubtedly could, too.

"Shall we?" said Daxton, and it wasn't a request. He strolled toward the hill nearby, where Mercer Manor had once stood. There was nothing left but charred stone now.

Greyson and I followed him up what had once been the sloping pathway. The gate had melted away, and part of me hoped it would be impossible to tell where, exactly, the manor had once stood. I didn't think I could take seeing the very spot where Knox had died.

Could have died, I said firmly to myself. There was still hope. There was always hope, and I wasn't sure which was worse—the pain of loss, or the pain of never knowing. Still, I clung to the possibility that someway, somehow, Knox had defied the impossible and escaped Elsewhere in time. Rivers had known about the tunnels, after all—maybe they had used them.

But that only brought up the horrible image of thousands of charred bodies deep below our feet, where no one would ever find them. I choked back a wave of nausea and dug my nails into my palms, forcing myself to push that image aside. There had to be a way.

As we grew closer, Daxton made a delighted sound and hurried forward, stopping in a specific spot. "Look at this. Of course this would survive—how could it not?"

With my insides in knots, I walked toward him until the guard put up his hand, indicating I was close enough.

I peered around. Daxton stood directly over an ornate *H* carved into the marble floor.

The foyer of Mercer Manor. Which meant—

I looked to my right, where Knox's office had once stood. Nothing remained but more ash and char, and I silently turned and marched back down the hill. I expected Daxton to call me back, to insist I stay and witness these horrors, but I wouldn't have gone. He could do whatever he wanted to me. I didn't care anymore.

Footsteps hurried after me, crunching against the ground, but to my relief, it wasn't Daxton or a guard. Instead, Greyson caught up with me and took my arm. "Are you okay?"

"How can you possibly—" I sucked in a breath and held it until we crossed the melted gate, where I burst. "I can't do this. I can't play this stupid game just to keep him happy. He's a monster. He knows *exactly* what he's doing, and he's *reveling* in it. Do you have any idea how many people died in this section alone?"

Greyson shook his head, his grip on me tightening. "You need to keep it together," he whispered. "Just for a few more hours. Please."

"I need to get out of here." I crossed over the spot where Jonathan Mercer had executed Scotia, who had been the rebel leader inside the prison camp before dying right before the Battle of Elsewhere. Everything was a memory. Everything was a reminder of my failure. And I couldn't do this anymore.

Daxton must have gotten what he wanted out of me, because the guards didn't stop us as we boarded the plane.

I spent the next twenty minutes cleaning ash off our shoes, and by the time Daxton finally returned, looking entirely too smug and satisfied, something inside of me had broken.

Maybe Lila had been the lucky one after all. She would never have to wade through the ashes of the people she'd cared about. She wouldn't have to put up with Daxton's sadistic games. She wouldn't have to look over her shoulder with every step she took, wondering when the ax was going to drop. No wonder she'd been so willing to take the risk of stepping onto that helicopter and putting her fate in Daxton's hands. For her, death *was* freedom. And a pardon from the life she would have had to live if she'd survived.

"Now that Elsewhere is gone, what will you do with citizens who commit crimes?" I said as Daxton passed us. I'd meant it as a challenge—as a way to point out one of the many flaws in Daxton's path toward a stranglehold on the country. Instead he paused halfway back to his private quarters at the tail section of the plane, and he regarded me as if I'd just told an amusing joke.

"They'll get what they deserve, of course."

A lump formed in my throat. "You'll execute them. Even the people who do nothing more than look at a Shield the wrong way."

He shrugged. "Laws must be enforced. Perhaps the Blackcoats should have thought through the consequences of their actions before overtaking Elsewhere."

My entire body went cold, and before I could stop myself, I snarled, "Burn in hell."

He flashed me a wink before turning on his heel. "No need. Your friends are doing a marvelous job of that for me."

Greyson grabbed me by the shoulders before I could leap out of my seat and claw Daxton's eyes out. Only once he was tucked safely away in the back of the plane did Greyson finally let me go. He sat beside me and took my hand, clasping it tightly between his. "You know that's what he wants from you."

"I don't care." Tears stung my eyes, and my breaths came in wet, noisy gasps. It felt as if a boulder was pressed against my chest, and even Greyson, with his steady gaze and warm touch, did nothing to help calm me down. "All those people—he doesn't care. Their lives are nothing to him as long as he's still in power."

"Their lives will never be anything to him," said Greyson gently. "It doesn't mean they weren't worth anything at all."

"As long as he's running the country, that's exactly what it means." I wiped my cheeks with the back of my hand. "When we get back to D.C., we have to find a way to get him alone."

"We will," he said softly, and though he was holding himself together far better than I was, there was a break in his voice that said more than words ever could. It would have been simple for him to go over to Daxton's side— to be his ally, his pet, his heir. He would have been safer. Happier, probably. And he would have had far more freedom than we did now.

Instead, he remained resolute in our mutual goals: to find a way to overthrow that monster, and to finish the war the Blackcoats had started. He was on my side—Lila's side, even though Lila wasn't here anymore. We were in this together.

I didn't remember much about the rest of the flight to D.C. Greyson remained beside me on the sofa, but neither of us said anything. Hours felt like minutes and minutes felt like hours, and when we finally landed, all I wanted to do was curl up in bed and never get up again.

As our chauffeured car drove through the streets of D.C., part of me realized I was expecting to return to Somerset, where I had spent my months as Lila. But it was gone now, too, and instead I looked at Greyson. "Where are we going?"

He looked up from the scribbles he was making on a notepad. "What? Oh. Daxton said something about—reclaiming Minister Creed's manor. That it belonged to the state now, and since we didn't have anywhere else to stay…" Greyson frowned.

I rested my head against the cool window, watching the buildings and pedestrians slide by. Creed Manor. Of course. Because he hadn't tortured me enough already.

Daxton's car was already parked and empty when we pulled into the wide circular drive. Knox's home was a sprawling brick mansion, and though the estate was as wet and gray as the rest of D.C., it had a warm, inviting feel to it that I resented. I didn't know what I'd expected from the place Knox had grown up, and where he had slowly been forged into a rebel, but this wasn't it.

The inside was cozy. Nothing like the cold, elegant starkness of both Somerset Manor and Mercer Manor, which had technically belonged to the Hart family anyway. The floors were made of wood, bright curtains opened up to wide windows, and artwork hung on the walls not to intimidate, but to complement. It was a beautiful home, but I couldn't shake the feeling that I was walking down the hallways with a ghost.

Greyson followed me with his arms crossed, looking as uncomfortable as I felt. "I've been here a few times. I know where the guest rooms are."

I wasn't interested in the guest rooms. Not yet anyway. "Can you show me his room?" I said, and Greyson nodded. Together we trudged up the winding staircase and into the bright and airy upper floors, where he led me down a maze of hallways until we stopped at a doorway toward the end of the wing.

"I'll be across the hall," he said, nodding to another door. "If you don't want to sleep in Knox's room, you can sleep in here, too. There are two beds."

I would have slept on the floor if it meant waking up and having instant reassurance that Greyson was all right. "Okay. I'll be in soon," I said.

He flashed me a sad smile and slipped inside, leaving me alone to face Knox's room and the questions and memories that would undoubtedly come with it. I took a deep breath and slowly turned the handle.

The musky scent of Knox hit me hard, and I stood in the doorway, struggling for air and gripping the handle so tightly I could feel the lock leave an imprint on my skin.

His bedroom—his suite, really—was decorated much like the one in Somerset; in rich golds and blues, with a leather sofa, desk, and an entire wall full of books that looked read and cherished, not just put on display. Even though I knew it was an invasion of privacy, I wandered into his bedroom as soon as I could make myself move. I sat down on his king-size bed and picked up one of the pillows, hugging it to my chest.

I'd never imagined where he'd lived when he wasn't at Somerset. He was there so often that I'd nearly forgotten he was a guest, rather than a permanent resident, and I racked my brain trying to think of any period of time where he'd been gone for longer than a day. He probably hadn't come back here, anyway, I reasoned, at least not for the night. Given the way Knox had spoken about his family, I couldn't imagine this had been a happy, welcoming place for him. It was hard to picture Somerset as a safe haven for anyone, but maybe that was exactly what it had been to Knox.

"Your pillow smells like you." The words slipped out before I could stop them, and my face grew warm, but there was no one around and no reason to be embarrassed, not really. Back at the Stronghold, during the few moments Greyson had left me alone, I'd caught myself talking to Knox every now and then, in the hope that he could hear me. Here, surrounded by his things, it felt as natural as breathing.

"It wouldn't have been that bad, would it?" I looked around the bedroom. A mahogany dresser stretched across one wall, along with a matching armoire, and a door led into what I assumed was a bathroom. Or a closet. "I know that wasn't the plan—that you probably never intended for us to ever actually get married, fake as it would've been anyway. But once we stopped trying to kill each other in our sleep, it wouldn't have been that bad."

I buried my nose in the pillow again and closed my eyes. With his scent came a rush of memories, and I let myself wallow in them for far longer than I should have. After losing the people I loved the most—Tabs, Nina, Benjy—I didn't understand why Knox's death had hit me so hard. But over the past several months, despite our differences, we had become inseparable. He had been there for me, guided me, protected me in his own way, stopped me from blowing everything on more than one occasion—he had become my compass, and I didn't know where to go without him.

Losing Knox wasn't just about him, though; it was also about losing the war. If Knox was alive, we would still stand a chance. But the more time that passed without word from him, the less I could convince myself to believe it. Whether he was alive or not, he wasn't here. He was gone. We were adrift—I was adrift—and the revolution was over. I mourned that as much as I mourned him. Or so I told myself, because nothing else made sense. We'd barely tolerated each other the past few weeks we'd been together. I had no right to mourn him like this.

But I remembered those last few moments in Somerset, before I'd been captured—the way he'd looked at me. The way he'd touched me. Everything we hadn't said, and everything we hadn't needed to say. I didn't know where we would have been if everything had continued—if Knox and I hadn't gone there that day. If I hadn't been captured. If I had returned to Elsewhere that evening and talked things out with Benjy.

Maybe things would have been different. Maybe they

wouldn't have been. But in the lonely quiet, I gave myself permission to wonder.

Kitty Doe would always be Benjy's. But Kitty Hart... I didn't know. And now it was looking more and more like I would never find out.

XII

ONE CHANCE

I didn't know how long I sat there, hugging Knox's pillow and trying not to drive myself crazy with uncertainty. The shadows in his room grew longer, and the light from the sun dimmed. Eventually, once I was stiff from sitting in the same position for too long, I considered getting up. But before I could talk myself into it, the bedroom door opened.

I flew to my feet, ready to defend my reasons for being in there to Daxton or any of the guards he might have sent to check on me. But to my shock, it was Benjy who slipped inside. As soon as he caught sight of me, he stilled, and the shirts he carried fell to the floor.

"I'm sorry, I—" Lila would have never apologized, but I shook the thought from my mind and hurried to help him pick up the laundry. I had barely dared to think about him since his execution had been stayed, not sure how many more times my heart could break and still remain a whole. But here he was, kneeling down next to me, and I didn't know what to say. Suddenly everything I'd been thinking about Knox felt like a betrayal, and I swallowed hard as my face grew warm. He'd caught me in Knox's bedroom, clearly upset. I didn't know if he had the right to be angry or not, not anymore, but I wouldn't blame him if he was.

But he didn't look angry. Benjy stared at me, his blue eyes wide and bright, and for the first time in what felt like my entire life, I couldn't read the look on his face. He wasn't angry, though. That was something. "I was hoping you'd be in here," he said, his voice barely a whisper.

"Is that why you're bringing clean clothes to..." To a dead man's room. But I couldn't say that, so instead I tried to refold a shirt. My efforts were uneven and laughable at best. Benjy gently took it from me and refolded it with perfect precision, and I bit my lip, not wanting to know why he'd been trained to do something so ordinary when he had a VI on the back of his neck.

Had a VI on the back of his neck, I remembered. Because just like me, he'd been sent to Elsewhere, too, which meant the VI he'd worked so long and hard for was now scarred over with an X. All because of me.

How much guilt could one person take? How many burdens could I live with until my mind and body simply gave up? Whatever that limit was, I was sure I would soon reach mine. It simply couldn't be possible to live with more than I already was, to hurt the people I cared about—to watch them murdered because of something I had done— and not crumble into dust.

Once the shirts were stacked neatly again, I stood and took a step back, not sure what to say. He opened and shut his mouth, no doubt struggling with the same problem.

"I know it's you," he finally said, even though I'd already known from what he'd said at the execution. "I just—I need to—"

"I'll wait," I said softly, and with a grateful look, Benjy disappeared beyond the door I'd wondered about only minutes earlier. It turned out to be a massive walk-in closet, even bigger than the one Lila had had at Somerset, and as I waited, I vowed that if Knox were somehow alive, I would never let him live that down.

A minute later, Benjy ducked back into the room, closing the closet door behind him. We stood there with only a few feet between us, but it might as well have been infinite. I didn't know what to say or what to do, which only disturbed me more. This was Benjy. He was my best friend. There should have never been any distance between us at all, even if we were half a world away from each other.

Apparently he was thinking along the same lines, because at long last, his eyes crinkled with a smile. "You know, just a few weeks ago, I would have gotten a hug by now. And been forced to make you a promise never to get myself almost executed again."

He hadn't meant it as a command, but I gladly took it that way, relieved not to have to make the decision for myself. I stepped forward and wrapped my arms around him, inhaling his scent. It was different from Knox's—less woodsy and musky, but tied to the best moments of my life. I hadn't realized at the time that my memories of the group home and Christmases with one cheap present and meals with forty other people would be the ones I'd miss so much. I'd spent my whole life up until the test looking forward to the future and the endless possibilities it held. I had been so sure Benjy and I would get our happily-ever-after, and now—this was it. Standing in Knox's bedroom, hugging Benjy and missing both of them. The Benjy I'd thought my future would hold no longer existed. Maybe he never had. He was still the kind, gentle, loving boy who had helped me with my homework and read to me and stuck up for me when no one else would. He was still all those things and more. But sometime in the past five months, ever since I'd been Masked, something had shifted, and we'd been too busy trying to hold on to the past to try to make sure we'd both be happy in the future.

"I love you so much," I whispered hoarsely. "If I'd lost you…"

"You'll never lose me," he said, and his strong arms tightened around me. "You're my family, Kitty, no matter who you have to pretend to be. And I will *always* be here for you."

He ran his fingers through my hair, and I squeezed my eyes shut, feeling like the worst person in the world. Benjy had nearly died. I'd been so sure I would never see him again. And here I was, sitting in Knox's room, missing him more.

"Look at me," he said gently, and he pulled away enough to touch my chin. "I meant what I said. It will be okay. *You* will be okay. And so will I."

I nodded, struggling to find a way around the lump in my throat. "We'll be okay together."

A sad smile flickered across his face. "Not that kind of together. Not anymore."

It took me a moment to fully realize what he was saying, and I stared at him, my eyes filling with tears all over again. It was one thing to think it to myself; it was another to hear him say it. It made my traitorous thoughts all too real. "But—"

"You will always be the most important part of my life," he said. "You're my constant, and I'll be yours for as long as you want me to be. I will never love you any less, and I will never *not* be here for you. And maybe, if things shift that way again between us..." He hesitated. "I don't think they will, though. I think we've both been holding on because we're familiar. Because it's all we've ever known, and change is scary as hell."

"That doesn't mean—that doesn't mean it was bad," I whispered, and his expression softened.

"It's never been bad, and it never will be." He pulled me into another hug, gentler this time. "But it's a different kind of love. My favorite moments with you have always been just—being together. Reading. Talking. Spending time together. The rest... I don't need it to love you. And after we...after being with you...that only confirmed it. That isn't our kind of love. What we have is stronger. More important. And I think..." He paused, and I could feel his head turning as he looked around Knox's room. "I think you feel the same, even if you don't realize it yet."

"Don't tell me how I feel," I said, my voice breaking. "You have no idea."

"Then tell me."

I searched for the words I wanted to say, but I couldn't find them. He wasn't wrong. I had loved and would continue to love Benjy unwaveringly for the rest of my life and beyond, but we would never have the future we'd dreamed of. We would never have our cottage in the woods, away from the rest of the world. I'd wanted that so badly—still wanted that, to break away from this poisonous society and just *be*, with no expectations and no one judging me. But while Benjy had always been a piece of that, he had never been the most important piece. Not really.

Besides, I would be Lila until the day I died now. And even if we'd wanted to stay together, with Daxton breathing down our necks, it would be impossible.

As soon as that excuse popped into my head—and it *was* an excuse—relief spilled through me, and I hated myself even more. I shouldn't have needed an excuse to feel comfortable with the honesty between us, but I did. And that only made it worse.

"You're always going to be my best friend," I mumbled into his shoulder. "And if—if anyone else feels threatened by that, then they won't be worth it, no matter how much I care about them. You're my family."

I felt the tension in his body melt away, and he pressed a kiss to the top of my head. "Damn right I am."

We stood there together for what felt like an eternity, and eventually my gaze settled on Knox's pillow. Even if I'd wanted to fight Benjy on it, he was right, and for more reasons than either of us would say aloud.

At last Benjy let me go, and he studied me for a long moment, his eyes moving from mine to my hair to my mouth, and I wondered what he was thinking. Maybe he was trying to memorize this moment. Or maybe he was trying to reconcile the person I was now with the person we'd both thought I would always be. At last he offered me a small smile. "Come on—Daxton's expecting me downstairs in a few minutes, but I'll show you to your room."

I hesitated. "I thought I'd stay with Greyson. Who's my brother," I added, more out of reflex to avoid hurting Benjy's feelings than anything else.

He chuckled. "Yeah, I'd put that one together, don't worry. You can sleep wherever you'd like, but they sent some of your things—Lila's things—here, and I thought you might like to know where they are. Clothes, jewelry, all of that."

I didn't care about clothes or jewelry, but I nodded anyway, because it was an excuse to spend a few more minutes with him, and I needed confirmation that we really were okay. That he'd meant the things he'd said as much as I did.

He led me down the hall to the next suite over, exactly the way it had been at Somerset, too. "Here," he said, opening the door for me. "I need to go, but I'll see you at dinner."

"Be careful," I said. The thought of him alone in a room with Daxton and those guards made my blood boil, but if Daxton had wanted to kill him, he would have let the executioner do it. For now, Benjy was as safe as any of us could be, and I had to take comfort in that.

He waved goodbye and disappeared around a corner, leaving me to explore the room. It was decorated in shades of purple and silver, but there was nothing out of the ordinary that stood out. Nothing that looked like it had belonged to Lila.

As soon as I wandered into the bedroom, however, I froze. Sitting on the nightstand, angled toward the bed, was a golden picture frame with a maze design. It was the frame Greyson had given me the night I'd been arrested. I hadn't seen it since the Battle of Elsewhere.

Sitting down on the edge of the bed, I picked it up and stared at the picture displayed. Greyson and I sat together in the library of Somerset, and we looked relaxed—happy, almost, despite the turmoil at the time. I found the button on the back of the frame easily, and I pressed it long enough for a second, hidden picture to show up—the one of me and Benjy, before I'd been Masked.

Seeing us together, happier than we'd likely ever be again—it made me ache with regret and loneliness. We'd made the right decision today. Clinging to the past wasn't going to help us get through the future, and while we would need each other now more than ever, it wasn't in the same way. But it still hurt like hell, and I wasn't sure it would ever be completely okay.

As I stared at my old face, however, suddenly it shifted again—this time into a photograph I'd never seen before. It was a picture of Hannah and I together in Mercer Manor, talking during a moment I'd long forgotten. Knox must have taken the picture—Jonathan Mercer sure as hell hadn't—but however it had gotten there, I was glad it existed.

I examined the picture closely. Hannah hadn't fully realized I'd been her daughter until after it had been taken, but Knox had managed to capture a moment when we'd looked comfortable together. Not quite mother and daughter, but likely the closest he'd been able to get.

Hannah was still out there somewhere, hidden where Daxton would never be able to get his disgusting hands on her. And suddenly, more than anything in the world, I wanted to find her. I'd lost enough. I wasn't going to lose my mother, too—not when I'd only just met her.

"She wanted you to have that," said Benjy from the doorway, and I jumped, nearly dropping it. "I'm sorry— Daxton's in a meeting with Minister Bradley. Told me to come back later."

And instead of doing anything else, he'd come back to see me. If I'd had any doubts that we would be okay, they were gone now. "You saw her?"

He nodded. "That's where Knox sent me. He thought I'd be safer there."

"But—they caught you." A bubble of panic formed inside me. "Is Hannah—"

"She's fine," he said. "I was caught when I left with a handful of other Blackcoats to go on a mission. It was stupid—we should have stayed put, but Elsewhere had just been destroyed, and our lines of communication were scrambled." He nodded toward the frame. "She talked about you all the time. Asked me a million questions. I repeated the stories so many times that even I got sick of them, but she never did." He grinned, but it faded quickly. "This isn't over, Kitty. There must still be Blackcoats out there."

"Even if there are, there's nothing we can do now," I said. "Daxton is constantly guarded. I would kill him—I *will* kill him—but it's going to be a long time before he trusts me enough to be in a room alone with me. If he ever does again."

"There are other ways to kill someone than stabbing them through the heart."

I frowned. "Poison?"

"That could work, but he has food tasters," said Benjy with a shrug. "Besides, that's not what I'm talking about. He's crazy, and all he wants is power. If we expose that—"

"We've already tried," I said. "If anyone says a word about what's really going on, he'll have them killed in an instant. And no one wants to take that risk."

"It's easy now, though. Don't you see? Winning this war. Once he's gone, the position will pass to Greyson, and then it'll be over."

"It's already over," I said, that familiar ache filling my chest. "If I could kill him, I would. In a heartbeat. But it's impossible."

"Nothing's impossible. You're proof of that." Benjy paused, drumming his fingers on his elbow. "What if I can get a gun?"

I stared at him. "No. Whatever you'd planning—absolutely not."

"It's worth a shot."

"I—" I blinked. "That's a terrible pun, and *no*. We're going to do this the right way. No taking chances that might not pan out."

He watched me for a long moment. "So you're in?"

I gritted my teeth. That was the plan anyway, wasn't it? Wait for Daxton to die. But Benjy wasn't supposed to get involved. And even though we might not be together in that way anymore, the instinct to protect him still roared inside me. "One condition. You let me do it. No stupid risks. No wasting your second chance on this. Greyson has to live to take over the title, and *you* have to live to help him. I'm the one who's expendable. Is that clear?"

His expression darkened. "You're not expendable."

"*Is that clear*, Benjamin?"

He worried his lower lip. "All right. But we come up with a plan. A good one. Solid, foolproof—"

"Nothing's ever foolproof."

"As close as we can get, then."

I nodded. "I have no intention of getting caught. Or dying."

"You'd better not." He gave me a look and glanced over his shoulder. "I need to go. For real this time. We'll come up with a plan, and we'll find a way. Even if we're the only two Blackcoats left, we will make sure it wasn't all in vain."

My mouth went dry, and all I could do was nod. "We'll only get one chance. You know that, right?"

"One chance is all we need." He flashed me another grin, and with that, I was alone again. But for the first time since I'd watched Elsewhere disappear, I didn't feel like I was on my own. Somehow, someway, we would find a way to kill Daxton, and we would end this once and for all.

XIII

BUGGED

Though we had moved halfway across the country, that night at dinner it seemed as if we were right back where we started. Greyson and I walked into the Creeds' dining room, which was large enough to seat all the former Ministers and their families with ease, and once again the servants escorted us to the foot of the table, beyond where we could be any real threat. Some part of me had held out hope that being back in D.C. would change things—that he wouldn't keep us on such an obvious leash. But of course Daxton had no reason to care about appearances anymore, not when the truth of his identity was out there, and no one had any power to do anything about it. So what if the servants returned to their families and gossiped about how the Prime Minister clearly didn't trust his own son and niece? He was untouchable.

It was exactly that arrogance I was counting on, though. Eventually he would give. Eventually he would make a mistake. And when he did, I would be ready.

I hadn't seen Benjy since his promise to procure a gun, but soon enough, he and the former Minister Bradley entered together. Neither of them spoke as Benjy joined us, but Daxton clapped gleefully.

"Bradley! Yes, do come sit here with me. We have much to discuss, and we wouldn't want to bore the children with the details, now, would we?"

Minister Bradley raised his chin, his handlebar mustache gleaming in the light, and with a pompous sniff, he passed us and made his way to Daxton. Good. They deserved each other.

"How is everyone enjoying our new home?" said Daxton as the servants hurried to set Minister Bradley a place nearby. "Greyson, Lila, you've had the pleasure of touring the property before, have you not?"

"We have," said Greyson in a painfully neutral voice. As much as I would have enjoyed watching him lash out at Daxton, it was safer this way. "Quite a few things have changed."

"Have they? I can't say I've noticed. Lila," he added in a faintly sinister tone, and I snapped my head up to glare at him. "Have things changed much from your memory of it?"

A test, whether he knew it was one or not. He had been acting as Daxton Hart long enough that he had undoubtedly visited Creed Manor several times. I had no idea if things had changed, or if Greyson was merely imagining it. But as long as Daxton seemed determined to pretend everything was perfectly all right between us, I would be determined to prove they weren't.

"It's soulless," I snapped, not bothering with any form of neutrality. "I'm not surprised you can't see it, considering you have no soul."

For a split second, everyone in the room seemed to tense. Bradley blinked and focused on Daxton, Greyson's fork stopped halfway to his salad, and Benjy stilled, staring at me as if he couldn't believe I'd said that to Daxton's face. But of course he hadn't been with us for the past month, so he had no idea that this was our version of normal.

I half expected Daxton to dismiss me from the room and find some twisted way to punish me later for embarrassing him in front of his guest, but instead, he merely chuckled. "Oh, I know exactly what soulless means, darling. We saw it earlier today, didn't we? In the ash of Elsewhere."

I clutched my fork so hard that it began to bend. If I'd had the skill to do so, I would have flung it across the dining room straight into Daxton's eye. Something to practice in my spare time, I mused.

Before things could get uglier, Minister Bradley cleared his throat. "Yes, about Elsewhere, Prime Minister. There are several replacements I would like to speak with you about, if you'll excuse the grisly talk over dinner..."

The pair of them bent their heads together, and though I could feel the heat of Daxton's stare every now and then, I purposely ignored them for the rest of dinner. Greyson, Benjy, and I remained quiet for the most part, only commenting on neutral topics when we spoke at all. The weather, the rebuilding of Somerset, how nice it was to be out of the Stronghold at last—we avoided any mention of Elsewhere, and none of us said a word about Benjy's near-execution. I couldn't be overly familiar with him anyway, in case I accidentally tipped Daxton off. However long this tightrope walk lasted, I would have to convince not only

Daxton that I was Lila, but myself, too. By the end of it, I wasn't so sure I would recognize this new me at all.

It was strange, looking at Benjy and knowing he wasn't mine anymore, not the way he had been before. I caught myself thinking of him as my boyfriend more times than I could count, but slowly I began to remove myself from that connection. I would have to, not only to be convincing as Lila, but because we weren't *Benjy and Kitty* anymore. We were just Benjy and Kitty. Separate. And I would have to get used to it sooner rather than later.

At long last, after the dessert course had been served, Daxton stood. "I hope you all have an enjoyable evening in our new home. It's only temporary, I assure you—construction on Somerset is due to begin any day now—but it's always best to be as comfortable as possible."

He winked, and a shiver ran down my spine. I didn't want to know what constituted *comfortable* for him.

Once he was gone, with Minister Bradley trailing at his heels, the three of us stood. "I need to finish up with the Prime Minister," said Benjy, but before he left, he hesitated and leaned toward Greyson and me. "Be in Greyson's room at ten o'clock."

Before I could ask what was happening then, he disappeared, leaving Greyson and I to exchange a look. There was no use speculating—a servant could overhear, and we wouldn't be any closer to the truth anyhow. But together we ascended the stairs, and once I'd changed out of my dinner clothes, I joined Greyson in his suite.

"What *is* that?" I said, making a face. Greyson stood beside a glowing three-dimensional blueprint of something that looked more like an insect than anything useful.

Sometime that afternoon, he had turned his sitting room into a makeshift laboratory, complete with the equipment he'd taken to the Stronghold with him—the only equipment he had left after the bombing of Somerset, I realized.

"It's a device I intend to start working on tonight, if I can get the mechanisms right," he said, his brow furrowed as he spun the image around, searching for something.

"It looks like a cockroach," I said.

"Excellent. That's what it's supposed to be. A bug." He motioned for me to join him, and I crossed over to his workstation. "It isn't a new concept, of course, spy devices that are hidden in plain sight. But this one's designed to move around exactly like an insect would. I wanted to attempt a common housefly first, but the wings are too complex for me to create with my limited equipment."

"But an exact replica of a cockroach is no problem," I drawled. He blinked, and I shook my head. "You're a genius. You know that, right?"

"Yes." He winked at me before peering at the insect again. "Once I get the leg movement right, I should be able to steer it around the manor without detection. I have a few subjects I caught in the cellar to give me an idea of what I'm missing."

He motioned to a jar nearby, and against my better judgment, I glanced inside. "You're keeping cockroaches as pets now?"

"There are a surprising number of them in the manor. But don't worry," he added quickly. "I only found them on the lower levels."

"Cockroaches don't bother me. We're already living with one," I muttered, sitting down on the sofa.

"Once I have this little guy up and running, we'll have a way to track every move Daxton makes without ever being seen."

"Unless someone spots your bug and tries to smash it," I said, and he shrugged.

"That's the beauty of it. Unless they're looking too closely, if they step on it or otherwise destroy it, it's designed to resemble a dead cockroach."

I shuddered. "Still a genius, but definitely twisted."

"It was a necessity. I'm not completely unaware of how the presence of a cockroach in the upper levels of the manor would be viewed."

He straightened, and once his eyes were on me instead of his new toy, his entire demeanor seemed to shift. It never ceased to amaze me how different he became in his workshop—how scientific and methodical and distracted he grew. He was wholly focused on his inventions, and though part of me was jealous that he had something to distract him, the fact that he was working on an actual bug made it clear he was still as determined as I was to reignite the rebellion and take Daxton down for good.

"You must be happy to see Benjy again," he said, and I nodded.

"It's—complicated. He's not—we're not together anymore. Can't be, not when I have to live as Lila completely."

"Oh." His face fell. "I'm sorry. That must be hard."

"He's still my best friend. He always will be," I said quickly. "But—yeah. It isn't fun. And being here where Knox grew up…"

I trailed off, and neither of us had to say anything. We both missed Knox. As hard as it was for me, being here without him, I couldn't imagine how difficult it was for Greyson, who had real memories of this place. Of Knox here, in his home. No doubt it felt empty without him.

"What do you think Benjy wants?" said Greyson at last, and I toyed with a loose thread on the sofa.

"He wants to help us kill Daxton," I said. "We can trust him. He would never betray us."

Greyson frowned, and he spun the hologram around again. "Maybe not on purpose, but he's going to be with him every day now, and Daxton's listening."

"Benjy's too smart for that," I said firmly. "He's a VI. Victor Mercer was only a V, remember?"

A ghost of a smile replaced his frown. "I thought the ranks were unfair and meant nothing."

"They don't, but—" I stopped and sighed. "Just let me have this, all right?"

"All right. Just this once," he teased. "Only because it's Daxton."

I watched him work that evening as we both waited for ten o'clock to come around. It was incredible, seeing what he could do with only a few tools and his hands. Bit by bit, he began to create his bug.

Even if this didn't work, I was confident the three of us would be able to come up with some kind of plan. We might not have had the resources and the manpower of the full Blackcoat Rebellion, but sometimes all it took was one small ripple to change the course of fate. And we were all determined to do exactly that.

At last, at the stroke of ten, a soft knock sounded on the door. While Greyson hastily hid his bug from sight, even though I'd insisted Benjy wouldn't tell, I stood and opened the door. Benjy stood on the other side, his lips pressed together anxiously, and I recoiled as soon as I saw why.

Minister Bradley hovered over his shoulder, his brow sweaty and his paunch heaving from the long walk.

"Can I help you, Benjamin? Minister Bradley?" I said stiffly, exactly the way Lila would had she been faced with the same pair. Behind me, I could hear Greyson scramble to clear the last evidence of his bug from the room.

"Don't worry, he's here to help," said Benjy, and I scowled.

"Help with what?"

"Killing the Prime Minister, of course," said Minister Bradley. I groaned inwardly. Of all the people to trust— Benjy must have known this was a trap.

"I have no idea what you're talking about, but if you say it any louder, I'm sure Daxton would be more than happy to torture the truth out of you," I said, starting to close the door. Benjy stuck his foot in the way, however, stopping it with his boot.

"Lila. Think about it. He wants to stop him as much as we do," said Benjy in a hushed voice. "He came to me, not the other way around."

Lila, not Kitty. So Benjy hadn't trusted him with everything. That was a small comfort in the face of the rest of it, though, and I gritted my teeth. "Did it ever occur to you how simple it would be for Daxton to tell him to do exactly that?"

"But he didn't," said Minister Bradley. I could hear Greyson approach, and he stopped directly behind me.

"Prove it," said Greyson simply, and as if this was what

he'd been waiting for, Minister Bradley opened his jacket, revealing a silver gun.

"This is for you, my dear Lila." Pulling it from the holster, he took it by the barrel and handed it to me grip-first. If I'd wanted to, I could have easily pulled the trigger. "I thought it might come in handy."

I stared at the weapon in my hand, my mind whirling. It had to be a trap. There was no reason for a greedy, selfish, disgusting pig of a man like Bradley to help us. If anything, he had every reason to betray us to prove his loyalty to Daxton, thus securing a position in the new government.

But here was a chance—a real chance—warm and heavy in my hand. No matter what tricks Daxton might have been willing to pull, he never would have given us a way to kill him.

My grip on the pistol tightened, and I pointed it directly at Bradley. "Should I see if it's a fake?"

"Oh, it isn't," he said, ducking his head with such speed that I knew it had to be genuine. I'd never seen him move so fast before. "It's very, very real, and very, very loaded. If you wouldn't mind, my dear Lila…"

"The safety's on anyway," I said, lowering it. To Greyson, I added, "What do you think?"

He shrugged. "It couldn't hurt to see what he has to say."

With the gun securely in my hand, I stepped aside, and finally Benjy and Minister Bradley entered. Neither of them made a move to sit down in the living area, and instead we lingered in a circle near the doorway. More beads of sweat formed on Bradley's forehead, and he dabbed his face with a handkerchief. No one could fake that kind of anxiety.

"I won't stay long," he began. "I'd like to help in any

way I can. There's a great deal of information out there regarding the remaining Blackcoats, and if you'd like me to pass it along—"

"No," I said instantly. Benjy and Greyson gave me strange looks, but I ignored them. "It won't help us in here, and if you're telling the truth, then we shouldn't know anyway."

"Right," said Greyson, catching on quickly. "The less we know, the better. That way Daxton can't get it out of us."

Minister Bradley exhaled. "All right. But if anything does become useful—"

"Why are you helping us?" I demanded. He fell silent. "You have everything to lose. Power, prestige, privilege, your prime position as Daxton's lapdog—"

"It is not what I have to lose, dear Lila, but what I have to gain." He lowered his voice several notches and leaned in, though the walls were thick enough that I doubted anyone trying to listen through the doorway could hear us. "Is it so strange a thought that perhaps I do not want the country run by a madman?"

"You didn't seem to think he was mad when you got everything you wanted," I said.

"Perhaps I was blinded by greed then, yes. But even I cannot ignore what happened in the Stronghold. I am not interested in a dictatorship, and though you may believe otherwise, I do care about this country. Deeply."

"What do you want in return?" said Greyson. "When I'm Prime Minister, what price am I going to have to pay for your help now?"

Minister Bradley sniffed. "I assure you I am doing this out of the goodness of my heart—"

"We don't trust the goodness of your heart," I snapped. "We trust your self-interest."

At last he sighed and wiped his forehead once more. "Very well. Allow me to have a place in your new government. I quite enjoy my job, and I do not want to lose it in the revolution. I promise I will look out for the best interests of the people, and I will follow your agenda."

"I don't want a puppet," said Greyson.

"And I do not wish to be a puppet," said Bradley. "That is what I am now, though, with your father. Or—the man claiming to be your father." He raised an eyebrow, and Greyson looked at his feet. "I do not want to give up my lifestyle, but I do not want to concede my morality, either, or what is left of it. It *is* possible to be selfish while looking out for the people, my boy. I do not claim to be perfect, and it has taken me a great deal to get this far. But I hope in time you are willing to trust me, or at the very least trust my desire to have a place in your new world, when the inevitable comes." He nodded to the gun. "Use it wisely."

Without another word, he ducked into the hallway, leaving the three of us alone. I strode over and locked the door, and once that was taken care of, I wheeled around to face Benjy.

"What the hell do you think you're doing?"

"What had to be done," said Benjy, and to his credit, he didn't flinch. "I believe him, Lila—"

"Kitty," I said. "Greyson knows."

"Good." He and Greyson exchanged looks before he continued. "We have the gun. That's what we need, right?"

Reluctantly I nodded, opening the cylinder to make sure it was full. "These could be blanks."

Greyson peered over my shoulder. "They're not. See the way the metal crimps?"

"I can do it," said Benjy as I inspected the bullets. "I'm with him every day. The guards search me, but I could find a way—"

"No." I closed the cylinder and set the pistol aside. "You're not taking that risk."

He scowled. "Kitty—"

"If you do it, you'll just be a rebel, and he'll die a martyr," I said. "If Greyson does it, people will speculate he only wanted his father's power. But if Lila does it—if the beloved mouthpiece of the Blackcoats does it—the people will be behind her."

Greyson bit his lip. "It'll have to be in public. On camera, if we can manage it."

"That's the only time we're allowed to get close to him anyway," I said. "You'll pardon me, won't you?"

That got a small smile out of him. "I think I can manage that."

"Good. And Benjy—" I looked at him. "Thank you."

Benjy crossed his arms, and the tips of his ears turned red. "I don't want you doing this."

"Doesn't matter. It has to be done. Everything will work out—we'll make sure it does." I touched his elbow. Part of me was hoping for the spark we'd been missing, but as reassuring as it was to have him there, planning and strategizing with us, that was all it was: a familiar comfort. The boost of confidence I needed to go through with this. If there was a hole in the plan—a real hole, and not simply Benjy's fears about losing me—then he would tell us.

"Okay," said Greyson, looking back and forth between us. "First chance we get."

I nodded, my heart racing. We could do this. We could really do this. "First chance we get."

That chance didn't come for weeks.

With Greyson busy tinkering with his bug, and with Benjy catering to Daxton's every want and whim, I was left largely on my own each day. Sometimes I sketched while Greyson worked; sometimes I watched the news. But mostly I explored Creed Manor.

There were parts I couldn't access—Daxton's quarters, mainly, which put a damper on things. And the vents were far too small for me to fit inside, much to my frustration. But I memorized every hallway, every room, every closet of Creed Manor I could find, until I knew it as well as I had known Somerset.

My knowledge of the manor's layout came in handy when, at last, Greyson managed to get his bug up and running. We weren't sure what we expected to get out of it, but it was comforting, having a way to find out what Daxton was really up to. And once the bug had the run of the manor, Greyson and I spent hours in his suite, watching the feed and waiting for anything telling to happen.

It never did. And the more time that passed, the more discouraged I grew. Daxton had yet to give us an opportunity to kill him, and though I was tempted to do it over yet another course of roast beef, I knew that would only put every other person in that room in danger. Greyson was right—it had to be public. All we could do was wait.

One morning, at the crack of dawn, a guard burst into

our bedroom. "Get up," he ordered. "The car leaves in an hour."

"We get to leave?" I said groggily, sitting up from the second bed in Greyson's suite. "Where?"

"Oversee reconstruction of Somerset," the guard grumbled.

Greyson and I exchanged a look, and my heart leaped into my throat. This could be it. This could finally be the opportunity we'd been waiting for.

Once the guard left, we got ready, and I carefully hid the gun inside the lining of my bulky winter coat. One shot. That was all I needed, and all of this would finally be over.

We took two cars to Somerset, with Daxton and Minister Bradley in the first while Greyson, Benjy, and I followed in the second. I checked to make sure the privacy screen was up, blocking our conversation from the driver. "Do you think the guards will try to protect him?" I said in a low voice as we drove down an avenue toward Somerset. Creed Manor wasn't far, but that only gave us a few minutes to talk, and I needed to be prepared for anything that could happen once I pulled the trigger. Having Greyson and Benjy there wasn't ideal, but with luck, I could separate from them. If the guards retaliated, I wanted to be the only one who paid the price.

"Maybe," said Greyson grimly. "If you think for a moment they might—"

"I'll stop," I lied. I knew I wouldn't, and they knew I wouldn't, either. But as willing as I was to die for this cause, I couldn't stomach the thought of dying today—of never seeing the light at the end of the dark tunnel that had become our lives—and I told myself again and again that it wouldn't happen. I would hide the gun in my coat. They wouldn't be able to tell it was me until Greyson was in charge, and he would pardon me. It would work out.

It had to.

When we arrived at Somerset only a few minutes later, there was a crowd of onlookers waiting for us at the gates, held back by armed guards. Daxton's car slowed, and he cracked the window to stick a hand out and wave.

A few members of the crowd clapped, but it didn't look terribly enthusiastic. Maybe public sentiment was turning against him more swiftly than we'd thought. Or maybe it was too cold out for anyone to feel particularly enthusiastic about anything. With that in mind, I rolled down our window.

"What are you doing?" said Greyson, trying to snatch my hand from the button. I gave him a look.

"Seeing how much fallout we're going to have to face."

Sticking my head out the window, I beamed at the crowd and waved, and a roar of applause and whistles began. Nearly everyone in the crowd lit up, and they began to shout and wave back. My smile grew genuine. Daxton was the only one feeling the cold, it seemed.

"Get back in here before someone shoots you," hissed Benjy, but I only slid back into my seat once the crowd was out of sight. Greyson hastily rolled the window up.

"No one's going to shoot me," I said. I was the one with the gun, after all. "Did you see that?"

"Yes," said Greyson, frowning. "It was unnecessary."

"No, it was exactly what they wanted," I said. "Daxton waved, and no one cared. I smile and wave, and they're practically crawling over themselves to get closer."

"It was still dangerous," said Greyson, and I shrugged.

"I've been shot at before. Besides, this was worth it."

"I don't see how," he said, but Benjy spoke up before I could.

"In the court of public opinion, Lila will win every time against Daxton. We can use that. We will."

When the white manor of Somerset came into view, my stomach knotted, and I had to force myself to breathe steadily. This was it. This was the moment we'd been waiting for. I touched the inside of my jacket, the metal cool and reassuring to the touch. I could do this. I *would* do this, and by noon, everything would be exactly the way it should be. I just had to pull the trigger.

In a stroke of inspiration, I secured my right sleeve in the pocket on that side, making sure it wouldn't accidentally fall out. This way, it looked like I had both of my hands in my pockets, but my right arm was inside my coat instead, within reach of the gun hidden in the lining. It wasn't the most graceful of plans, but it would give me a way to shoot Daxton without giving the appearance of pointing a gun directly at him. It might buy me the few precious seconds I would need to keep myself alive.

As we piled out of the car, Daxton watched me coldly from the other side of the drive, and it took me a panicked moment to realize it wasn't because he had noticed my empty sleeve. He must have witnessed my impromptu rally. I couldn't decide whether to feel smug about it or worry about his potential retaliation. But what could he do? As long as I did my job, he would be dead in a matter of minutes, and the country would be ours. If I survived that long.

I swallowed that thought and steeled my spine against the

fear washing over me. Too many people were counting on that bullet for me to change my mind, but it was far more difficult to find my courage now than it had been in a room far from Daxton and his guards and the consequences of my actions. I bit the inside of my cheek. This was exactly the version of me Knox would have been thrilled to see— someone thinking her actions through before taking them. Only now, that hesitation could blow things all to pieces.

As we had hoped, a camera crew had gathered to record our observation of what remained of Somerset. They likely planned to show this clip on the six o'clock news as a fluff piece about how the Hart family was rebuilding after the war; they had no idea this would become a shot that, with any luck, would go down in history. My palms began to sweat. I could do this. I *had* to do this.

Construction crews had cleaned up the worst of the wreckage in Somerset, and they had already built scaffolding around the parts that had to be reconstructed, including the residential wing. Seeing the destruction from the outside made me wonder how anyone had survived at all. As we all gathered on the brown front lawn, a foreman in a construction hat joined us, and he and Daxton shook hands.

"It's a pleasure, Prime Minister," he said, and I caught a glimpse of the V on the back of his neck.

"The pleasure is all mine," said Daxton with grace and charm I'd nearly forgotten he was capable of. "I hear you're planning on remodeling the residential wing completely."

"We are," said the foreman, and he launched into a description of the new amenities. My heart pounded, and blood rushed in my ears as the world outside my mind grew noiseless. One twitch of the finger. That was all it would take.

Under the guise of getting a better look at the manor, I shifted my stance, giving me a clear shot. I was only a couple feet from Daxton—even without aiming, it would be hard to miss him. Guards surrounded us just off camera, ready to jump in at the first sign of trouble, but none of them were watching me. Despite Daxton's abundance of caution, none of them seemed to expect an inside job.

At last I screwed up my courage and moved the gun in the right position. At the edge of my vision, I could see Greyson watching me, and as our eyes met, he gave the slightest hint of a nod.

With my expression as impassive as I could manage, I took a breath, steadied my hand, and pulled the trigger.

Bang.

Daxton cried out and collapsed. A chorus of shrieks rose up from the crowd, and several people ducked. At the last second, I remembered to duck as well, and I twisted around wildly, pretending to search for the shooter. But I didn't have to fake my pounding pulse or the fear in my eyes.

In an instant, the guards turned toward us, and several flung themselves over Daxton protectively, but it was too late. He lay still while the rest of us remained close to the ground.

All of us...except Minister Bradley.

"Is he—?" Bradley's eyes widened, and rather than backing away, he stepped closer to the pile of guards. Even as close to the ground as I was, I could see the faintest hint of a smile on his face.

Idiot. *Idiot.*

But there was nothing I could do in the chaos of the moment without giving myself away. I replaced the gun in the lining of my coat and, as the remaining guards rushed to protect us and guide us safely back to the car, I looked over my shoulder at Daxton. He lay motionless on the grass, and though I could already hear sirens in the distance, it was too late.

I'd done it. I'd pulled the trigger.

And now it was over.

XIV

ROOM OF HORRORS

The car sped back to Creed Manor with Greyson, Benjy, and me in the back. Two guards had come with us, squeezing in on either side of Greyson, and no one said a word throughout the journey. I didn't trust myself to speak without giving the game away, but mostly I was shocked I'd managed to do it. Greyson and Benjy looked equally stunned, as if they, too, hadn't been sure this would happen.

Good. Better to fool the guards, then. And when the truth came out—when I confessed to killing Daxton in the memory of the Blackcoats and for the good of the country— Greyson would have the power to pardon me.

Everything would be fine.

Except, as the three of us were rushed inside Creed Manor, the slightest suspicion began to bloom in the back of my mind. I heard our protectors' earpieces crackle, and one gave a grunt in reply. Something wasn't right— not that anything could be *right* for the men who had just failed to protect their charge from being assassinated, but it was something more than that. Benjy was ushered off to Daxton's office, while the pair of guards joined Greyson and me upstairs.

"You're to remain in separate rooms," said a gruff man with cropped hair who reminded me far too much of Strand, and he stepped in front of me, blocking my way into Greyson's suite.

"On whose orders?" demanded Greyson, standing up straight and radiating confidence. Maybe he was faking it, or maybe power suited him—either way, he was right. They should have been listening to him, not anyone else.

"On the Prime Minister's orders," said the guard.

"Greyson is the Prime Minister now," I said sharply, but he didn't so much as blink.

"Separate rooms. Those are the orders."

I stared at Greyson, desperation coursing through me—not because we needed to be together, but because if the guards were still taking orders from Daxton, that meant one of three things:

One, Victor Mercer wasn't the only person Masked as Daxton Hart.

Two, he'd planned for this and, in the event of his death, we were to be executed.

Or the third and most frightening possibility: somehow, someway, Daxton had survived my bullet, and now we would all be facing the consequences of my actions.

I didn't know which option was worse. At least if Daxton were dead, others could steer the country toward the Blackcoats' ideal, no matter what happened to me and Greyson. But if he had been Masked again—if there was an endless supply of Daxton Harts sitting around in a facility somewhere, ready to take the old one's place—then we were never going to win.

"If you will, Miss Hart," said a second guard, taking my arm and leading me to my suite down the hall, which I hadn't slept in since arriving. I dug my heels in and tried to return to Greyson, but the guard's grip was incredibly strong.

"Greyson!" I shouted, yanking so hard that I was sure my arm would be bruised in the morning. "Let me *go*. I'm staying with my cousin."

"No, you aren't." The guard opened the door and unceremoniously flung me inside. I stumbled and landed on the floor, but he didn't seem to care. He slammed the door shut firmly behind me, and I sat there in silence, my head spinning. Whatever this was, it was clear something had gone horribly wrong.

All I could do was wait.

The first thing I did was hide the gun.

I tried to open a window to get rid of it, but they were all firmly locked, and I wouldn't be able to control where it landed anyway. It was entirely likely it would bounce into the open grass, and even if I did manage to make it land in the shrubs, a gardener would find it eventually, and it wouldn't be difficult to guess where it came from.

Instead I hollowed out a thick book with the blade of a razor. It was crude, but it worked, and I returned the book to its place on the shelf. It wasn't the best hiding spot in the world, but it was better than underneath my bed.

I waited for Greyson to contact me on the ear cuff, but the crackle of static never came through. Maybe he'd forgotten about it, though that seemed unlikely, and the more time that passed, the more anxious I became. I tried everything I could think of to escape that room and get to Greyson, even if all I could do was make sure he was okay, but there were guards stationed at my door constantly, and I had no doubt the same was true for his. Days passed, and my meals were brought to me on silver platters, but no amount of finery could disguise the fact that once again, I was a prisoner.

No one answered my questions about the state of Daxton's health. If he was dead, if he was alive but barely hanging on, if he was perfectly fine and playing yet another sadistic game—no one said a word. Over and over, I pictured the shooting in my mind, trying to figure out where he'd been hit. Or if he'd been hit at all. I hadn't seen any blood, but we'd been ushered out of there so quickly that it was impossible to say for sure whether there had been any or not.

At last, five days after I'd tried to kill Daxton—or succeeded, and didn't know it yet—my door burst open. I sat on the couch with my sketch pad, expecting a servant with my lunch. Instead, two guards strode in and immediately took me by the arms, hauling me to my feet.

"What the hell do you think you're doing?" I growled, struggling against them, but they swiftly yanked my hands behind my back and handcuffed my wrists. Neither of them offered an explanation as they half led, half dragged me out of the suite and down the hall. I twisted around in time to see the guards standing in front of Greyson's door, and the knot in my stomach lessened. At least Greyson was still all right. Or as all right as he could be when he probably hadn't left his room in days, either.

The guards led me down the grand staircase and into the wing that had, until this moment, been completely off-limits to me: the master-suite wing, where Daxton had spent all his time holed up away from us, scheming and plotting and doing whatever it was he did each day. Coming up with more ways to destroy the lives of innocent people, I supposed. He wasn't good for much else.

His wing was double the size of my suite, Greyson's, and Knox's put together, and it was decorated in the same warm woods and colors as the rest of the house. But the deeper we went down the hallway, the colder the air seemed to grow, until at last the guards opened a door near the end of the corridor.

It was a plain room with white walls, but the stench of human waste, blood, and fear punched me in the gut, making my stomach heave. "I'm not going in there," I said, nearly choking on the putrid air.

"Oh, yes, you are," said a voice inside. Daxton appeared from behind the door, wearing a black apron over his suit and holding what looked like a curved saw. The blade dripped with fresh blood. "Surprised to see me, Lila?"

I gaped at Daxton, my mouth dry and the edges of my vision going dark. I searched for any sign that he was a replacement, but no one could mimic the coldness in his voice and the sadistic glint in his eye. I hadn't done it. I hadn't killed him.

Failure and shame and pure self-loathing washed over me, squeezing me in a vise grip from which there was no escape. That was twice now I'd failed to murder the man known as Daxton Hart. At least this time, it wasn't from lack of trying.

"I'm thrilled you're still alive," I said through a clenched jaw, my mind racing. Whose blood was that? I glanced into the room, but most of my view was blocked by Daxton and the door. Who else was at the manor with—

All the air left my lungs, and suddenly it was all I could do to remain standing. I'd been so busy worrying about Greyson that I hadn't given Benjy's safety a second thought.

No. I couldn't lose control. I couldn't forget who I was supposed to be. Benjy was nothing to Lila. Daxton would have no reason to hurt him for my sake. And if I asked about him—if I gave even the slightest hint he was my top priority—

"Where's Greyson?" I managed, forcing the words out. "What the hell did you do to him?"

"Oh, don't worry. Greyson is quite safe," he said, and he stepped aside, giving me room to enter. "He doesn't have the courage to pull the trigger anyway, does he? No, no—once I reviewed the footage from the incident, it became crystal clear who the perpetrator was."

My head buzzed with fear and pure adrenaline, and I staggered forward, hardly daring to let myself think it. It couldn't be Benjy. It couldn't be Benjy. It couldn't be Benjy.

I exhaled sharply when I saw the body lying prone on a steel table. Or at least I thought it was a body—the skin was nearly all gone, revealing the angry red muscles below, and the hands and arms lay in pieces on nearby trays, clearly sawed off bit by bit. The massive belly was sliced open, and another bowl of organs had been placed beside several fingers.

I turned away and was sick on the floor, heaving up what felt like everything I'd eaten in days. I'd been right. It wasn't Benjy. Even though it was nearly unrecognizable, the body was too big to be him. But I did recognize the handlebar mustache attached to what was left of the face.

Minister Bradley.

"Is he—?" I managed once there was nothing left to come up. For once, I hoped the answer was yes.

"No, not yet. He will be soon, though, don't worry. To his credit, it did take several days to break him," said Daxton, setting aside the saw and moving to admire his handiwork. I'd seen evidence of it before, I realized—in the basement of Mercer Manor. At the time, I'd assumed it was only Jonathan Mercer. But of course his brother had enjoyed himself, too.

"You think—you think Minister Bradley tried to kill you?" I said, gagging again as the smell of vomit mixed with the rest of it.

"Oh, no. The public does, of course—it's easy to spin the footage from the event to make it seem like that's the truth—but I know exactly what happened." Daxton selected a particularly long knife from his collection of tools, testing his thumb on the tip. "Even without Bradley's confession, Greyson doesn't have the courage, and Benjamin would have done it privately, no doubt. Or at the very least, he's competent enough to recognize a bulletproof vest underneath a suit when he sees one."

But he hadn't. None of us had. In the dead of winter, with the bulky coats we were all wearing, it would have been impossible to tell a vest from an extra sweater. I cursed myself again and again for not considering that possibility. I should have aimed for his head.

"So you think it was me," I said, too shaken to fake Lila's usual haughtiness. I wanted to believe that, faced with the torture Minister Bradley had spent the past five days enduring, she wouldn't have been able to keep it up, either.

"I know it was you, Lila. Bradley admitted he gave you the gun. My guards are searching your room now. I have no doubt they will find it soon."

There was no point in denying it. He knew Lila had wanted to kill him; he knew we all did. And whether I admitted it or not, my sentence would still be the same. "Is that why you brought me here? To execute me?"

Daxton laughed as he traced the tip of the knife over Bradley's exposed chest. Though he had been still and silent until now, the former Minister suddenly trembled, and a soft moan escaped. My stomach contracted again, but there was nothing left to purge.

"Execute you? My dear Lila, why on earth would I do something so foolish? No, no. Your allegiance, feigned or not, is far too precious. I only wish to demonstrate to you exactly what will happen to Greyson and anyone else alive you love should you ever attempt something this heinous again."

He shoved the blade into Bradley's chest, right where his heart must have been. At once, Bradley's moans stopped, and grim relief filled me. Five days. It had taken him five days to break and betray me. No one could blame him for that, and if Daxton hadn't put him out of his misery, I would have found a way to do so before leaving the room.

"You are mine, Lila. Do you understand? You and

Greyson—you are my pets, to sit and stay and roll over as I please," snarled Daxton. "Dogs do not bite their master unless they want to be euthanized. Is that what you want?"

"The dogs wouldn't bite at all if their master didn't abuse them." My voice trembled, but at least I'd found some drop of courage. "The master is always at fault."

"Maybe. But the master is the one who holds the leash, so in the end, does it really matter?" He pulled the knife from Bradley's body with a sickening, wet sound. "Let this be a warning to you, Lila. There is no escape, and the harder you try, the direr your circumstances will become. You are dismissed."

I couldn't get out of that room fast enough. With my hands still cuffed behind my back, I lurched back through the doorway, and the guards caught me by the elbows, steadying me so I didn't fall over.

"Oh, and Lila?" called Daxton through the doorway. I didn't turn around. "I expect to see you at dinner tonight."

Over my dead body, if I'd had any choice, but I didn't. This was it. This was going to be my life from here on out—existing merely to give legitimacy to Daxton's rule and to buy him the sympathy of the people. And if he ever did decide to kill me, there were a million ways to do it that wouldn't lose him either of those things. Hire someone else to murder me in front of an audience, for instance, the way I'd tried to do to him. Poison me until I was so weak that my heart gave out. Stage some sort of accident that couldn't be traced back to him. My life was at his mercy, but then again, that's exactly how it had been since my seventeenth birthday. This wasn't anything new. The noose around my neck had only tightened, and now Daxton wasn't bothering to feign civility anymore. It should have been refreshing to know precisely where we stood, with no pretenses between us. But when I was the one directly underneath his boot, that wasn't much of a silver lining.

When the guards finally led me back to my room, it had been ransacked so completely that nothing was where it should have been. I wasn't the least bit surprised to discover they'd found my hollowed-out book, but if Daxton was going to kill me for the assassination attempt, he would have already done it. He didn't need the proof, and my punishment was continuing to live under his rule.

I spent the rest of the afternoon cleaning up, taking my time returning books to the shelves and clothes to the closet. It was busywork, but I was grateful for something to do. Still, no matter how many trinkets I picked up and returned to their original spots, I couldn't shake the image of Bradley's mutilated body, and I couldn't stop hearing that single pathetic moan. I could have lived a hundred more years, and I would never forget those few minutes I'd spent with Daxton in that room of horrors.

My picture frame was, thankfully, unbroken, and I set it back on the nightstand. It was almost a form of torture in and of itself now, having those memories so readily at my fingertips. But I needed something to keep me sane, and if Daxton was going to deny me everything else, then those few pictures were all I had left.

At dinnertime, a knock sounded on my door. I was sitting on the sofa once more, staring at the wall of bookshelves. I couldn't read any of them, but I'd thought about opening one up and pretending. "Come in," I called, expecting the guards. To my surprise, it was Benjy who opened the door.

"Hey," he said with a tight smile, and I scrambled to my feet. He didn't step inside the room, however, and I stayed put, too. Seeing him alive and well was a balm I hadn't known I'd needed, but now that he was standing in front of me without a scratch on him, everything inside me seemed to deflate.

"Is it time for dinner?" I said, and he nodded, pressing his lips together.

"The Prime Minister asked me to escort you." A flicker of uncertainty passed over his face, and I knew without a doubt that something else was going on.

"Very well," I said with a sniff, another image of Bradley flashing in my mind. No matter how much perfume I sprayed, the stench of that room still lingered in my nose. "Will Greyson be joining us?"

"Not tonight." He must have sensed my silent question, because he added, "Daxton and I visit him regularly, and he's all right. Bored, and he asks about you every time we see him, but he's okay."

Relieved, I took Benjy's arm and let him lead me into the hallway. The fact that they hadn't insisted on handcuffs this time surprised me, but I doubted Daxton would ever let me get close enough to him again for that to be a problem.

When we arrived, two servants opened the doors to the dining room for us, and I stopped when I saw the spread laid out on the table. Whole hams and chickens, a mountain of colorful fruit, and a maze of vegetables and soups. More kinds of bread than I'd known existed. And along the edges of the room, waiting to be served, sat tray after tray full of decadent desserts.

"What...?" Never before had I seen such an opulent display of food, not even at the endless stream of parties I'd attended as Lila before the war.

"Lila!" Daxton clapped his hands on the other side of the room, where he stood examining a roast pig. "How lovely it is to have you join us."

"Is it somebody's birthday and I missed the memo?" I said warily. Benjy left me at the foot of the table while he took a seat toward the center, between Daxton and me.

"Oh, no, but we *do* have a special guest." He gestured, and another door opened.

Her wrists were shackled to her ankles, her clothes were dirty, and her tangled black hair hung in her face, but as she entered the dining room, she looked up, and our eyes met.

Celia.

XV

GILDED CAGE

"Mom?" I croaked. It had been a long time since I'd had to pretend Celia was my mother, but now even she had no idea I wasn't her daughter.

Her expression crumpled, and for a second, I thought she was going to cry. "Lila," she said in a choked voice. "You're okay. I've missed you, honey."

"I've missed you, too," I said. I wanted to go to her, to hug her and tell her everything was okay, but I could feel Daxton's beady eyes on me, and I didn't dare show an ounce of weakness.

"Family reunions always make me so happy," he said. "Please, everyone, sit—this feast won't eat itself."

Between the horrors I'd witnessed that afternoon and seeing Celia in such awful shape, I wasn't sure I'd ever be hungry again, but any insubordination on my part would only make things worse for her. Obediently I sat and let the servers fill my plate with a variety of foods, but none of it looked appetizing. Instead I stared at the woman who had helped me impersonate her dead daughter from the beginning. She had been through more than any of the rest of us, first losing her husband to the brutality of her family, and then not only losing her daughter, but being forced to train her replacement only days later. In the middle of it all, she had formed a rebel group to fight her family, and never, not once, had I seen her wallow in her grief at the expense of what needed to be done. That kind of strength and bravery couldn't be learned. It was something innate inside her, something irreplaceable. She was the reason I had survived this long. Together, she and Knox had made sure I'd been as safe as possible, and now there was nothing I could do to return the favor.

"So." Her voice was hoarse, and her hands shook as she picked up a fork with fingers that didn't bend properly. A chill ran through me as I pictured the things they must have done to her, but despite her condition, she wore a mask of indifference. "How long will you play with your food before putting me out of my misery, Victor?"

"It's *Daxton*. One would think you would recognize your own brother," he said with a wave of his knife.

"One would think," said Celia mildly. He sniffed.

"I've already made plans to have you executed in the morning. It should be a good show."

"I thought the war was over," I said hollowly, stabbing a piece of lettuce. "Won't another execution stir up discontent all over again?"

"Hardly," he said. "The people deserve closure, and Celia is the missing link. Once her body is burned and there's nothing left of her, then and only then can we have peace."

My insides seized, and despite her hard shell, even Celia paled at that. "Burning at the stake? Isn't that a bit medieval?"

"Rather suitable for a witch, wouldn't you say?" he said. "Or would you rather be drawn and quartered?"

"I would have thought family would show each other mercy," she countered.

"You've made it painfully clear, dear sister, in your multiple attempts to kill me, that you have never had any intention of showing *me* mercy," he said. "Why should I return the favor?"

"Because it would make you look benevolent in front of the entire country," I said with as much strength as I dared. "You don't want the people to see you as sadistic, especially when Celia has never been pinned as directly responsible for any specific murders."

"She's responsible for the whole damn rebellion." Daxton slammed his fist into the table. "I will not show mercy when she deserves none."

"Then you're going to make half a billion people sympathize with her and hate *you*," I said, refusing to be rattled by his outburst. "Either way, she's going to die. You don't want to make yourself look like the monster you really are in the meantime."

The dining room fell deathly silent. Daxton sat at the head of the table, shaking with rage and turning a strange shade of purple. I could only hope he gave himself a stroke, or better yet, a heart attack; instead, as the seconds passed, he began to calm down, and his face returned to a normal color.

"You're right, Lila," he said all too calmly. "You're absolutely right. Very well. A merciful execution it is. A hanging, or death by firing squad—I'll let you know in the morning, Celia."

Of course he would. That would give her all night to worry about it. "I'd like to stay with her," I said. "She's my mother, after all. I have a right to say goodbye."

"I was just about to suggest the very same thing myself," said Daxton in a dangerously cheerful voice. Whatever he had planned, it couldn't be good, but I would deal with it when it happened. "Now enjoy yourselves, both of you. This is, after all, a celebration."

If I had been in Celia's position, I wouldn't have been able to eat a bite. As it was, I could barely keep my dinner down, but she feasted on everything in sight. Plate after plate, entrée after entrée, as if she hadn't eaten in a month and never would again.

But she wouldn't, I realized. This was her last meal.

After that, I didn't touch the rest of my plate, even avoiding the desserts that the servers brought around for us to sample. Daxton seemed abnormally happy throughout the rest of the meal, and he continued to chat about the execution as if it were some party we were all looking forward to. Celia focused on eating, while Benjy also stared at his plate, barely touching a thing. As much as I hated knowing he had to see this, too, at least this time I wasn't the only witness to Daxton's depravity.

At last, once even Celia couldn't eat another bite, Daxton stood. "Make sure Celia is comfortable," he said to Benjy. "It is, after all, her last night."

"She can stay in my room," I said, trying to give my voice as much authority as I could muster. Daxton tilted his head, considering.

"Well, it's a bit more luxurious than the cellar, but why

the hell not. I'm feeling generous tonight." He bowed. "Ladies. Benjamin. Enjoy your evening."

As soon as he was gone, everyone in the room seemed to exhale with relief. Benjy stood. "I'll escort you both back to Lila's room," he said. "And I'll make sure the guards undo your shackles, Celia."

"Thank you," she said, and the guards took their places on either side of her. I joined them, and together we trooped upstairs and back to Lila's suite. True to his word, Benjy instructed the guards to remove Celia's binds, and as she walked into the room, it suddenly hit me that I would have to spend the next twelve hours convincing her that I was, in fact, her daughter.

Benjy touched my shoulder, and I looked at him, more scared than I'd been in ages. He didn't say anything, but he held my stare for a split second and nodded slightly. I could do this. He knew I could do this.

The problem was, I didn't want to.

As soon as the doors closed and the lock clicked into place, trapping Celia and me for the night, she crossed the room and embraced me, her frighteningly skinny arms wrapping around me with what must have been all the strength she could muster. Silently I hugged her back.

We stood like that for minutes—hours—I couldn't tell, and it didn't matter. I would stay like this for the rest of the night if she wanted me to. But eventually she let go and touched my face, gazing into my eyes. Lila's eyes.

"When—" Her voice caught in her throat, and a tear rolled down her cheek. She didn't bother wiping it away. "When did it happen?"

I opened my mouth to ask what she meant, but it suddenly hit me, and the words retreated. She knew. Of course she knew. "Late December," I whispered. "It was instantaneous. She felt no pain, and she didn't know it was coming."

Celia took a long, deep breath and released it slowly before capturing me in a hug again. "Good. At least she didn't suffer."

"Not even a little," I promised. "How did you…?"

"Lila is my daughter. I know her better than anyone in the world." Celia ran her fingers through my hair. "As soon as I knew he had you, too, it was obvious he was only going to keep one of you alive. I've been watching your appearances. You're good. You're very, very good. But you aren't her."

No, I wasn't. "I'm sorry."

"Don't be. It isn't your fault, and you've done a wonderful job keeping her alive. But, Kitty…" She paused and took my hand, leading me to the couch, where we sat down beside one another. She wrapped her arms around me again, holding me like I really was her daughter, and she kissed the top of my head. "Don't lose yourself in this, all right? The Blackcoats are down, but they aren't defeated. The people are unhappy, and eventually the revolution *will* happen. When it does, you need to be there to believe in the impossible. That's the only way change happens—when someone dares to think differently and does whatever they have to in order to make that a reality. You can't do that if you've lost yourself in the meantime."

"I'll try not to," I said, curling up against her. "We haven't given up."

"Of course you haven't. You're a Hart. Not giving up

is in our genes." I could hear the smile in her voice, and I allowed myself to relax. If she could smile right now, then I could, too. "I'm sorry about everything that's been done to you, Kitty. Truly."

"I'm not." As soon as I said the words, I knew they were true. "You and Knox gave my life meaning and purpose. I won't lie and say it's been easy, but nothing worth having ever is, right?"

"My husband used to say that all the time," she murmured.

"Benjy did, too. It's how he tried to get me to do my homework when we were in school." I paused. "I'm sorrier for all you've been through. You're the strongest person I've ever known."

Her arms tightened around me. "I could very well say the same about you. You'll make it through this—you and Greyson both. I'm only sorry I won't be there to see Victor's face when he realizes he's lost."

I swallowed thickly. "I'll make sure he loses everything."

She smiled. "Good girl."

We sat together on the couch for the rest of the night, neither of us bothering with sleep. She told me her life story, about growing up as a Hart and slowly realizing how wrong and twisted the world really was. About what the real Daxton—my father—had been like, and Jameson, my half brother. She told me stories about the good memories she had with her family, even her mother, Augusta, and she lingered on the memories of Lila. I had already heard a number of her stories when she'd been educating me on her daughter's life back in October, but this time, she told me personal ones—like what holding Lila for the first time had felt like. Seeing her first steps. Her first words, her first birthday, and the last time she'd seen her. Little moments I hadn't needed to know when I was pretending to be her, but now that Celia knew she was about to die, I supposed it was cathartic to remember. Or maybe she just wanted to make sure the best moments of her life didn't die with her.

"When I was younger, I always thought death was the worst possible thing that could happen to someone," she murmured as the horizon slowly turned gray. We didn't have much time left, but she didn't speak any faster. Instead, she seemed to slow down, her gaze growing distant. "And then my husband was murdered, and they tried to kill my daughter, and I realized death isn't the worst thing. It's just the last thing. And endings are hard, that's all." She took a deep, shuddering breath. "I hope every day there's something more."

"More?" I said.

"Something after this life, in whatever form it takes. And that's why I'm not scared," she added. "Because the worst that can happen is nothingness. And while that's a frightening concept, if there *is* something more—maybe they'll be there. Maybe I'll see my husband and daughter again, and that's worth the risk any day. It's something to look forward to."

It was a small comfort as she faced her own death. But keeping her alive in a world where her family was long dead—that was the worst kind of cruelty I could think of. No matter how Daxton killed her, it would still be a mercy kill. We would all die one day, and at least she wouldn't have to live to see another without her husband and daughter.

When the knock sounded on the door at sunrise, she held me to her once more, close enough for me to feel her steady pulse. "Remember what I said. Don't forget yourself, Kitty. Don't forget your bravery. You're not alone in this fight, and when the time comes, don't hold back."

"I won't," I said, my voice breaking. "I promise."

She tucked my hair behind my ears and brushed her fingertips against my cuff. "That's pretty," she murmured. "You should wear that to my execution."

My hand flew to my ear. Did she know what it was? If she did, she gave no more indication of it, and instead she stood and smoothed her dirty clothes. A pair of guards stood at the door with her shackles, and as she crossed the room toward them, I walked with her. My eyes welled as they secured her again, though her expression was strangely calm. I tried to remember what she had told me—that death wasn't the end to her; it was a possibility for the re-union she'd been waiting for. But a lump formed in my throat anyway.

"They'll be there," I managed, embracing her one last time. "I'm sure of it."

Her chains rattled as she hugged me back as best she could. "So am I."

The guard cleared his throat, and at last we let each other go. Our eyes locked, and I remained absolutely still as the guards led her away, her neck twisted so she didn't lose sight of me until the last possible moment. No—not me. Her daughter. Lila.

Once she was gone, I shut the door and tried to move back to the couch, but my legs gave way underneath me, and I collapsed to the floor, sobbing harder than I had since this whole mess had begun.

I don't know how long I sat there, choking on my own tears, but suddenly a pair of familiar arms wrapped around my shoulders, and I leaned against Benjy, clinging to him. He held me, not saying a word as I cried myself out. There was nothing to say anyway. No magic formula of words to make it any better. It was what it was—the end for her. The end of all her possibilities, and despite what she said, it was the end of the Blackcoat Rebellion.

"Daxton wants you there," whispered Benjy, rubbing my back. "I'm sorry."

"Don't be," I said hoarsely, and he helped me up. I'd known this was coming. The real Daxton had forced Lila to watch her father's execution; there was simply no way Victor Mercer would let me miss Celia's.

I splashed cold water on my face and dressed in all black. Daxton might have considered this a celebration, but no one would mistake me for a reveler. My eyes were still red and puffy, so I found a pair of sunglasses and put them on, too. When I returned, someone had brought me break-fast, and I stared at the ham and eggs like they were made of plastic.

"You need to eat something," said Benjy, who sat on the couch waiting for me. "You barely had anything at all last night. The kitchen tried to give you steak, but I made them switch it out for ham."

Feeling more like a robot following commands than a real human being, I managed a few mouthfuls of eggs. They tasted like nothing, even though I didn't doubt they were seasoned to perfection.

"Good. And a bite of ham. Just one," encouraged Benjy, and reluctantly I cut off a piece. I stabbed it with the tip of the knife hard enough for the metal to screech against the china, and I winced. They may have traded steak for ham, but they'd left the sharp knife on my plate.

"There," I said, once I'd eaten it. "Happy?"

"Yes. Thank you," said Benjy, and he offered me his hand. "Let's go."

I started to reach for it, but I was still holding on to the knife. A guard poked his head into the room, and Benjy turned away. He was still on my side—he would always be on my side. But that was the moment I chose to slide the knife into the sleeve of my leather jacket before taking his hand.

Greyson waited for us in the car, and he too wore all black. He offered me a tiny, watery smile, and I slid in beside him, hugging his arm and resting my head on his shoulder. I didn't dare say anything, not when I knew the driver could be listening, but there was nothing to say anyway. Though Greyson hadn't been present at dinner the night before, he must have known what we were doing here, and talking about it wouldn't make any of this any easier.

Minutes later, we arrived at the edge of a park near Somerset, and though it was barely dawn, thousands of people had already braved the freezing morning air to gather around and watch the execution. I didn't know how many were there to celebrate the end of the rebellion and how many were simply chomping at the bit to see Celia die, but whether they were here for entertainment or out of morbid curiosity, I hated them all.

Camera crews lined the front, blocking most of the audience's view. Security cleared a path for us to make our way to the stage, where Daxton already waited. It was the same kind of platform Mercer had used in Elsewhere to kill Scotia and her Blackcoat supporters; the same kind of platform I'd stood on while giving my speech to the entire country, revealing my real identity and exposing Daxton's. D.C. was really no different from Elsewhere, in the end. At least the Mercers had been open about their brutality and the consequences of straying an inch out of line. Here, the people gathered had no idea how little control they had over their own lives.

"Good morning, Lila," chirped Daxton. He was dressed in a blue suit and red coat with an American flag pinned to the lapel, but he didn't comment on my outfit. I couldn't fathom him expecting anything else. "Ah, Greyson. So pleased to see you could join us."

Neither Greyson nor I responded. Instead we stood together, side by side, and waited in the frigid morning as sunlight began to sneak across the park. A chorus of shouts echoed from the edge, and I turned in time to see the guards forcing a path again, this time with Celia between them.

She'd been cleaned up and dressed in a blue jumpsuit, and she walked with her head held high, not making eye contact with anyone in the crowd. But though they were loud, I didn't hear any boos—instead, several of them reached for her, trying to touch her as she passed.

At last she reached the stage, and the guards escorted her up the steps to the center. Though she was only minutes from death, her eyes were bright, and she looked happier than I could ever remember seeing her before.

"Celia Hart," called Daxton, and his voice echoed throughout the entire park. "You have been charged with treason against not only your country, but your family. Your mother, your brother, your nephews, your daughter—you have committed grievous and unforgivable acts against us all, and now you will face the consequences of your actions. Do you have any last words?"

"Yes." Her voice also echoed across the crowd, and she smiled. "Checkmate."

For the briefest moment, confusion flashed across Daxton's face. He quickly covered it with a smile that might have looked benevolent to the cameras, but to me was full of malice and hatred. "Yes, dear sister. Checkmate."

A guard brought him a silver pistol—the same model I'd used to try to kill him. Knowing Daxton, it was probably the exact same gun. He would have found poetry in that, in some sick and twisted way. Once he'd expertly checked the chamber, he pointed the barrel toward Celia's forehead, and I held my breath, staring at my feet. I couldn't watch this.

"Oh. How rude of me," said Daxton, and he lowered the weapon. I looked at him, wild hope fluttering through me. "Your daughter asked for a merciful killing on your behalf, and I agreed."

Holding the gun by the barrel, he offered it to me instead. I stared at him uncomprehendingly.

"Go on then, Lila," he said, stretching the gun closer to me. "I will grant you the privilege of giving your mother the painless death you believe she deserves."

All the air left my lungs, and I couldn't breathe.

He wanted me to kill her.

He wanted Lila to kill her own mother.

Daxton leaned in, and I noticed a button he held in his other hand. He lifted his thumb, and the light flickered off. "Lila, dear, your mother is going to die today one way or the other. If you do not do this, I will have her doused in gasoline and burned alive in front of all these people. She will die in one of the most painful ways possible, and you will never get her screams of agony out of your head. Is that what you want for her? For yourself?"

His voice only passed to me. The button must have controlled the microphones, but I hardly cared. I couldn't kill her. I couldn't.

"This is what you asked for, yes?" said Daxton, and he placed the gun in my hand. "I am offering her a swift, painless death out of the goodness of my heart. Don't force her last few moments to be in agony."

"Lila." Celia's voice drifted toward me, and I looked at her, my eyes wide with panic. "It's okay. None of this is your fault. And I want it to be you."

My fingers curled around the handle as a choking sob bubbled up inside me. I could pull the trigger and shoot Daxton now and end this whole damn thing. That was exactly what I should have done, but before I could work up the courage, Daxton leaned in again.

"If you get the urge to try again, don't. There are snipers pointing their weapons directly at you and Greyson," he whispered. "If you so much as think about killing me, you will both be dead."

I would have been happy to die if it meant taking Daxton with me, but Greyson had to live. He had to be the one to put the country back together. Daxton must have known that, because he flashed me a wide smile and stepped back. "At your leisure, my dear."

It took every ounce of strength I possessed, but I lifted the gun, holding it the way I'd learned on the ranges in Elsewhere. The way Knox had taught me in Somerset. The way I'd shot Augusta Hart over and over and over again, until there had been no bullets left in the chamber and the white carpet had been soaked with her blood. My finger rested on the trigger, but no matter how hard I tried, I couldn't pull it.

Celia held my stare for a long moment, and she smiled. "Sometimes you have to sacrifice your queen to capture the king."

My lower lip trembled, and I had to grab the gun with my other hand as well to hold it steady, lest it accidentally slip toward Daxton. The crowd was silent, and my heart pounded in my ears.

"I can't," I whispered.

"Yes, you can," she said, and her smile grew. "I'm looking forward to it."

The sob I'd been holding in finally escaped, and at last I squeezed my eyes shut and pulled the trigger.

XVI

CHECKMATE

The gunshot cracked through the air like a whip, and as I stood there in shock, my eyes shut and my entire body trembling, several things happened in quick succession, faster than my muddled mind could follow.

A roar rose from the crowd, the sound of it unlike anything I'd ever heard before. Hundreds of voices joined together, enraged and ready for war.

At the same time, someone cried out in pain, and I opened my eyes to see Celia press her hand to her temple, where a streak of red spilled down her cheek. I stared at her, stunned. I'd put a bullet in her brain. How—

That was when I noticed the camera behind her. Several reporters had ducked, and the camera was a smoking mess with a shattered lens. Though I'd grazed Celia, I'd missed doing any real damage to her, hitting the camera instead. Around us, the crowd began to riot, and the Shields who had been so focused on the stage now faced outward, pointing their weapons into the audience. Several people screamed and tried to run, but others only climbed over them, getting closer and closer to the platform. Fear seized me. I didn't know if they were coming for me or Daxton or both of us.

"Give me that," he snarled, and he grabbed the gun from me, loading it with another bullet. It must have only had one. "Stupid bitch. Might just shoot you next."

"I—" I stood there dumbly, frozen in place, but Celia screamed, an animalistic sound that made the hair on the back of my neck stand up. With inhuman speed, she hurtled toward Daxton, crashing into him before he could close the chamber. They tumbled off the stage and onto the ground, knocking over a pair of Shields in the process.

I started to move toward the edge of the stage to help her, but Greyson grabbed my elbow. "Come on, we have to get out of here," he shouted over the noise, and he pulled me toward the staircase instead. I looked over my shoulder, desperate for any sign of Celia, but she was in the middle of a knot of Shields now, all clamoring to break them apart. No doubt they couldn't risk killing her without killing Daxton, too. And though it would mean losing Celia, I hoped like hell they would try anyway. It was undoubtedly what she wanted.

Greyson and I pushed our way through the crowd, and a few startled guards from Daxton's protection detail joined us. Faces blurred together, and I had no idea where we were going. Greyson seemed to know, however, and he led me down a zigzagged path, avoiding the worst of the crush.

As we neared the cars, a shot rang out from the platform, reverberating through the park and down my spine. I slowed, trying to see who had taken the bullet, but the crowd had swallowed the stage whole.

"Celia—" I began, but Greyson tugged me along. I

stumbled, and a guard scooped me up, narrowly avoiding a collision with a pair of young men brandishing sticks. They were running for the platform, not us. They were after Daxton.

When we reached the car, Greyson skidded to a stop. "That's going to be useless," he said, and I forced myself to focus long enough to see the four shredded tires.

"We'll take the Prime Minister's car," said a guard, and he ushered us to another black limousine ten yards down the road. The tires on his were still intact, and the guard opened the door, shoving both of us inside. "Wait for the Prime Minister," he shouted to the driver before slamming the door and running back toward the melee.

"It must have killed him to protect us instead of Daxton," said Greyson as we climbed toward the front of the limousine. His coat was rumpled, and his hat was askew, but he was unhurt.

"Do you think Celia killed him?" I said breathlessly, my brain still trying to process everything.

Greyson bit his lip. "I hope so," he finally said, even though the driver was listening. "If there's any justice in the world."

He set his hands over mine, and it was only then that I realized I was trembling. Swallowing hard, I dug my nails into my legs, trying to regain control. Though the fighting continued in the park, with shots ringing out and screams rising above the fray, it was all oddly muffled in the car. "Why are they rioting? The Shields are going to kill them."

"Because he tried to make you kill Celia." He leaned in closer. "You did exactly what you should have done."

"I didn't—" I clenched my jaw. I couldn't admit that I

hadn't meant to only graze Celia. Even if Greyson wouldn't have judged me for it, I was judging myself. I should have never pulled the trigger. "He isn't back yet. Do you think...?"

Greyson fell silent, and together we stared out the window, waiting. Every muscle in my body felt like a tightened coil, ready to spring at any moment. Celia had been so determined—and if anyone deserved to take out Daxton, it was her.

At last a knot of Shields three deep pushed through the rioters, and my heart dropped. "They wouldn't be protecting her like that," I whispered, hope draining out of me. Greyson squeezed my hands.

Sure enough, once they reached the street, Daxton emerged from their protective circle and tumbled into the car. Four long scratch marks ran down the side of his face, and he favored his left shoulder, but the worst of it was the blood that had soaked through his suit, turning his white shirt crimson. I shifted to sit next to Greyson and made myself as small as I could while Daxton composed himself, running one bloodstained hand through his salt-and-pepper hair.

"Ah, yes. They told me about the other car." He settled his hands in his lap, and only then did he seem to notice the blood. He held up his palm and grinned. "Your mother's. Feisty, wasn't she?"

He had killed Celia after all, then. My eyes burned, and I traced the handle of the knife I had slipped inside my coat. One stab to the heart, if he had one. That was all it would take.

But Greyson wrapped his arms around my shoulders to hold me in place, and I took a deep, shuddering breath. If I attacked now, Daxton would know it was coming, and no doubt he would overpower me. Wherever we were going, there would be a smarter time. I hoped.

The car sped down the avenue, and I blinked back tears, staring out the window. Something had happened in that park—something huge. But I didn't understand it yet, and I wondered how Daxton would spin it this time. A bunch of leftover rebels wishing their leader goodbye. A riot incited when I tried to kill him instead. Whatever happened, there had been more cameras there than I could count. It had to have been broadcasted live. The people had to know what Daxton had tried to do, and they had to have seen citizens fighting back. I refused to believe anything different.

"You're taking us to Somerset?" said Greyson as we pulled up the long, winding drive and approached the remains of the Hart family home. Scaffolding covered the hole in the residential wing, but it was far too early for the construction workers to be on-site.

"The rioters are heading toward Creed Manor, and the Prime Minister's protection detail rerouted us here. Until they can rejoin us, you're to take cover in the safe room," said the driver.

"Fine, fine. Make it quick, before they come here, too," said Daxton with a trace of nervousness in his voice. The driver parked the car and hopped out to open the door for us. Daxton climbed out first, not seeming to care that he left a trail of blood wherever he moved, and I followed several seconds later, keeping my distance from both him and the blood.

"Miss Hart," said the driver, holding out his arm for me to take. I did so, still too unsteady to trust myself to stay balanced. But when I looked up, I caught myself staring into the same blue eyes I saw every day in the mirror, no matter whose face I wore.

My mouth fell open, and Rivers winked. "Do you need an escort to the safe room?" he said. "A guard is expecting you."

"They will not be joining me," called Daxton, already hurrying through the front doors. As soon as he disappeared into the remains of Somerset, I caught Rivers in a hug, burying my nose in his blond hair.

"What's going on?" I said, stunned, as I finally let him go. He cleared his throat, and I glanced over my shoulder. Greyson stood directly behind me, his eyebrows raised.

"Friend of yours?" he said, and I nodded.

"Greyson, this is Rivers. Rivers, this is Greyson," I said. The pair of them shook hands, but as soon as they let go, Rivers ushered us toward the doors.

"No time to waste. You spoke with Celia?" he said.

I nodded. "What—"

"Make sure she didn't die for nothing," he said. "Hurry, before Daxton tries to close the door himself."

No doubt that was exactly what he would do, and I gave Rivers a quick, grateful smile. "I'll see you soon, right?"

He winked again. "Sooner than you think."

Taking Greyson's hand, I hurried into Somerset and headed directly for the nearest staircase. The bombs hadn't flattened the atrium like they had the residential wing, and to my relief, the steps were still in one piece.

"Explain that to me," said Greyson as we raced to the lowest level. "Who's Rivers?"

"He's a lieutenant with the Blackcoats. If he's here, something's going on. Something big."

"I gathered as much," said Greyson. When we reached the basement landing, he stopped, and I pitched forward, barely catching myself on the railing. "Do you realize what we're about to do?"

"I—yes," I said. "We're about to get in the safe room."

"With Victor Mercer. Alone." He stared at me. "That's suicide, Kitty."

"But—" I paused. "Rivers is planning something. He said to make sure Celia didn't die for nothing."

"She didn't die for nothing. I—" He tugged off his hat, and his hair stuck up like he hadn't bothered to brush it that morning. "I can't let you go in there, Kitty. Not when I know you won't come out."

"Greyson, I have to—"

"You have to what? To give him exactly the opportunity he needs to kill you? He can say you died in the riot. He can say a stray bullet hit you, and the public will believe him."

"Did you see that out there? Did you?" I gestured wildly toward the ceiling. "They don't believe a word he says. And if we're going to end this, we have to do it *now*. It's the only chance we'll get."

"You don't know that." His Adam's apple bobbed, and his grip on my hand tightened. "I'm sorry, Kitty. I can't let you do this. Even if there is a plan, no one bothered to tell us what it is."

Suddenly my cuff crackled, and out of nowhere, a familiar voice sounded in my ear. "Tell him Daxton isn't armed, and the vest he's wearing isn't nearly as bulletproof as he thinks it is."

The ground seemed to move underneath my feet, and it was all I could do to stay upright. "Kn-Knox?" I whispered, touching my cuff.

"Knox?" said Greyson, his eyes widening, and I nodded, stunned. He fumbled through his pockets, presumably for his own transmitter.

"Sorry for the radio silence," said Knox. "Couldn't let you in on anything while you were under Daxton's thumb."

"But—you're not— Elsewhere is gone—"

"As soon as you were captured, Rivers insisted we use the tunnels to move everyone out of the sections," he said. "We figured Daxton would try to torture information out of you, and with the supply lines choked off, there was no point staying anyway. By the time the bombs hit, we'd been gone for days."

I had no idea what to say to that. Everyone was okay. No one had died in that pile of ash that was now Elsewhere. And Knox was *alive.*

"I'm going to kill you," I said in a choked voice. "All this time, and you were really okay." I paused as realization hit me. "Wait—that means—you heard *everything*—"

"I did. I'm touched, truly."

I let out several curses. Greyson leaned in closer, apparently unable to find his transmitter. "What's he saying?"

"I'm saying you need to get in that safe room, Kitty," said Knox. "Just you. We need Greyson alive, and if things don't go as planned…"

I swallowed. "Right. I'm the pawn."

"You haven't been a pawn for a very long time." I heard

the smirk in his voice, and for a split second, I couldn't help but grin. He was alive. He was actually alive.

I quickly relayed Knox's message to Greyson, whose frown only deepened. "No. I won't let her go in there, Knox. He'll kill her."

"He's unarmed," I said. "And I have a knife."

Greyson shook his head, his grip on my hand almost bruising. "No. *No.* You're it. You're the only family I have left. I'm not letting you go."

"Greyson—"

"Kick him in the shin, and then run like hell toward the safe room," said Knox. "There's no time. I'll explain while you run."

I winced. "I'm so sorry," I said, and before Greyson could move, I did exactly as Knox had instructed and kicked him. Hard.

Greyson cried out, and his grip loosened enough for me to yank my hand back and make a break for it. I raced down the hallway toward the safe room, gripping the handle of the knife in my sleeve. This time, I wouldn't fail.

"Kitty, listen to me," said Knox in a low voice. "We've planted cameras in the safe room. Before you do anything else, you need to get Daxton to confess. Preferably not under duress. As much as you can get out of him—make it happen. But most important, make sure he admits to being Victor Mercer. Can you do that?"

"Don't have much of a choice, do I?" But even if I did—even if Greyson could have done it, or Knox, or anyone else, I would have still been running at breakneck speed toward that room. Because Lila was the one with the real power. She was the one the people loved. And that was worth more than control through fear ever would be.

"The connection will probably break up as soon as the door's closed," said Knox. "I'm on my way, and I'll be there as soon as I can. Just remember—no matter what else happens, make him confess. The entire country will be watching."

"Got it." I turned a corner and saw a burly guard standing in front of the doors to the safe room. I expected a fight—no doubt Daxton had given him the order not to open the door for anyone—but he immediately punched a code into the keypad and tipped me an enormous wink. Another Blackcoat, then. Suddenly my world seemed to be full of them. "The Prime Minister is waiting for you, Miss Hart."

I brushed my wild hair from my eyes. "Thank you," I said. Taking a deep breath, I threw out a silent, wild hope into the universe that I would make it out of this alive, and finally I stepped inside.

XVII

DEATH BY A THOUSAND CUTS

The safe room wasn't very big—the size of a generous living room, maybe, with the walls covered in cabinets and drawers that held enough supplies to keep the entire Hart family alive for months. Several couches stretched across the room, and there was a small private bathroom in the corner. Claustrophobia aside, it wasn't a terrible place to spend the night, as I'd done during the Blackcoat bombings my first evening in Somerset.

I searched the walls for any sign of a camera, but I didn't see so much as a red light. It didn't matter. I had to trust Knox. I had to believe he was right, and this was the chance we'd been waiting for.

Daxton stood pacing a circle in the center of the room, his hands clasped behind his back. When I slipped into the room, he stopped, his face twisting into a snarl. "Who said you could join me?"

"Your protective detail made me," I said, lingering near the door as the guard pushed it shut. It was at least two feet thick and made of impenetrable metal—supposedly strong enough to withstand even a nuclear bomb. "Greyson—he refused to come."

"He always was smarter than you." Daxton resumed his pacing. "I should kill you myself. Do you have any idea what you did out there?"

"I didn't do anything. The crowd was ready to rip you apart the second you tried to make me kill my own mother. That's twisted even for you, Victor."

He pushed his bloodstained hair back from his eyes, glowering at me. "It's *Daxton*."

"Who the hell are you kidding down here?" I waved my hand toward the empty room. "It's just me and you, and we both know exactly who you are."

"Yes, we do." He took a step toward me, his shoulders squared. "I am the Prime Minister of the United States of America. I am the most powerful man in this country. And no matter what my name happened to be two years ago, today it is Prime Minister Daxton Hart."

That was as much of a confession as I would probably get out of him, but I had no doubt it wouldn't be good enough for Knox. The few supporters Daxton had left could spin it, and we would be left at square one.

"How did she pick you?" I said. "Augusta. Did you two know each other? Did she come to Elsewhere one day and see you there with eyes exactly the same color as her real son's? I know how you found Kitty, but how did Augusta find you?"

He took a deep breath, his chest rising and falling as he stared at me wordlessly. For a moment I wondered if he'd cracked—if he was so deluded into thinking he really was

Daxton now that he couldn't handle any memories of his life before, believing they would negate his new identity.

But instead a wicked smile twisted across his face, and he took another step toward me. I had nowhere to go in the safe room, which only seemed to grow smaller and smaller as the seconds passed. My fingers tightened around the knife's handle. Let him try to hurt me. We would see how far that got him.

"Victor Mercer knew the family intimately," he murmured. "Daxton was a friend of his, you see. He would stay with Victor and his brother while he visited Elsewhere, and they would help Daxton partake in his particular... proclivities. Augusta didn't visit as frequently, but she did drop by from time to time, and one day, she approached Victor with a proposition. She liked him, you see. He was resourceful, driven, and he took pride in his work—all qualities she needed in a double for her son."

"And you jumped on the chance to seize power for yourself," I said.

"Naturally. Victor wasn't stupid." He took another step closer to me. He was within arm's reach now, but he kept his hands at his side, instead towering over me. "Do you want to hear something funny?"

"Bet it won't make me laugh."

"Mmm, but it *will* make you think." He closed the distance between us, his body inches from mine. I could smell the blood on his clothes, and it made my stomach turn. "Victor Mercer was Masked *months* before the original Daxton Hart died."

I stared at him, my heart pounding. "What?"

He grinned and raised his bloodstained fingers, brushing them against my jaw. It took everything I had not to stab him through the gut right then and there. "Perhaps Augusta knew Celia was targeting Daxton, or perhaps her son was misbehaving, and she wanted him out of the way. Perhaps she wanted a puppet she could control. Or perhaps it was simply a coincidence."

Nothing was a coincidence in the Hart family, and my mind reeled. Daxton, his wife, and his elder son, Jameson, had all been in the car that had exploded, killing them instantly. But it had been Daxton's car—he was the only one who was supposed to die. I didn't know for sure who had bombed it, but before that moment, all signs had pointed to Celia. Now I wasn't so certain.

"Guess Augusta gave you your lucky break," I said shakily. "Now look what you've turned it into. A dictatorship, with you at the top of the pyramid."

"It is rather beautiful, isn't it?" He brushed his thumb against my lips, and I nearly gagged. "Just like you."

"You know what my favorite part was? How you killed Minister Creed and Minister Ferras in cold blood and forced the other Ministers to sign the amendment that gave you absolute power," I said. "Managing a coup in your own country with only two bullets—it's actually sort of impressive. But I bet the real Daxton could've done it with one. Are the surviving Ministers still being held prisoner in the Stronghold, or have you flayed them alive and butchered them the way you did Minister Bradley?"

"Mmm. I had no idea you had such an admiration for my techniques. It's a shame—if I'd known sooner, perhaps we could have made the most of it. Though I suppose there's still time." He slid his other hand over my hip. "I don't have to kill you right away."

"You don't have to kill me at all," I said, suppressing a shudder at his touch. "The people will revolt."

"They already are. I hadn't wanted to declare war on my own country, but if I must..." He shrugged. "So be it."

My lips curled in disgust. "You don't care about the people at all, do you? Just power and what it can do for you."

"That's all any successful politician cares about," he said. "You would do well to remember that, Lila."

"I care about the people. Greyson cares about the people."

"And look where that's gotten you."

"Held prisoner against our will and forced to do your bidding so you don't kill us," I said. "I'm aware, thank you. But you know what we have that you don't? The people's support. They're out there rioting for *us*, not you. And they will keep rioting until you're no longer a problem for them."

"What, do you truly believe I'll ever allow you or your idiot cousin to take my place?" he said, then chuckled. I could smell stale coffee on his breath. "You were never going to outlive me, Lila. You or Greyson."

"What was your plan, then? To live forever?" I spat.

"All great men do."

I choked out a laugh. "You think you're a great man? Celia was great. Knox is great. Greyson will be great, and they will all be remembered as heroes. But you are nothing more than a weak, scared little man who had to step into the shoes of a tyrant in order to be anything in this world. History won't remember you as a great man. History will remember you as a coward."

He hissed, and his hand flew to my throat, squeezing until I couldn't breathe. My eyes widened, and I clawed at his hands while fumbling the handle of the knife, struggling to slip it out of my sleeve.

"That's it, Lila," he murmured, his dark eyes dancing with sadistic joy. "Fight me. Go on. Try to show me which one of us has the real power."

The edges of my vision grew dark, and his grip tightened even more. But I refused to let this be the end. He had killed Celia, he had killed Lila, and he had done his best to kill Benjy and Knox. But he wasn't going to kill me.

I kicked him in the knee as hard as I could, and his grip immediately loosened as he cried out. I stumbled away, gasping for air and finally pulling the knife from my sleeve. Blood rushed to my head, and the room spun, but I gripped the back of the couch and forced myself to hold it together.

"You stupid, *stupid* bitch. I could have made it infinitely less painful for you, but you're out of luck now, aren't you?"

He surged toward me, his hands reaching for my throat again, but this time I was ready. I ducked and thrust the knife as hard as I could into his belly. It slid in far more easily than I imagined it would, and the handle slipped from my grip.

Daxton stopped and looked down at the knife sticking out of his stomach, his expression strangely calm. "Well. That hurts, doesn't it?" Slowly, with a pained wince, he pulled the blade out of his body and examined it. "A steak knife? That's not terribly creative of you, Lila."

I stumbled backward against the door, unarmed and

dizzy from strangulation. He had to be in agony, but he walked toward me with ease, holding the knife like a toy.

"I've always loved your face. So even, so perfect—you're practically Aphrodite," he murmured. And in a blur of motion, he slashed the blade across my cheek.

I felt the skin split and warm blood pour down my face, and burning pain followed. I bit my lip, refusing to cry out. I wouldn't give him the satisfaction.

He slashed my cheek again, this time deeper and barely half an inch from my eye. "The ancient Chinese had a flair for execution. My favorite in particular is the death of a thousand cuts, where piece by piece, the flesh was removed from the body. How many cuts do you think it will take to kill you, Lila?"

"I don't know," I rasped, my voice barely recognizable. "But I know how many cuts it takes to kill you."

"Oh?" he said. "Do tell."

"Two. One to your belly, and one to your legacy." Red-hot pain seared my cheek, but I forced a grin. "Smile, Victor. You're on camera."

He twisted around wildly, pressing one hand to his abdomen while the other gripped the knife. "What are you talking about?"

"I'm talking about the game you and Celia have been playing," I said. "You've lost. The entire country is watching all of this, and they've heard every last word. No matter what you do to me now, you're dead."

Daxton scrambled toward the nearest cabinet, throwing open the door and ripping through the supplies. Blood dripped to the ground where he stood, but he didn't seem to notice or care. "You're lying."

"Go ahead and try to convince yourself of that, but I'm not," I said. "You're a dead man walking, Victor Mercer."

With an enraged cry, he pulled a pistol from his jacket—the same one he'd given me to execute Celia. "Then I might as well take you with me," he snarled.

I ducked as he pulled the trigger. The bullet ricocheted off the metal door behind me, and a cabinet across the room exploded. Daxton swore and, with trembling hands, dug through his pocket and produced another bullet. "Nowhere to go," he said in a nervous singsong voice. The color drained from his face, and the puddle of blood beneath him grew larger. "I already told you, Lila. You will never outlive me."

Suddenly something beeped, and the door to the safe room groaned and creaked open. Standing on the other side, his hair windswept and his face flushed, was Knox, a semiautomatic weapon in his hands. At least he'd had the sense to bring more than one bullet with him.

"Lila, move," he ordered, and I jumped out of the way, giving him a clear shot at Daxton. It occurred to me half a second too late that I had also given Daxton a clear shot at Knox.

Another shot rang out, reverberating through the safe room, and Knox swore. He dropped his gun and clutched his shoulder, and Daxton dived for the loaded weapon. Panic and adrenaline surged through me, and I scrambled toward it as well, grabbing it an instant before he could and pointing the barrel directly at his head. This time I wouldn't miss.

He laughed, a crazed, unhinged sound that turned my insides to ice. "You got me," he said as he slowly stood, wincing as even more blood gushed from his belly. "You've won, Lila. Congratulations."

"Can't win while you're still alive," I said, finger on the trigger. "Now tell everyone what you did to Kitty."

"What I—" He chuckled again. "Who cares? She was a nobody."

"I care," said Knox, stepping toward him with his hand still pressed against his wounded shoulder. "She may have been nobody to you, but the country loved her. So tell them what you did to her."

"I—" Daxton sighed. He was ghostly pale now, but other than a slight tremor in his hands, there was no other sign he was injured. "I told her I would let her go. And I did."

"And then what?" I growled.

"And then…and then I may or may not have had her helicopter blown to bits." He shrugged. "Couldn't say for sure."

I swallowed hard. I could have told him it was Lila, and maybe I should have. The country had a right to know she was gone. But I couldn't bring myself to do it. Lila deserved better than to die in the mountains, her body buried by snow and never recovered. She deserved this legacy. After all she had been through, she deserved to be remembered as one of the greats, too. Not me. I would have been nobody without her. But she was the reason behind all this. She was the reason the Blackcoats would now celebrate a hard-won victory, and she was the reason half a billion people would now have the freedom to live the lives they chose. Not the lives the government gave them.

I couldn't take that from her. I didn't need the glory. I didn't *want* the glory. All I wanted was for this to be over.

"Victor Mercer." I could barely speak. My voice was broken and hoarse, and every word felt like I was swallowing glass, but I forced them out. "You have been found guilty of treason, conspiracy to commit treason, and the murders of Kitty Doe, Celia Hart, Minister Creed, Minister Ferras, and Minister Bradley, among countless others. You are hereby sentenced to death. Do you have any last words?"

He considered me for a long moment. "Yes, as a matter of fact, I do."

And faster than I would have ever thought he could move, faster than I could react, he leaped toward Knox and pressed the knife against his throat.

"You will pardon me. You will get me medical treatment. And you will release me, or I will kill your fiancé."

Knox fought back, but Victor dug his finger into the bullet wound in his shoulder, and Knox cried out in pain.

"It's your choice, Lila. If I die, Knox dies with me. There will be no second chances this time." Victor shifted, his chest shielded by Knox's shoulder. There was no way I could kill him without shooting Knox, too.

I stood frozen in place as my heart pounded and my vision grew blurry. "Even if I let you go, you have no way to know for sure that I'll stick to my word."

"But the country is watching, remember?" He inched the knife across Knox's throat, and pearls of blood formed at the blade. "Surely you wouldn't lie to them."

"They want you punished for your crimes. No one would blame me for having you arrested, no matter what promises I make."

He sighed. "I suppose you're right. I guess that means I'll just have to kill him after all, won't I?"

His hand holding the knife twitched, and I didn't think. I didn't breathe. I did exactly what he'd urged me to do less than an hour before, standing on that platform in front of thousands of people, with Celia kneeling in front of me, ready to die.

I pulled the trigger.

XVIII

SCARS

The bullet hit Knox in the spot where his shoulder met his chest, half an inch below where Daxton's shot had landed.

The force of it pushed him backward, and the knife went flying as Victor slammed against the wall. Together they lay in a crumpled heap, and I hurried over, my heart pounding.

"Knox?" His name came out choked, and I dropped to my knees beside him. "Please don't be dead, please don't be dead—"

"I'm not dead," he managed, wincing. "I think Victor might be, though."

Knox sat up, revealing Daxton underneath him. His dark eyes were wide, his mouth slack, and fresh blood blossomed from the bullet that had traveled through Knox's shoulder into his chest. He wasn't moving.

"Looks like the bastard had a heart after all," said Knox, and I held out my hand, helping him to his feet. The world seemed to tilt on its axis, and I stared at Daxton's body, trying to absorb what had just happened.

He was dead.

Finally, at last, Daxton Hart—Victor Mercer—was dead.

"I should—I shouldn't have killed him," I whispered. "I should have shot him in the knee."

"You're not that good of a shot. Besides, he was already minutes from dying," said Knox. "Look at how much blood he'd lost. There was no saving him."

"He should have had to stand trial for his crimes. He should have—he should have had to look his victims' families in the eye and lived to face the consequences. Death was too easy. I *had* him. I should have—"

"Lila." Despite his injuries, Knox hunched down in front of me, staring me straight in the eye. "You did exactly what you should have done."

I threw my arms around him, hugging him as tightly as I dared without causing him more pain. He embraced me in return, rubbing slow circles on my back.

"Come on," he murmured. "Let's get out of here."

Knox hadn't been bluffing. The Blackcoats had once again hijacked the broadcast system, and the entire country had seen the showdown in the safe room between me and Victor Mercer. Before Knox and I even made it to the atrium, a team of paramedics ran down the steps directly toward us. I stepped aside, expecting them to race to the safe room to see if there was any hope to save their Prime Minister, but instead they stopped.

"Miss Hart—Mr. Creed—please sit and let us examine you," said a woman. I glanced at Knox, and he nodded. Together we sank down, and the paramedics got to work inspecting my throat and the bullet wounds in Knox's shoulder.

I insisted on walking to the ambulance, but much to his chagrin, Knox was forced onto a stretcher and carried out, the paramedics threatening to withhold painkillers if he didn't stay put. Greyson waited for us outside with Rivers at his side, and as soon as I stumbled out, a blanket wrapped around my shoulders and a paramedic holding my elbow to make sure I didn't fall, they both raced toward us.

"Lila—are you—what happened?" Greyson skidded to a stop on the gravel drive.

"Victor's dead," I croaked. The more I spoke, the harder it became. "Knox—"

"I'm fine," he called as the stretcher appeared. "Did the whole thing get on air?"

"The whole thing," said Rivers with a grin.

I refused to be split up from Knox, so we rode to the nearest hospital together in the same ambulance, with Rivers driving Greyson behind us. Through the back windows, I spotted hundreds, if not thousands of people gathered at the gates of Somerset, watching us drive off. A cheer rose up, loud enough for us to hear through the ambulance walls, and the sob I'd been holding in all morning finally escaped. We'd done it. We'd actually done it.

"It's really over, isn't it?" I whispered. Knox, who'd so far spent the ride arguing with the paramedic, nodded.

"Yeah," he said, his expression softening for a moment. "It's over. You did it. *Hey.*" He caught the paramedic's hand. "What did I say about shots?"

A team of doctors waited at the entrance to St. George Hospital, and as soon as the ambulance doors opened, they rushed to help us. Knox was immediately carted away, but just as I began to panic, Greyson appeared.

"I'm right here," he said, taking my hand as they loaded me onto a stretcher. "I'm not going anywhere."

True to his word, Greyson stuck by my side for the rest of the day, even as reporters descended on the hospital, begging to speak to him. Benjy somehow managed to find us, and he brought with him a protection detail for Greyson and me—all Blackcoats, he promised. And all immeasurably loyal to us.

Doctor after doctor inspected my face and throat, and though it didn't seem like much of a big deal to me, they insisted strangulation had dangerous lingering effects, and they couldn't be too careful. Every time I started to protest, Greyson shushed me and told me to let the doctors do their jobs, and reluctantly I did so. After kicking him in the stairwell and abandoning him, I owed him this.

"We've done everything we can to prevent severe scarring to your cheek," said a doctor with a thick black braid hanging over her shoulder. "But I'm afraid without more—advanced measures, there will always be scars."

I'd had enough *advanced measures* done to my body to last me a lifetime. "It's okay," I said tiredly. "They're fine the way they are."

"You're sure?" said Greyson, and I nodded.

"I earned those scars. I'm keeping them."

He touched my chin and examined the stitched-up lines running down my face. "They suit you," he said. "Make your outsides match your insides."

"What, damaged?" I teased. He blushed.

"No, I mean—tough. Strong. Fierce. A fighter."

"A regular badass," said Benjy, who lingered nearby, and I gave him an amused look. I could live with that.

At last the chaos of the day subsided, and night set in. As soon as Knox was out of surgery, we were given private hospital rooms side by side. With Greyson's help, I snuck out of bed and into Knox's room, pulling my IV along with me. Together Greyson and I sat on the sofa while Knox slept off whatever they'd given him, and I couldn't help but notice a little trail of drool running from his mouth to the pillow. It would have been cute if he wasn't snoring so loudly.

"So," I whispered. "You're Prime Minister now."

Greyson took a deep breath and released it slowly. "Guess so," he said. "I'm going to put together a council tomorrow."

"Like the Ministers of the Union?"

"Something like that. I want you to be on it. You, Knox, Benjy, Rivers, the other leaders of the rebellion who survived—you all won this war. I want to honor that and turn this country into something to be proud of."

"You will." I rested my head against his shoulder, my gaze lingering on Knox. "Thank you. I know being Prime Minister was the last thing you wanted."

"Being my father was the last thing I wanted," he corrected quietly. "Making a difference in this country— giving people their lives back and making sure all of this wasn't for nothing—that's an honor. Besides," he added, "if all goes as planned, I'd like to hold elections eventually. Real elections, where there's more than one name on the ballot. And term limits. No one will rule this country indefinitely again, and the people will have a voice— a real voice."

That sounded almost too good to be true, but wasn't that exactly what we'd spent all this time fighting for? "America's lucky to have you."

"No. They're lucky to have *you*."

I pressed my lips together. "I'm sorry for kicking you in the shin."

He chuckled and pulled me closer. "I'm sorry for trying to stop you. But I meant what I said, Kitty. You're it. You're the only family I have left now. I'm never going to let anything bad happen to you again. I promise."

"Bad things happen all the time. Maybe not war and death and maiming, but—little things." I looked up at him and offered him a lopsided smile. It was all I was capable of at the moment. "It's okay. I don't mind them, as long as I have you."

Knox let out a particularly loud snore, and my shoulders shook with laughter.

"You, too," I added, giving him a look. He was still fast asleep, and I turned back to Greyson. "We're through the worst of it. We'll get through the rest together."

Greyson sighed. "I hope so." After a moment, he added, "Can I ask you something?"

"I think you already did."

He smiled vaguely before it dropped from his face completely. "Why didn't you tell Daxton who you really were?"

I hesitated, not sure how to put it into words. "Lila gave up her entire life for this rebellion. She risked everything time and time again. And maybe she had her moments of weakness, but we all do. I wanted to honor her. I wanted to make sure her name goes down in history as the reason this all happened. If I told the country who I really was— it wouldn't matter that she started it. They would only remember that I finished it, and I couldn't do that to her. She deserves to be remembered."

Greyson took a deep, shuddering breath and wiped his

eyes quickly. "Thank you. I know she would have appreciated it. And thought you were crazy for not wanting credit."

"It's not about the credit," I said. "It's about making a difference. And we all did that together."

"We did. And even if everyone thinks you're Lila, I can find a way to have you returned to your original appearance," said Greyson. "We have all the doctors in the country at our disposal. I can make it happen."

For months, I'd wanted nothing more than to look in a mirror and see my real face staring back. Round and freckled, with a button nose and dirty blond hair several shades darker than Lila's. But I was more than my appearance. I was more than what people thought when they looked at me. And no matter whose face I wore, I would have to find a way to accept that.

"Kitty Doe is dead," I whispered. "I'm Kitty Hart, and somehow, even though I shouldn't be, I'm still here. And this is what I look like, scars and all. I don't want to change a thing."

"Okay," he said softly, running his fingers through my hair. "You're perfect exactly the way you are."

I smiled again and let my eyes fall shut. "Damn straight."

Sometime in the middle of the night, I awoke with a jolt. A nurse stood over me in the dimly lit room, silently checking my vitals. When he noticed I was awake, he winced, clutching his tablet apologetically. "Are you sure you wouldn't be more comfortable in your own bed, Miss Hart?" he said quietly. Beside me, Greyson had also fallen fast asleep.

"No, I'm good here," I mumbled. "Can I have something to drink?"

He fetched me a glass of ice water, and I sat up. Swallowing was a torture unlike anything I'd ever experienced, but I managed to get some down by taking tiny sips. As soon as he was done checking me over, the nurse exited, leaving me alone in the darkness.

"How's the throat?"

I jumped, nearly spilling the water all over my lap. Knox's eyes were open, and he watched me from his position prone on the bed. "It's fine," I lied. "I'll live. How's your shoulder?"

"It's fine," he said. "I'll live."

We stared at one another for a long moment, and finally he cracked a grin.

"You look like hell."

"And you don't?" I said hoarsely. With effort, he sat up.

"No worse than you do. Come over here. I don't want to wake Greyson."

Reluctantly I untangled myself from my brother and crossed the room to sit in the chair beside Knox's bed, shoving a small pillow behind my back. It wasn't the most comfortable piece of furniture I'd ever encountered, but it would do. Being this close to Knox without the fear of Daxton killing us both felt like a dream, and given the fuzzy state of my mind, I wasn't so sure it wasn't. He was really here. "I can't believe you didn't tell me you were still alive that whole time."

"You figured it out well enough on your own," he said. I glared at him, my cheeks burning.

"And I can't believe you let me ramble on like that when you were listening the whole time."

"Would it make you feel better if I said I wasn't?"

"Were you?" I said cautiously, and he grinned.

"Of course I was. Had to make sure you two were all right."

I pulled the pillow out from behind my back and hit him in the thigh. "You're awful and I hate you."

"Only one of those is true." He reached for my hand with his good arm, his touch warm and heavy and comforting, and his expression softened. For a moment I thought I saw a flicker of something more, but it was too dark to be sure. "You did great, Kitty. I can't tell you how proud I am."

I didn't know how to respond to sincerity from him. Not like this, not when I wasn't prepared for the feelings coursing through me like lava, overwhelming my senses. Anger, relief, desire, pure and desperate joy—there were too many to name, let alone make any sense of. So instead I replied like we always did, with just enough bite to let each other know we cared. "Of course you can't, because that would be admitting I did something right for a change."

Knox smirked, and though he could have let the moment pass, his thumb brushed against the back of my hand, sending sparks through me. "So what's next, now that you've saved the world?"

"I didn't save the world," I said, my overworked voice breaking.

"Close enough. Are you and Benjy getting a cottage in the woods together? Going to run off and be a happy little couple?"

"I—" I stopped. If he'd been listening, he should have known. Maybe he did. Maybe he wanted to be sure. "Benjy broke up with me." The words hurt less than I thought they would. "He's still my best friend, and he'll always be around, but—it's better this way. We weren't as good together as we both deserved. Not like that."

Knox raised an eyebrow. "Oh? And how good can it get?"

"I—" I took another sip of my water. My throat burned, but it gave me time to think. I didn't know how good it could get. That was the problem. I thought Benjy was it, but he wasn't. And the evidence was currently staring at me.

"You...?" said Knox, waiting for me to continue. I shook my head. He knew. He knew he knew, and I'd given him the confirmation he needed. Now he was just being a jerk.

"Don't make me say it. Today's been traumatic enough for both of us."

He seemed to consider that, leaning back against his pillows without taking his eyes off me. I held his gaze, and for the space of several heartbeats, neither of us said a word. My pulse raced. He knew. And so did I, without him having to say a word.

"You should get some sleep," he said at last. "Save that voice of yours. The next few days are going to be rough and confusing, and the people are going to need some guidance."

I nodded, both relieved and dismayed at the shift in conversation. The last thing I wanted was to go on national television yet again, but he was right. The people would need a leader, and I had already given them everything else. I could give them this, too. "Will you do me a favor?"

"Anything." He seemed to realize how earnest he sounded, because he added with a smirk, "Within reason."

I gripped my glass, running my thumb through the condensation. "I'm tired," I whispered.

"I told you, you should get some—"

"Not that kind of tired. I'm exhausted. Wrung out. There's nothing left. I just need—I need a break. I need to get away. Not forever. But just for a little while."

Knox was quiet for a long moment. "I can make that happen."

"Really?" I said, and he nodded.

"I know exactly where you should go."

The next day, the hospital released me into the care of a private physician. Walking out into the bright sunlight, so incongruous with the turmoil we had all survived—it didn't feel real, but nothing did anymore. And I was okay with that. The instant it felt real was the moment I would start appreciating it all a little less, and I never wanted that moment to come.

Greyson assembled his council in the dining room of Creed Manor that afternoon, along with a camera crew and an order for my speech to be broadcast on every channel across the nation. My throat was in bad shape, and more than once, Greyson asked me if I was sure I wanted to do this, but I was. He would do most of the talking anyway. I just had to make sure the country knew he was nothing like his father or the madman that had impersonated him.

With Knox still hospitalized, the council consisted of seven members: me, Greyson, Benjy, Rivers, and three other surviving leaders from the rebellion. Together we sat at a round table—it was symbolic, according to Benjy—and as the red light clicked on, I took a deep breath.

"My name is Lila Hart." My voice was barely above a whisper, and the microphone was turned up as loud as it would go, but I knew subtitles would be running across every screen. "Yesterday, you all witnessed the undoing of Victor Mercer, who had been terrorizing our great nation as Prime Minister Daxton Hart for over a year. You heard him confess to treason, murder, and countless other crimes, and for the first time, you had the veil pulled back from the people who have been running your country and your lives. You saw the corruption. You saw the greed. You saw the madness my cousin Greyson and I have been witnessing for months, and you also saw your Prime Minister die at my hands. I'm sorry for taking his life, and that's something I'm going to have to live with for the rest of mine. But I am not sorry for doing what I had to do in order to protect the people—in order to protect *you* from his tyranny.

"I won't pretend everyone watching this supported the Blackcoats," I continued. "We were a country divided in more ways than one. Not just by our beliefs, but by the tattoos on the back of our necks, too. By a corrupt, imperfect system that, while providing the very basic necessities, has also ruined many lives and stopped far too many from reaching their full potential.

"But I will say that everyone watching this—you are now free in a way you have never been before. This is a freedom our ancestors fought to protect, and it is a freedom our families, friends, and loved ones fought to restore to us in the Blackcoat Rebellion. And from this day forward, I and the people at this table will make sure their sacrifices were not in vain. We will make sure your rights are protected, and we will make sure that everyone has a chance—a *real* chance—to live their lives to the fullest. My cousin Greyson may not have been a Blackcoat, but we both believe in freedom and democracy. We both believe in letting you, the people, decide who governs you. And while he will remain Prime Minister during this transitional period, during the restructuring and rebuilding of our government into something the people control, as soon as this country is ready for a fair election, he will relinquish his title to your chosen representative."

I met Benjy's gaze across the table, and he gave me an encouraging nod. Taking another deep breath, I continued. "Change won't happen in a day, or a week, or even a month. It may take years to fully restructure ourselves into something our forefathers would be proud of. We will make sure it happens as fast as possible, but we won't do so to the detriment of any of you. Your lives will continue much as they are, with the exception of wages and rations being increased for the lower ranks. But to those of you who haven't taken your test yet—" I paused and looked directly into the camera again. "You will not be ranked. You will be assessed, and you will be guided, but you will not be forced into a life you haven't chosen. I—" I stopped, my voice tired and my throat aching, but I pushed on. "I know it will be difficult, and things won't be perfect right away. But please give us a chance. I swear we will make you proud."

The others sitting at the table applauded, and when it faded, I squared my shoulders. "And now, allow me to introduce your new Prime Minister, Greyson Hart, who will explain our preliminary plan."

"Thank you, Lila," he said gently, and while he talked about things like representation, elections, and his plans for change, I let my mind wander toward the possibilities of what this country might be like in five years. It seemed crazy to think about a time without ranks. They had become so ingrained in our mind-set that it would take far more than a few years to shake it completely. But in a generation or two...maybe by then, the people really would feel like equals.

Benjy nudged a piece of paper across the table toward me, and I took it. On it he had drawn a beach with the sun beating down on the waves, and a stick figure with shoulder-length hair building a sandcastle. Me.

With the knowledge that the camera was focused on Greyson, I picked up a pen and drew him a sketch in return. It was once again a stick figure, but this time I stood in a cottage in the woods, and I wasn't alone. Another stick figure stood beside me, her hair in a braid and a smile on her face.

I pushed the paper back to Benjy, and he examined my drawing. Looking up at me, he tilted his head questioningly, and I nodded.

I would be there for Greyson. I would be Lila Hart. I would be a member of this council, and I would do whatever I had to do in order to help make sure this country became everything the Blackcoats wanted it to be. But for now, just for a short while, I would be someone else, too.

I would be me.

XIX

COTTAGE IN
THE WOODS

One week later, I sat in the middle of a meadow beside a lake, my head tilted back as the sun warmed my face in the chilly February breeze. I had been out here for nearly an hour now, breathing in the fresh air and the smell of the dormant forest. I couldn't wait for spring, when the grass would grow and flowers would bloom and I could spend all day outside without worrying Hannah.

As it was, she stood in the doorway of our cottage, holding a wooden spoon as she watched me. "Kitty, you're going to freeze to death out there."

"It's not that cold." My voice was still rough, but I could speak without pain now, and a doctor came by every few days to make sure my recovery was going well.

"The tip of your nose is red, and I don't doubt that cuff has frozen to your ear by now," she said. "Besides, you have someone waiting for you."

"What? Who?" I stood and headed toward the cottage, brushing the dirt off my pants. The metal cuff *was* cold against the cartilage of my ear. But while Greyson didn't use his, and I hadn't heard a word from Knox since I'd last visited his hospital room the day I'd left D.C., I couldn't bring myself to take it off.

"Benjy. He's on the monitor."

Hannah held the door open for me, and I stepped into the warm cottage. It was small, with only a living room, a tiny kitchen, two small bedrooms, and a bathroom we shared, but it was all the space Hannah and I needed. At first we'd tiptoed around one another, not entirely sure what to do or say, but as the days passed, we slowly grew more comfortable with one another. I wasn't sure I would ever be able to call her Mom, and it was undoubtedly difficult for her to think of me as the baby she'd been forced to give up all those years ago, but we were working on it. And that was the important part.

"I set a mug of hot chocolate on the desk for you," said Hannah as she helped me out of my coat and hung it near the crackling fire to warm it for the next time I decided to go outside—which, admittedly, would probably be as soon as my call with Benjy ended. After spending so many months trapped in one way or another, I loved the freedom of the lakeshore. The cottage was inviting, and I never felt like an intruder, but it also didn't quite feel like home yet.

"Thanks," I said, flashing her a grateful smile. I headed to the desk, where Benjy's face appeared on the monitor as he waited for me.

"Took you long enough," he said. "What were you doing?"

"I was outside," I said. "What's going on? Did something happen?"

"What, I'm not allowed to call twice in one day?" said Benjy.

"I—" I eyed him and picked up my hot chocolate. "You're sure nothing's going on?"

"Positive. My dinner plans fell through, and I just thought you'd like me to read to you for a while."

This had become our daily ritual: Benjy would call after the morning council meeting had ended, and once he updated me on everything they had discussed, he would read to me. It wasn't the same as it had been before, but it was enough for now. "As long as the story isn't boring," I said. It never was.

"Can't say for sure—I bought a few new books today, and I thought we could read them together." Benjy held up an orange-and-turquoise cover I couldn't read, and his smile grew goofy and huge. "The girl at the bookstore said this was a good one."

"The girl at the bookstore?" I leaned toward the monitor. "Do tell me more, Benjamin."

He turned red. "It's not like that—"

"Uh-huh. I know that look on your face. That's how you looked at me for ten years."

"I'm looking at you now, aren't I?" he said.

"That's not the expression you wore when this call started. Spill, Doe."

At last Benjy caved. "Okay, fine—she's cute. Brunette. Glasses. We talked about books for a while."

"Did you ask her out?" I said, and he nodded.

"This weekend. To talk about this book."

I laughed. "So that's why you want to read it to me," I said, and he shrugged sheepishly.

"We can read something else, if you want."

"No, no. I insist on this one." I curled up in my seat, cupping my hot chocolate. "She better not be a better kisser than me."

"I'll let you know." Benjy waggled his eyebrows and opened the book. "Chapter one."

He read to me for the next twenty minutes, and Hannah joined us, standing behind me. She ran her fingers through my hair, her fingertips accidentally brushing against the X scarred into my neck, but neither of us said a word about it. Soon enough, it wouldn't matter.

A knock sounded on the door in the middle of chapter two, and I looked up. "Benjy, hold on, someone's here." Greyson had visited twice so far, but he was usually good about telling us when he was coming.

"Oh, I sent you a present," he said, and I stood.

"A present?" While Hannah tended to the stew that was beginning to bubble over, I headed toward the door.

"Yeah, thought you could use it," he said mischievously, and I opened the door.

"What—"

I stopped. Knox stood on the porch, his arm in a sling and a bag hoisted over his good shoulder. He wore a thick woolen coat and at least three days' worth of stubble, but he looked healthier than I had seen him in a long time.

"Hi," he said, his smile growing as he looked at me. "I hope I'm not intruding."

His voice sparked something deep inside me, warming me from the inside out. He looked happy, too. Happier than I'd ever seen him before. And suddenly I couldn't help but feel exactly the same.

"No, never," I said, moving aside to let him in. As he stepped into the cottage to join us, his hand brushed mine, and our eyes met. And I knew, without question, that I was home.

★ ★ ★ ★ ★